'Sayrid, I marry a woman—not a man. Find a dress.'

Sayrid stared at Hrolf uncomprehendingly. 'A dress?'

'You do own a dress…don't you?'

She released a breath and offered a prayer up to all the goddesses in the Aesir and Vanir. At last—a way to postpone the evil day with dignity. Somehow she'd discover what he truly wanted before she started believing that he wanted her. She could use this to buy time and find a solution to the mess. It wasn't over until the ceremony was done.

'My best dress is at home. What a pity. We will have to name another day, when I can be attired in the sort of clothes fit for a sea king's bride.'

'Borrow one.' A glint showed in his eyes as he raked her form. 'Or come naked. But I marry a woman. Today.'

AUTHOR NOTE

This story came about because I love seeing how women survived in male-dominated professions in bygone eras. So when I discovered it is highly probable that there were Viking shield maidens—aka female warriors—I knew what my next heroine Sayrid Avildotta would be.

While I was writing this book I was able to visit the Viking exhibit at the British Museum and see some of the artefacts there, such as ships, swords and several hordes of gold and silver. All exciting stuff. However, the Viking skull with filed teeth did make me wince…

The book from the exhibit—*Vikings: Life and Legend*—which details the latest research on Viking life, was also useful in answering several questions about the current thinking on certain aspects of Viking culture (for example, the misidentification of various pendants as Valkyries when they could easily be a depiction of real shield maidens).

I do hope you enjoy this tale of a shield maiden and the warrior who shows that she can be a woman as well as a warrior.

As ever, I love hearing from readers. You can contact me through my website michellestyles.co.uk, my blog michellestyles.blogspot.com or my publisher. I also have a page on Facebook—Michelle Styles Romance Author—where I regularly post my news. And I'm on Twitter as @michelleLstyles

TAMING HIS VIKING WOMAN

Michelle Styles

First published in Great Britain 2015
by Mills & Boon, an imprint of Harlequin (UK) Limited,
Large Print edition 2015
Harlequin (UK) Limited, Eton House, 18-24 Paradise Road,
Richmond, Surrey TW9 1SR

© 2015 Michelle Styles

ISBN: 978-0-263-25550-8

Harlequin (UK) Limited's policy is to use papers that are natural,
renewable and recyclable products and made from wood grown in
sustainable forests. The logging and manufacturing processes conform
to the legal environmental regulations of the country of origin.

Printed and bound in Great Britain
by CPI Antony Rowe, Chippenham, Wiltshire

3387444

Michelle Styles was born and raised near San Francisco, California. She currently lives near Hadrian's Wall with her husband, a menagerie of pets and occasionally one of her three university-aged children. An avid reader, she became hooked on historical romance after discovering Georgette Heyer, Anya Seton and Victoria Holt. Her website is michellestyles.co.uk and she's on Twitter and Facebook.

Previous novels by the same author:

THE GLADIATOR'S HONOUR
A NOBLE CAPTIVE
SOLD AND SEDUCED
THE ROMAN'S VIRGIN MISTRESS
TAKEN BY THE VIKING
A CHRISTMAS WEDDING WAGER
  (part of *Christmas By Candlelight*)
VIKING WARRIOR, UNWILLING WIFE
AN IMPULSIVE DEBUTANTE
A QUESTION OF IMPROPRIETY
IMPOVERISHED MISS, CONVENIENT WIFE
COMPROMISING MISS MILTON*
THE VIKING'S CAPTIVE PRINCESS
BREAKING THE GOVERNESS'S RULES*
TO MARRY A MATCHMAKER
HIS UNSUITABLE VISCOUNTESS
HATTIE WILKINSON MEETS HER MATCH
AN IDEAL HUSBAND?
PAYING THE VIKING'S PRICE
RETURN OF THE VIKING WARRIOR
SAVED BY THE VIKING WARRIOR

*linked by character

And in Mills & Boon® Historical *Undone!* eBooks:

THE PERFECT CONCUBINE

Did you know that some of these novels are also available as eBooks? Visit www.millsandboon.co.uk

For my aunt Sandra K Erickson

Chapter One

AD 830—north-east Sweden

Sayrid Avildottar stood in the ice-cold pond, fish spear raised, her eyes on a particularly large sea trout.

She and trout were old adversaries. Fishing helped to hone her eye and her hand when she was at home as well as providing food for the table. And out here in the pond, no one ever complained that she was far too tall, too clumsy or too unwomanly. Not that anyone did much these days. She'd proved her worth with five seasons of profitable sea voyages.

It was amazing how quickly people fell silent when you had gold in your purse, a reputation as a canny trader and a sword by your side that you knew how to use.

The *jaarl* would surely relent and allow her

to lead a *felag* further east where fortunes truly could be made, instead of always trading with Birka and having to pay tribute to the various sea kings who prowled the sea lanes. And after that, she would never need to go on a voyage again. She would be able to stay at home and make sure her lands were safe. It would give her half-brother, Regin, time to become the capable warrior that she knew he could be and give her half-sister time to choose the warrior she married, instead of being forced into an unwise alliance with a man who had little respect for her.

She simply had to work out a way to make the *jaarl* see it was in his best interest.

The trout spun round and started back towards her, making its final bid for freedom. Sayrid balanced on her toes, waiting for that precise heartbeat when her spear would be most effective.

'Sayrid! Sayrid!' Her half-brother's voice resounded about the pond at the very instant she was about to thrust the spear.

The spear fell harmlessly into the pond and the fish flashed away.

'This had better be good, Regin,' Sayrid called back, retrieving the spear and vowing that next time the old trout would not get away so lightly. 'You've cost me a fish supper.'

'Blodvin has sent an urgent message about the marriage.'

'What can be important about that?' Sayrid peered into the water, trying to spot the trout again. 'The bride price was sworn last jul-tide. It was more than it should have been, but dewy eyes, honeyed curls and a sizeable portion of land come at a price.'

Svear custom dictated that before any marriage could take place, the groom paid a bride price to his intended's family to show that he was capable of supporting her and any children in the appropriate manner. In return her family paid a dowry which he could use during his lifetime, but which reverted to the woman and her children at his death or after a divorce. The amount exchanged usually cancelled each other out.

'Sayrid. Is that all you can think about—how much gold my marriage will cost this family? It is my future happiness at stake here.'

Sayrid rested her elbow on top of the spear. Gods save her from her family. Ever since her younger brother, Regin, had fallen for Blodvin, he'd changed and become more apt than normal to stare off into space.

'I'll forgive you supper, but stop panicking. Come the next Storting you'll be married. Even Ingvar Flokison the Bloodaxe would not dare cross our family, not after the bride price has been agreed. That's all I'm saying...' She detected a slight movement in the water. 'Now if you don't mind, I have a bone to pick with this trout.'

'Sayrid, look at me instead of dismissing me. Please.'

Sayrid turned around and winced at Regin's tragic expression. Thankfully their father was no longer there to mock.

'Regin, what is wrong?' she asked in a far gentler tone. There was little point in rehearsing her old arguments against a match with Blodvin. Regin had made up his mind and his stubborn streak rivalled her own. It was why they had been able to face their father down years ago when he had tried to use his fists on their sister, Auda, when she could barely walk. 'What new demand has Bloodaxe made? Whatever it is, I'll deliver it. You know me and my ways. I always hate being disturbed when I'm fishing.'

'She is marrying someone else.'

Sayrid froze. 'Who? Who thinks they can cross this family without retribution?'

'Hrolf Eymundsson. Her father doesn't dare refuse him as he is a sea king with half a dozen ships under his command.' Regin clutched his hair with both his hands. 'I can't lose her, Sayrid.'

'What?' Sayrid stood up straighter. 'Whose idea of a joke is this? Hrolf Eymundsson isn't here. The *jaarl* would have informed me. He would have requested my help in defending our village.'

'Hrolf and our *jaarl* exchanged peace rings at Birka. They are allied against Lavrans and his Viken raiders.'

'I heard about that.' Sayrid scowled. If she had been there, she'd have counselled against it. Once a marauding sea king, always one. But she had been in Ribe with the Danes, seeing whether that market was any better than Birka, and the *jaarl* had followed his instincts. She had to hope that Hrolf the Sea-Rider would honour his pledges and deal with the threat from Lavrans. However, she suspected given time he'd prove the same as every other sea king she'd encountered—an oaf with an overinflated opinion of his self-worth and an insatiable desire for gold, leading to demands for more tribute. The *jaarl* had been less than pleased when she had voiced her opinion on the subject.

'Hrolf arrived for a visit to cement the alliance two weeks ago.' Her brother gave her a sharp look. 'I thought you saw the *jaarl* when you returned.'

'We spoke of other things.' Sayrid concentrated on keeping her face blank. There was no need for Regin to know how badly the interview had gone and how she'd stormed out. 'What does this alliance have to do with Blodvin?'

'Eymundsson spotted Blodvin as soon as he stepped foot on our shores and made an offer that day. Her father wants the better match.'

'Better match indeed! The dirty scoundrel! We have already paid part of the bride price!' Sayrid gave vent to her anger and frustration at being kept in the dark about the sea king's visit and threw the spear with all her might. It stuck deep in the mud, quivering. 'No one cheats Ironfist's children.'

'Because of you, not me.' Her brother plucked the spear out of the mud and held it out to her. 'I'm the one she is supposed to marry. I'm not even head of the household. You hold that title by being a shield maiden.'

'An agreement is an agreement.' Sayrid crossed her arms and silently willed her brother not to cry any more. 'Blodvin chose you above all her other suitors.'

'Hrolf Eymundsson is another proposition altogether. You know his reputation as well as I. He came from nothing in a few years to commanding ships and a horde of Byzantium gold.'

'Fortune's wheel can turn sour just as quickly,' she said. 'Maybe his time has passed and yours is about to begin.'

Regin hung his head. 'You know what I'm like in personal combat.'

'That is all in your mind. Because of what happened when you were ten.' Sayrid climbed out of the pond. 'There is very little to wonder why your opponent won. He was a full-blooded warrior and you a mere boy. Far should never have forced you.'

Her father had a lot to answer for. He had been too quick with his fists and tongue, taking particular pleasure in tormenting her younger brother. He had only stopped when she had stood up to him, waving a sword in his face and threatening to use it. He'd retaliated by beating her until her back was bloody, but he had left Regin alone.

It wasn't his fists she had feared, but his cruel tongue. The worst was when he had proclaimed that any man could have her and all his property as her dowry without paying the customary bride price if they could defeat her in combat.

What a start to her career as a shield maiden it had been! Fighting off a fat drunken imbecile while everyone laughed. The jeers had turned to respectful silence when she met the next contestant, a respected but elderly warrior and disarmed him as well, followed by a young warrior. After that, the challenges had dried up.

'But Far said—'

'Far said a lot of stupid things,' Sayrid couldn't help but reply. 'Now he is dead from drinking far too much ale. He can't hurt you again. Ever.'

'But…but…' Her brother swallowed nervously.

'Our family prospers. Didn't Jaarl Kettil say how pleased he is with the amount of gold we brought back from our latest trading voyage?' Sayrid attempted a bright smile. 'You contributed to it.'

Regin shrugged. 'I'm still not a great warrior like Far wanted. Kettil will eventually demand a seasoned warrior, one who can lead *felags* and hold this land, not just a shield maiden.'

'You've other talents,' Sayrid said before Regin listed his perceived failings as a warrior or Kettil's stubborn refusal to allow her to lead a *felag* to the East. 'You acquitted yourself well in Tønsberg. You saved the lodestone from being washed overboard on that wave.'

He gave a sad smile. 'That was pure luck and we'd never have been near those rocks if I'd paid attention.'

'You're skilled at languages.'

Regin's nostrils flared slightly, reminding Sayrid of a high-strung horse who was about to refuse to get on board ship. 'Hrolf will challenge with the sword, not with verses of poetry.'

Sayrid stared at her brother. Where had his backbone gone? If he loved Blodvin as he claimed, he should be willing to fight for her. 'Panicking never solves anything. You're seventeen now, not an untried lad attending his first assembly. Every man has a weakness. Study him, find it and exploit it if you want the woman.'

'Blodvin thinks she might be pregnant.'

Sayrid froze. 'Yours?'

Regin went pink about his ears and he gave a

slow nod. 'Three months ago at the summer festival. It was the only time, I swear it, but she was so sweet in my arms.'

'Blodvin's father is a snake and not to be trusted, which is why you should have exercised restraint,' she said between gritted teeth before Regin could give her the intimate details. 'Wait, I said. Wait until you were safely married because of the possibilities of complications. Did I have to spell out what those complications were?'

'Blodvin expects me to face down Hrolf and claim her and the babe.' A nervous tic began in Regin's right eye as it always did when he contemplated fighting. 'Or I'm not the warrior she thought I was. She wants me to do it when they marry.'

'Marching into a wedding and snatching the bride will cause a major feud, assuming you even get out alive. I forbid it.' Sayrid concentrated on breathing. That woman would get her brother killed or, worse, start a feud which lasted generations. 'Why wait until I was fishing to tell me?'

Regin hung his head. His blond curls fell forward, hiding his face. Unlike Sayrid, who took after their tall, strong father, Regin took after his mother and was far shorter. Their father used to say he'd been doubly cursed—his eldest daughter was taller than most men and his only son prettier than most women.

'The message arrived this morning.' The sunlight streamed on Regin, giving him a halo of golden curls. 'Blodvin makes me feel like I have the strength of ten men.'

'Blodvin can send the child here when it is time. I would never turn one of your children away.' She held out her hands and willed her brother to take them. She knew her words were harsh, but the last thing she wanted was for her brother to be declared outlaw or worse over a flighty woman. 'In time, you will see that this was the best course. The Norns will have a different woman in mind for you.'

Regin turned his head away. 'There won't be other women for me. I love Blodvin with all my heart.'

'So speak all lovers until they meet the next woman.' She waited for Regin's sheepish smile.

His eyes burnt with a bright flame. 'It's only because you've never been in love that you make jokes.'

'Me in love? Gods forbid. I have a household to run and hungry mouths to feed.' Love was something that happened to women who didn't tower over all the men and who knew how to dance prettily and pour the drink with the right amount of simpering deference. Her father's scorn for once had held a ring of truth.

'Some day, Sayrid, you will know what it is like to have your heart ripped out.'

'I'm a shield maiden. First and foremost. I won't marry unless the man can defeat me in combat. The *jaarl* agreed to my pledge.' Sayrid made a practice throw of her fishing spear. She'd turned her father's cruel jest around and had made it a virtue. 'Don't distract me with discussions about my future. What do you intend to do, if you won't challenge Hrolf for the fair Blodvin's hand? Sail east?'

The pleading expression on Regin's face became truly heartbreaking. 'This is also an insult to the family. Bloodaxe will say he broke the agreement because...'

'Because I am unnatural and lead this house with my sword arm. Should I be sticking to my spinning and weaving, and wringing my hands when we lose everything to some arrogant sea king who sails into the harbour demanding tribute?' Sayrid finished before Regin had a chance to say the words. 'Because I am talented at the arts of war instead of those of love?'

'Going Viking isn't what women do.' Regin coughed. 'You have to admit my mother had a point.'

White-hot anger flashed through Sayrid. She had rejoiced the day her stepmother had remarried and moved more than a week's march to the south, taking her poisonous tongue with her. 'Funny how *that* excuse springs so readily to people's lips. They like to forget the trade and wealth our ships bring.'

Regin drew a line with his foot. 'Her father disapproves of you, but I don't. That is not what I was going to say. He will claim it is because I delayed the marriage and he worried about the agreed price being paid. If we had done as he wanted, I would have married at jul.'

'His wool sacks were light and I won't pay good gold for less than the full measure. A man who will cheat on such things, will cheat on his daughter's dowry.' Sayrid put her hands on Regin's shoulders and looked down at his watering eyes. 'We delayed the marriage because Bloodaxe had difficulties with the dowry and Blodvin wanted to have her dress properly embroidered. Not because of anything we did wrong. The *jaarl* knows the truth.' She paused. 'It is something to unsettle you so that we will accept a lower dowry.'

Regin slammed his fists together. 'I will marry Blodvin with or without your help...or die trying.'

Sayrid pretended to fiddle with the fishing spear. 'After I've forbidden it?'

Her brother's face took on his stubborn look. 'I'll go anyway.'

'I won't rescue you.'

His face fell. 'Maybe this time I won't need rescuing.'

A brief laugh escaped her throat. 'Regin! Think!'

'I love her, Say. I can't stand aside and let her be married to someone like Hrolf Eymundsson.'

Sayrid mentally said goodbye to a quiet few weeks fishing and planning how to be put in charge of a *felag*. 'If it means that much to you, then we will see *if* Blodvin needs rescuing. But if the lady wishes to be married to Hrolf Eymundsson, we leave her there and walk away. Agreed?'

Instantly, her brother's face became wreathed in smiles. 'I knew you'd do it. I told Auda you'd help.'

'And, Regin, this is the last time...'

* * *

Hrolf Eymundsson watched his host and hostess from under his hooded eyes. They were hiding something from him. He could tell from the way they kept glancing at each other and then glancing at the door. 'Is there some reason why you want the marriage to happen tomorrow?'

The sweat had beaded on Ingvar the Bloodaxe's forehead and he signalled to his wife that he wanted his horn of ale refilling. 'An agreed bride price and my daughter is everything you could wish for in a wife—accomplished and beautiful. Why wait?'

Hrolf inclined his head. When he'd returned from his latest *felag* to find Inga's mother dead and Inga barely able to speak his language, he'd known that he had to take steps. He required a wife with land, particularly land with good access to the sea, but more than that he wanted his daughter brought up by a woman who understood what it meant to be Svear. It was why he'd returned to this land, rather than marry one of the women along the Rus trading route. As his uncle had explained many years ago, wives had a defined role and purpose. And although he had never particularly wanted to marry, it was the only way to keep his daughter and growing empire safe.

The bride price was slightly steeper than he would have wished, but Bloodaxe's daughter had a number of suitors, according to the mother. Taking a bride from this area would demonstrate to Kettil that he was serious about their alliance—these shores would be protected from the menace that was his rival sea king, Lavrans. Unlike Lavrans, who continually demanded more tribute if he felt an ally was weak, Hrolf prided himself on honouring agreements to the best of his ability.

He had spied Blodvin looking after some children when he disembarked from his ship. She was pretty enough, with a vague look of Inga's mother about her, and had responded to his query with a sweet smile. When he learnt her name and that she was unmarried, it seemed the Norns had blessed him. Bloodaxe and his father had been close once in the old days before his father lost his lands and his title... Hrolf gripped the drinking horn tighter.

He had righted old wrongs and paid off the debts he owed. He was now a sea king who ruled the waves. And Bloodaxe was right—what more did he want? His daughter was the correct woman to mother his Inga.

'Blodvin is the proper sort of woman to be on a sea king and future *jaarl*'s arm!' the mother said with a loud sniff. 'I knew the Norns had a special future marked out for her.'

Hrolf took another draught of the indifferent ale. 'Your daughter has no objections? We've barely spoken.'

The man and his wife exchanged quick glances.

'Blodvin is quite shy.' Bloodaxe slapped his chest and emitted a loud belch. 'But she will make the ideal wife. She has spent years stocking her wedding chest. She knows all there is to know about housekeeping. Children adore her. Once she knows the match has been finalised, she'll be more than eager to have her wedding night.'

Every sinew of his body urged caution, but there was no reason to suspect anything was amiss with the woman.

'You, of course, know your daughter best.'

The faint sound of a creaking door caused Hrolf to stiffen. Instinctively he grasped the hilt of his knife. But neither Bloodaxe nor his wife appeared to take any notice of the sound. Hrolf forced his shoulders to relax. He'd lived for too long amongst warriors and raiders where any unusual sound could mean an enemy attack.

'I'd like to meet your daughter formally before we finalise the agreement.' He inclined his head. 'For courtesy. I'm sure she is as you describe her.'

'Get her, Wife. The time is right.' Bloodaxe's smile widened. 'You'll see that I speak the truth, Hrolf the Sea-Rider. Tomorrow night, you'll have your bride warming your bed.'

Bloodaxe's wife made a quick curtsy, but there was a nervous tic in her right eye. 'Blodvin has longed for this day.'

She scurried from the room. Deciding he'd exhausted Bloodaxe's limited range of small talk, Hrolf wandered over to the small window. In the fading light, he spied two cloaked figures entering the yard.

An owl hooted and the first figure hurried off. The other cloaked figure stood still in the shadows, listening, clearly up to no good.

Three heartbeats later, a woman's scream echoed around the room. Hrolf drew his sword.

'Husband! Blodvin has escaped from her room!'

'I locked her in the barn myself after she heard

about the rumoured match,' Bloodaxe thundered. 'This is the last time she behaves in this fashion! She will obey me.'

'Shall I go and check the barn and see if my bride is still there?' Hrolf enquired in a silken tone.

The gods were with her on this venture. Sayrid released the breath she'd been holding all the way from the river as the entire farm yard was bathed in silence except for the noise coming out of the barn.

Bloodaxe was utterly predictable in his hiding places. Blodvin was locked in the barn, loudly bemoaning her fate.

'Blodvin, it's Sayrid. Can you be quiet while I get this door open? You are making it impossible to think.'

'Sayrid! Why are you here?'

'Your maid delivered a message to Regin, begging for help.' Sayrid struggled with the bolt. 'Your prayers have been answered.'

'My father is about to marry me off to Hrolf Eymundsson. I overheard them plotting the other night and just had time to send Tove off before he locked me up. Hrolf is nothing but a grizzled old sea king! Rescue me, please!'

Sayrid put her weight into the bolt and it shot free. She opened the door with a loud creak. 'If you want to leave, then go and find your life.'

Blodvin rushed forward and gave Sayrid a crushing hug. 'I'll be your devoted follower for-ever, if you get me out of here unscathed. They want to marry me off before the next Storting, so Far can have the gold to pay his debts. Hrolf the Sea-Rider agreed to pay double what you were going to pay. Can you imagine?'

Sayrid stepped out of the overly familiar em-brace, feeling overgrown and awkward around the much smaller woman. 'I sent word asking for an emergency gathering of the Assembly.'

'You're far too good to me.' Blodvin gave a long sigh. 'Where is my beloved? Where is Regin?'

Sayrid stepped backwards and accidentally kicked a bucket over. Why was it that she could lead her men in battle and never put a foot wrong, but in the company of other women, she always seemed to be the one to make the mistake?

Blodvin covered her mouth as the bucket rolled.

'We go now.' Sayrid gripped Blodvin's arm. 'Regin waits on the river for you. He has a rowboat and will get you to our ship. I'll take care of any problems.'

Blodvin tried to peer around Sayrid. 'But Regin is with you? My beloved who pledged his life to me?'

Sayrid fought against the urge to be sick. She had forgotten how sickly sweet Blodvin was. Love was truly a condition she never wanted to suffer from.

'Regin loves you,' she said roughly. 'But I'll not have his hide nailed to the barn door.'

Blodvin nibbled her bottom lip. 'I wanted my future husband to rescue me.'

'Either you come with me and be Regin's wife or I leave you here.'

'I'll come! I want to!' Blodwin linked her arm with Sayrid's. 'We'll be sisters and it doesn't matter what anyone says about you. You're saving me from a fate far worse than death.'

Sayrid hooted like an owl. Instantly Regin returned the call. The tightness in Sayrid's shoulders eased. Everything was going to plan. 'There is Regin's signal. He waits for you.'

They had rounded the corner when a woman's scream rent the air. Blodvin froze.

'They've discovered I've gone! We're doomed.'

'Run, Blodvin, run!' Sayrid grabbed the woman's arm and started to pull her along. 'Now is not the time to have second thoughts.'

'But they'll catch us.'

'Not if I've anything to do with it. Go to the river. Tell Regin to cast off. I can swim.'

Sayrid shoved Blodvin forward, drew her sword and started to retreat. Each backward step was another victory. With any luck, Bloodaxe would not think to look in the river until it was far too late.

The sound of heavy footsteps caused her to freeze.

'Who goes there?' a commanding voice called out.

'A stranger going about her business.' Sayrid winced. She should have just said nothing, but she had to give Blodvin time to reach the river and safety. And she was willing to bet that at any more than the slightest hint of trouble, Blodvin would collapse in a heap. 'What is it to you?'

In the dull light, an unfamiliar Northman stepped forward. His blue eyes gleamed. Hrolf Eymundsson, perhaps, or one of his men? He was far too well dressed to be one of Bloodaxe's servants.

'You have taken something which does not belong to you.'

Sayrid shook her head to clear it. Now was not the time to notice his broad shoulders or the way his light brown hair flowed. Or that his height was equal to hers. Or to wonder about his name. Now was the time to save her life and to get out of there without encountering Ingvar the Bloodaxe.

'Why would I have done that? I've every respect for those who dwell here.'

'A mystery to me, but here you are on this moonlit night.'

'Perhaps I fancied a stroll?' Her voice was a bit too breathless for her liking. She gave a little cough. 'Walking after supper is good for you.'

'Unlikely. I've no time for games.' His gaze raked her form, making her aware of her slight curves. 'Even with a Valkyrie such as yourself.'

Sayrid pulled the cloak tighter about her body. Normally she never thought about such things, but the way he looked at her made her intensely aware that she was a woman.

The faint sound of oars slapping the water gave her courage. Blodvin and Regin were safe.

'No idea what you are talking about.' Sayrid made a steady shrug, but her heart thrummed.

Encountering a legendary sea king had not featured in her plan, but she could still make it work if she kept calm. 'If you'll forgive me, I've business elsewhere.'

'I would speak with my intended bride. Fetch her.'

Sayrid sucked in her breath. Blodvin definitely needed her eyesight adjusting if she thought Hrolf Eymundsson grizzled in any shape or fashion. He might not be in the first flush of youth, but he was very easy on the eye.

'Find a willing bride.'

The dimple in his cheek increased. 'Are you offering to take her place?'

'Hardly!' She slowly curled and uncurled her hands to stop them trembling. 'Next time, make sure the bride has not irrevocably pledged her heart to another.'

'Her father claims she is free.'

Sayrid rolled her eyes upwards. 'Ask him who else has paid the bride price.'

'Shall we ask him together? You and I, Valkyrie?'

Time to melt into the shadows. Sayrid took another step backwards. All her muscles tensed, ready for the final piece of her escape. All she needed was one more step. 'Another time.'

The warrior reached out and grabbed her arm, dragging her back against him. 'The truth… Valkyrie. Why have you kidnapped my bride? What grudge do you hold against me?'

She matched his furious blue gaze with one of her own. 'Ask Bloodaxe why he sought to cheat my family.'

He looked puzzled, but then a wide smile broke out over his face, transforming it. Her heart skipped a beat and her entire being was aware of him as a man. Sayrid angrily damped down the feeling. 'Your grievance is with Bloodaxe, not me. But you should take this to the Storting and allow the *jaarl* to resolve it.'

'You expect him to rule in your favour, Sea King? The *jaarl* is a man of law who won't rule in favour of whoever pays him the most gold.'

Hrolf froze. The split heartbeat of hesitation allowed Sayrid to twist her arm out of his grip and start sprinting for the river.

Behind her, she heard the pounding of his footsteps, but she kept on running.

Five steps from the river, a heavy weight landed on her shoulder and spun her around. 'Try that again and I won't be responsible for the consequences.'

His furious face was inches from hers. Their breath laced and she was aware of his muscle-bound arms imprisoning her.

Sayrid forced her shoulders to relax as she scanned the darkened river. She spotted her brother's rowboat, moving downstream. All she had to do was to let the current take her—the backup plan she'd worked out with Regin.

She leant forward. Her breasts accidently brushed his chest, making her body tingle. For one long heartbeat, an intense awareness of his lips filled her. If she slanted her head slightly to the right, their mouths would meet. She checked the movement with less than a breath to spare. 'I will take the consequences.'

Ducking, she wriggled free from his now-slack arm and tore the few yards to the river. Wading into thigh-deep water, she executed a perfect dive.

Hrolf stared at the dark river, willing the woman to resurface. He'd miscalculated badly. His entire being had wanted to taste her deep red lips and he'd allowed her to escape. He had no business calling himself a sea king if he behaved like an untried warrior who had never bedded a woman before.

Then he saw her head break out of the water as she drifted towards a small rowing boat. Someone pulled her aboard. Over the water, the sounds of laughter floated back.

Hrolf tightened his grip on his sword. 'This is the beginning, Valkyrie, not the end. No one plays me for a fool.'

Chapter Two

Sayrid's soft kid boots made a satisfying sound as she strode towards the Assembly Hall. She wore her new leather trousers with the dark green tunic Auda had made for her last birthday belted over them. Her cape swung slightly. Everything was designed to give the impression of supreme confidence, even though her insides churned.

She had considered all eventualities. Blodvin wore her morning gift of two arm rings and a necklace. At Sayrid's insistence, Blodvin had arranged her clothes so the pregnancy was evident to even the most casual observer. Blodvin and Regin were both prepared to swear a solemn oath that Regin was her chosen husband and she wished for no other. Surely Bloodaxe would do the decent thing and not demand Regin be declared outlaw for stealing away his only child.

Once the *jaarl* had declared in her favour, she would invite everyone to the wedding feast. Even now, the servants prepared the meat under Auda's expert direction. And it would be a celebration of the joining of two families, not a lament for Regin's death.

'I'd wondered if you'd show, Valkyrie.'

Sayrid missed a step. The trouble was that she had momentarily forgotten about *him* and the probability of his being at the Assembly. And now the man who had recently featured in her dreams leant against the side of the building. Why was he not sitting quietly next to Ingvar Bloodaxe or, better still, departing from these shores in search of another bride?

'Hrolf Eymundsson.' She met his dark blue gaze without flinching. 'Little point in arriving early and wasting my time.'

'Sayrid Avildottar.' He inclined his head so that his light brown hair flowed down his face, hiding his eyes. 'Valkyrie suits you better. After all, you are the shield maiden who controls the magically secured harbour. How many raiders have lost their ships trying?'

'Three came to grief after my father's death,

but it was more poor seamanship on their part than magic on mine.'

'That is not what the gossips say.'

Her heart gave a little flutter, but then it sank. She knew what the gossips said about her and her lifestyle. 'I'm flesh and blood, not one of Odin's handmaidens. A series of blockades guard the harbour.'

'Yet you swim. I hear rumours of your skill with the sword as well. Bloodaxe curses your name and fabled prowess on a daily basis.'

The rumours normally never bothered her, but a small part of her wished that he had remarked on her skills as a trader or navigator. She shook her head. Next she'd be hoping he found her attractive. Her limitations in the dainty and feminine part of life were as legendary as her skill with the sword.

'I was never very good with the needle. Far too big and clumsy. My stepmother used to despair,' she said, forcing her neck muscles to relax. If Hrolf thought he was going to humiliate her, he had another think coming. She'd long ago left behind the stringy girl who hid in the shadows praying that no one would notice her. She courted notoriety as it kept her ships and men safe. 'The sword suits me better.'

He pushed off the wall, causing the dark blue velvet cloak he wore to swirl about his narrow hips. On his arms, there were at least three heavy gold arm rings. Everything about him proclaimed that he was indeed as successful as the gossips implied.

'Was that what the other night was about, adding to your legend?'

'Preserving my family's honour.' She paused. 'Perhaps a foreign concept to a sea king, but it counts for much in Svear.'

His eyes filled with ice. 'Why did you kidnap Bloodaxe's daughter?'

'Harsh, when the woman went freely.'

'People whisper that with one wave of your hand, the locks fell open and you used the full moon to cast a spell on her, turning her into a swan so she could escape undetected.'

'If I'd done half the things claimed of me, I doubt I'd be standing before you. I'd be flying through the air to Constantinople on a pair of wings, as Kettil consistently refuses me a large enough ship to make that voyage,' she said crisply, giving him the stare that normally managed to send men running for cover.

'Why did you do it?' he asked in a low voice. 'The truth, because any games you choose to play, I will win. I make you that promise.'

Her mouth went dry and she bit back the words asking him what sort of games he had in mind. Instead she settled her features into a scowl. 'My brother and his chosen bride deserved to be together.'

'Any particular reason?'

She jerked her head towards where Blodvin and Regin stood waiting to hear their fate. 'They make a handsome couple.'

'Your brother should have challenged for the right. What good is a man if he cannot protect his wife and children?'

'Blodvin made her own choice.' Sayrid ignored his remark. 'No man cheats my family.'

Hrolf's eyes became deadly. 'Strong words. How did precisely Ingvar the Bloodaxe cheat?'

'When a bride price is agreed and paid, one expects the bride to remain available as long as she is willing.'

'Payments can be returned.'

Sayrid gave a soft cough. 'Next time ask

around. Better still, ask the woman if she wants to be married to you.'

He slammed his fist against his open palm. 'Bloodaxe swore there was no impediment.'

She rolled her eyes. It amazed her that a warrior such as Hrolf Sea-Rider would be inclined to believe Ingvar Flokison. But he'd been away in the East for a long time and perhaps had not thought to listen to gossip.

'A man who constantly delivers light sacks of wool should always have his word tested.' She poured scorn into her voice. 'Didn't you think to listen to the rumours and gossip before entering into negotiations? And you, a sea king with a reputation for quick thinking.'

A dimple flashed in the corner of his mouth. 'Women's talk around the distaff and weaving loom?'

'Men gossip far more than women. They just like to think they don't.'

'Truly?'

Sayrid ground her teeth. Hrolf was precisely like any other Northman—women were there to provide food, drink and pleasure only. She clenched her fists and regained control of her temper. 'Listening and heeding dockside chatter saved my ship on my first voyage. We went a different way home and avoided the sea raiders.'

He instantly sobered. 'What else did you learn, Valkyrie?'

Even now the hardship of that first voyage rolled over her—the storms at sea, the lodestone being washed overboard and the men who had tried to cheat her simply because she was a woman. And the others who gawped at her height.

'Things far too countless to mention.' She lifted her chin and adopted her no-nonsense voice. 'I wish you good day, Hrolf Eymundsson. My family needs me to make this right.'

'You care for your family more than your life.'

Sayrid shrugged. 'You'll find another bride, particularly as I've arranged for a feast after the Assembly to celebrate the marriage. I can suggest a name or two—women who are not spoken for and whose kinsmen are honest. I wouldn't want you to make the same mistake twice. Feuds ruin families.'

His piercing blue gaze locked on her mouth. 'I make my own choices. Without interference.'

Her stomach flipped over. Nearly kissing him the other night had been a mistake. She should have gone for another approach like stamping on his foot. 'I had only meant to be helpful.'

'I look forward to speaking more after the Storting…if you intend on being *helpful.*'

Sayrid frowned. What sort of game was he playing? Men didn't flirt with her. Perhaps he did really want introductions. Her heart panged slightly.

She made a breezy gesture. 'We've no quarrel, you and I.'

His hand descended onto her shoulder. The touch seared through her wool tunic, making her insides do a giddy loop. 'I'm glad to hear it.'

She moved away from him and sought to dampen down the bubbly feeling. This warrior was the same as the rest of them, worse even. Her father's long-ago words about how she had little to recommend herself even to a desperate man echoed in her brain. 'May you find the bride you truly desire, Sea-Rider. I wish you a long life and prosperity.'

'And you, Shield Maiden.'

The large hall teemed with people. After so many years being in the East, Hrolf was pleased to be amongst his own people again. He'd done

the right thing to come here and strengthen his
alliance with Jaarl Kettil. This was the sort of
place where a man could put down roots and
where his daughter could be brought up safely.

'Where did you get to?' Bragi, Hrolf's best
friend and helmsman, asked in an undertone.
'Jaarl Kettil remarked on your absence. I thought
we were here so you can identify the man who
stole your bride as Ingvar the Bloodaxe requested.
We want this resolved.'

Hrolf made a temple with his fingers. Sayrid was correct. Unfortunately. He'd forgotten
his father's story about Bloodaxe and his failure
to provide promised weapons on the battlefield
until Sayrid mentioned the light wool sacks. And
Bloodaxe's daughter was very obviously pregnant. There was much more to this than he'd first
considered. What was really going on? 'I'm making sure that I understand the truth before I decide which cause to support. A man's life is at
stake.'

'Who is that?' Bragi asked as Sayrid marched
to the front. Her cloak swung slightly, revealing
a few curves, if one bothered to look. 'Can anyone introduce me? Pray to the gods she is single.'

Hrolf frowned. Bragi would barely come up to Sayrid's shoulder.

'Sayrid Avildottar, shield maiden and in charge of the largest estate in the area after mine.' Kettil spoke before Hrolf had a chance to answer.

'Then she is single.'

'Her father declared that she will marry no man unless he first defeats her in combat.' The *jaarl* smiled slightly. 'It suits my purpose to have her sword under my command, but she grows bold and makes demands. She wants to lead a *felag* to Byzantium. Imagine.'

'Thor's beard, she is tall,' Bragi answered and added a slightly crude remark about the shape of her legs.

Hrolf fought against the urge to pummel his friend to the ground. It made no sense why he should feel protective of Sayrid. He barely knew the woman. For him, women were objects of beauty to be enjoyed while on shore. His uncle had taught him that lesson after his father's death. The way to prosperity was never to allow a woman to interfere with the important business of making a fortune.

'Only a brave or extremely foolish man makes remarks like that in her hearing.' Kettil moved his finger in a slitting motion across his throat. 'She takes offence easily. Her first voyage saw her defend her honour more than once.'

Bragi blanched. 'I will remember that.'

'Have many tried to win her hand?' Hrolf asked. 'Or was it only old men and beardless boys who tried?'

'What, and face the ignominy of losing to a woman?' Kettil shook his head. 'If all my warriors were like her, I would be king of Svear and Götaland, instead of a *jaarl* in a backwater.'

'There is good...but I'm exceptional.' Hrolf permitted his lips to turn up. Sayrid the Proud was about to learn an important lesson.

The flock of butterflies that had settled in Sayrid's stomach had turned into a herd of rampaging reindeer now that the Storting had started. Ingvar the Bloodaxe and his wife certainly looked the part of distraught parents. She risked a glance at where Hrolf Eymundsson sat with an impassive face.

'Regin Avilson stole my daughter from me,' Bloodaxe began with a distinct whine in his voice. 'He took her from my farm without my permission. He had no right to set foot on my property. He should be declared an outlaw and my daughter returned. Hrolf Eymundsson was there. He will confirm that Regin Avilson forced my daughter to leave against her will.'

'Objection!' Sayrid cried. 'Regin Avilson never set foot on Ingvar Flokison the Bloodaxe's property. How could he have stolen her?'

'If he didn't, who did?' Bloodaxe asked. 'Who else set my daughter free from a locked barn?'

'Why was your daughter locked up?'

'I asked the question first! Who released my daughter from my barn? Who undid the lock?'

'I did,' Sayrid answered in a firm voice and stepped out in the centre of the room. All eyes turned towards her. She stood taller with her shoulders back, never allowing her gaze to falter. 'I wanted to see if there was any truth to the rumour that Ingvar Flokison had decided against honouring our agreement of last spring. Going towards the farmhouse, I heard a cry for help. I unbarred the door. Blodvin Ingvardottar then ran out of the barn and down to the river. What happened after that, I couldn't say, but she found her way to my farm and my brother, demanding sanctuary!'

'Did anyone see you?' the *jaarl* asked, giving her a hard stare. 'Can anyone verify this?'

'Hrolf Eymundsson did. We spoke briefly.' Sayrid focused her gaze on Hrolf. 'He can confirm my story. And once Blodvin was safe, I sent word to you. I've not attempted to hide anyone or anything.'

'Time to hear from the independent witness,' the *jaarl* declared. 'What happened on that night, Hrolf Eymundsson? Give your impartial account.'

There was a sudden intake of breath and everyone turned towards Hrolf. His dark blue velvet cloak shimmered with self-importance. The torchlight caught the gold of his arm rings. Everything about him proclaimed that here was a man who was accustomed to power. Sayrid concentrated on his face and willed him to tell the truth.

'I encountered Sayrid Avildottar,' he said, inclining his head. 'There was a woman with her who ran off, but it was dark and I could not see her face. Later Sayrid went to the river and I lost her. These are the only people I encountered before Ingvar Bloodaxe arrived. I swear this on my sacred honour.'

Bloodaxe started bleating and whining about

how it had to have been Regin, but the *jaarl*'s face grew ever more stern. Sayrid's shoulders relaxed. Hrolf had told the truth. Regin was safe. And Bloodaxe would not start a feud with her.

'If Regin Avilson did not capture your daughter and she ran away of her own accord, you're not entitled to a fine,' the *jaarl* pronounced. 'Who among you believes that Blodvin Ingvardottar ran away of her own accord?'

Everyone except for Bloodaxe and his closest companions raised their hand.

'Your request for compensation is denied, Bloodaxe.'

Bloodaxe stroked his chin. 'As my daughter has run away, she is dead to me. I shouldn't have to provide a dowry for her.'

'She has married Regin Avilson. There was a prior agreement that they would wed and the bride price was paid,' Sayrid argued. 'The dowry includes all of the next bay.'

'Why would anyone pay a dowry for a dead woman?' Bloodaxe said as his wife sniffled noisily next to him. 'My daughter ceased to exist the instant she decided to run. And her maid has been dealt with.'

Sayrid clenched her fists and concentrated

on breathing steadily. Silently she promised to have the maid found and brought to her hall. She longed to draw her sword and start the feud for real, but if she did, she'd be made into an outlaw and all her lands would be forfeit. Some day she'd make him pay for the insult. 'If that is the way you wish it. I would ask that Ingvar Bloodaxe pays me passage for the wool sacks my ships carried this summer as part of the bride price. Who would pay a bride price for a dead woman?'

The *jaarl* nodded. 'A fair request. You will do this by the next Assembly, Ingvar. The matter is now closed and justice has been done.'

Bloodaxe muttered under his breath.

Sayrid raised her chin and carefully kept her face blank. Smug satisfaction would only rub salt into the wounds. Bloodaxe knew he'd lost. But the old miser would take his own sweet time in paying the amount owed. She'd be willing to wager gold on that.

Time to start making friends. Creating enemies benefited no one. She'd won. Regin was safe. She only hoped Blodvin was worth it.

'I would like to invite everyone to a feast to celebrate my brother's marriage to Blodvin the Fatherless.'

A loud cheering broke out in the hall, even amongst Bloodaxe's supporters. Sayrid carefully schooled her features. Her instinct was correct. Everyone loved a marriage feast.

'A word, Kettil, before the feasting begins.' Hrolf prevented the elderly *jaarl* from rising as the hall cleared.

'Your well-timed intervention prevented a bloody feud between two powerful families in this district.' The older man inclined his head. 'I salute your wisdom.'

'I told the truth.' Hrolf gave Kettil a hard look. 'Something you should have done when I first enquired about Bloodaxe's daughter. You encouraged me in the match when the woman was clearly besotted with another.'

'Until a woman is married...' Kettil waved a vague hand. 'It can be, Sea-Rider, that maintaining peace is far harder than simply leading a *felag*. I was aware of the complications of the match, but not the depth of feeling between the pair. Young Regin is far from the sort of warrior I'd have chosen for my daughter if I had been blessed with a child instead of being cursed to love barren women.'

'Is that so?'

'After her father's death, Sayrid promised he would become a good warrior, but I see little evidence of it.'

'My problem remains. I desire a wife and land with a bay to keep my ships.'

'You will have to seek her elsewhere.'

'And the Shield Maiden? What is her dowry? Avil Ironfist was a considerable landholder.'

Kettil gave a short laugh. 'Seek elsewhere. The maiden does not require a husband. She assures me of this every time she returns from one of her voyages. And she'd make a terrible wife. I doubt she knows one end of a loom from the other.'

'How hard can it be to defeat a woman?' Bragi asked. 'Who has she fought in defence of her property? A few old men and beardless boys? If you won't challenge for that prize, old friend, I will take the honour.'

'Leave it, Bragi. Some things make poor jests.'

'Do not think you are the first to covet Ironfist's lands. She holds them well.' Kettil raised a brow. 'Sayrid is perhaps the best fighter I've seen. She's quick and has a brain which is more than can be said for many warriors.'

Hrolf ground his teeth. The *jaarl* appeared to

think that he was a green boy just returned from his first voyage, not a grown man who had spent years honing his battle skills. 'Which goes to show that they are worth fighting for.'

Kettil clapped him on the back. 'A solution will present itself. For now I will enjoy the time we spend together before you go in search of the land you seek. In time our mutual enemy Lavrans will be defeated but, I think, far from these shores.'

Hrolf schooled his features. Kettil had always intended this outcome. But he was disinclined to walk away from a challenge, particularly when the prize was attractive as Sayrid Avildottar.

Sayrid breathed in the still evening air. She twisted first one way, then the other, attempting to loosen the tight muscles in her back. The sounds of the feast echoed out on to the quiet street. The *skald* started the first verse of the saga of 'The Sword Tryfling and the Shield Maiden'. It was apparently one of Blodvin's favourites, but Sayrid hated everything about it. Shield maidens never found true love except in stories.

It had been a spectacular feast, despite Bloodaxe's and his wife's non-attendance. Although there had been the usual niggles of people objecting to the seating arrangements and several questioning the quality of the ale, by and large the meal had passed without incident. She wished that the feeling of foreboding would go and that she could relax.

A movement in the shadows made her start. She crouched, instinctively reaching for her knife. 'Who skulks in the shadows? Show yourself!'

'I do my best thinking in the shadows.' Hrolf stepped forward. The torchlight picked out the planes in his face and the curve of his bottom lip. 'You should be in there, toasting the happy couple, listening to the *skalds* and basking in the glory. Your impassioned plea for the lovers carried the day, Sayrid.'

Now was not the time to explain that such gatherings always unnerved her. Everyone always seemed to stare at just the time she knocked over the ale or laughed too loudly or accidentally banged her fist on the table. 'Regin and Blodvin are fully capable of enjoying it without me.'

'And what do you plan to do next?'

'Fish, and try to convince Kettil to allow me to go east and down the rivers to Constantinople, instead of returning to Birka. You have been there, haven't you?'

His face hardened in the dim light. 'A hard journey. Many I've travelled with fell on distant shores.'

'We need to go to the markets ourselves, instead of paying a premium for other traders to go. The Viken give an even worse return than the Götalanders.'

'And Kettil disagrees?'

'He refuses to fund me.' She winced the instant the words emerged from her throat. It sounded like she was begging to be part of his next *felag*. She straightened her shoulders. 'But one day, I will go as the leader of my own *felag*. I will get enough gold for the proper-sized ship.'

'You are very determined.' His soft voice curled about her insides. Sayrid concentrated on breathing. Hrolf was used to women falling at his feet.

'Have you seen any pretty women to assist in your quest for a wife?' she asked to distract her thoughts from the shadowy hollow in his throat.

He gave a rich laugh and took a step closer. 'What is it about feasts that brings out the matchmaker in every woman?'

Sayrid carefully shrugged. 'You must be seeking a wife or you would not have offered for Blodvin.'

'I can find my own wife,' he said without moving away. 'My requirements are very exacting.'

His gaze honed in on her mouth as sure as an arrow shot from a hunter's bow. The very air between them crackled with energy. She knew all she had to do was to lean forward and she'd see if his lips moving over hers matched her dreams.

A loud laugh punctuated the air and broke the spell. Sayrid rapidly stepped back. She hoped the shadows hid the burn in her cheek. If she'd given in to her impulse and kissed him, he would have recoiled in horror or, worse, laughed at her folly. How could she ever forget for a heartbeat what she was and what people thought of her?

'Then I wish you every luck with that. I…that is we…should return to the feast. The *skald* has finished with the Tryfling saga.'

'Together? Aren't you afraid people will talk?' His voice rippled over her skin, doing strange things to her insides.

'About us?' She made her voice drip with scorn. 'Please give me some credit for knowing my reputation. Stealing kisses in the dark with a sea king would be dismissed as far too fantastical to be credited.'

'Some people are blind.' He put a firm hand on her back. 'After you, Shield Maiden.'

The noise fell to a deafening silence as everyone turned to look at them. Several people's mouths fell open and three women started whispering, putting their heads together and pointing.

One of the more drunken guests called out in jest that Hrolf the Sea-Rider was seeking to bypass the required challenge for her hand. Someone else took up the cry and the word 'challenge' reverberated from the rafters.

Sayrid's cheeks burnt fire. She bared her teeth in a fierce scowl designed to silence the crowd.

When the jesters fell silent, she started towards her place. However Hrolf grabbed her elbow, pinning her to his side.

'Keep still,' he commanded.

'Why? These people are best ignored. I am going to walk back to my seat and forget this ever happened. There will be no challenge.'

Hrolf held up his palm, calling for silence. The room became a sea of expectant faces. 'There is something I wish to declare.'

Sayrid frowned. Hrolf couldn't take these jibes seriously. A great hollow opened in the pit of her stomach. She knew what was coming next—

humiliation as he made it clear that he had no interest in her. She twisted her elbow.

'Let me return to my seat in peace.'

His face became hardened planes. 'You might wish to stay.'

'Doubtful. You have had your fun, now let me go.' She took another step towards the high table.

'Have it your way, but I did warn you.'

'Go on, Hrolf the Bold. What does a sea king want with this feast?' Kettil called from the high table where he sat with his wife. 'What does he want from the Shield Maiden?'

Hrolf reached out and captured her wrist, pulling her towards him. She missed her step and went tumbling against his hard body. 'I wish to take up Avil the Ironfist's challenge and fight for the hand of his daughter.'

Sayrid stared at the large Northman in disbelief. She had to have heard wrong. He wanted to marry her? He desired her? What new form of torture was this?

'Now I know you have had too much ale!' she gasped out, pulling away from him.

'There is only one way to win the hand of fair Sayrid,' someone called out. 'Fight her.'

He inclined his head, but the traces of an ironic

smile touched his lips. 'Any challenge of this nature needs to be issued in front of everyone. I'd no wish to disrupt proceedings earlier, but I've waited long enough. I will win the prize your father promised all those years ago.'

A hard knot formed in the base of her stomach. Her father's words had been designed to teach her the ultimate lesson in humiliation. Was that what Hrolf desired also? She longed to see his arrogant face humbled.

'Why? Because your chosen bride preferred another?' she asked in a furious undertone. 'Go ahead. Have your boorish joke, laugh about it with your friends and comrades, but I don't fight with ale-soaked warriors. There is no sport in it.'

'I assure you I'm quite sober.' He tapped his fingers together. 'But you do bring up a good point. You were responsible for me losing a bride. I require retribution. Will you fight and prove yourself worthy of the title or no?'

'You think you can defeat me?'

'There is one way to find out.' His stone-cold eyes met hers. 'Fight me.'

Sayrid stared at him in disbelief. This could not be happening to her. No man had wanted her. Ever. How many times had her father told her that? How many times had she heard the whispers which followed when she entered a new market town?

'How do you answer, Sayrid Avildottar? The entire hall waits,' the *jaarl* said. 'A warrior such as Hrolf Eymundsson deserves a proper response when he issues a challenge.'

Sayrid swallowed hard. She hated that her pulse raced at the thought that Hrolf might want her. She rejected the idea instantly as absurd. Standing there, all arrogant in his sea-king finery, he was confident of victory and clearly planned to reject her as a wife after she'd lost. He'd then lay claim to the lands as the better warrior.

She jutted her jaw out. She knew how to fight and how to win. She could defeat any man, but she also knew about choosing her battles.

'And your answer, Shield Maiden?' Kettil enquired in a silken tone.

She took a deep breath. 'My father died four years ago. That particular challenge has no relevance under our laws and customs.'

The entire hall erupted in pandemonium as people took sides. Kettil rapped his staff on the floor. 'The maiden is within her rights. A dead man's challenge does not have to be honoured.'

'Then I make another.' Hrolf's eyes sharpened to daggers. 'Sayrid Avildottar, I challenge for all the land you command against my ships and gold.'

Sayrid blinked. 'What are you saying?'

'If I win, your lands become mine. If you win, I go into your service and my entire fortune will be at your disposal for one year.'

The entire feast went silent. No one moved. Even the servants stayed still like frozen statues.

Sayrid clutched her hands together. Hrolf was offering her gold and ships. Enough to go to Byzantium? This was her opportunity if she was brave enough to take it. But…there had to be a catch. 'No man wagers such a thing. Your entire fortune on one contest? Are you mad?'

'Are you afraid to lose?' Hrolf stood there, muscles taut, his face seemingly carved from ice. 'Are you willing to admit I am the better warrior?'

Sayrid examined the floor. If she refused, Kettil would have grounds never to entrust her with a *felag*. He might even take the lands away on the pretext that Regin would never be as good a warrior as Hrolf. She could almost hear Kettil forming the words now.

How could she make sure her family was safe then? And if she accepted? Her heart beat a little faster. She could wipe the floor with him. Her earlier hesitation had been nerves.

'Give me a moment. I need to consider.'

'The offer is only good for tonight, Shield Maiden.' Hrolf gave an arrogant laugh. 'Time to test your powers against a real warrior, or are you afraid of the truth?'

'The truth?'

'You won't fight because you know you will lose.' He lowered his voice. 'Because you have been living on a misplaced reputation and are past your best.'

She raised her head and met his stare head-on. 'I've never run from a fight in my life. I accept with pleasure and I look forward to putting your ships to good use.'

His proffered hand was well shaped with long fingers and well-groomed nails, but it was also the muscular hand of a warrior. Sayrid gulped and returned his clasp with all her strength. She could defeat him, just as she had defeated every other man who tried. This time, she hoped that he wouldn't hate her for it.

'It is settled, then. We meet after dawn has broken.'

She started. 'Why not now?'

'I'd hardly wish to be accused of taking advantage of you...in the dark.'

Her face burnt as laughter rang out from the crowd. She balled her fists. That warrior would be laughing on the other side of his face when she was through with him.

'In the morning, after the crow crows five times will be the proper time for the match,' Kettil declared. 'Sayrid has choice of weapons.'

'I choose the sword and shield,' Sayrid said.

Hrolf inclined his head. 'The sword it shall be. I should warn you, Sayrid, I've never lost a bout which counted. Should you wish to withdraw before the match, we can agree terms.'

'Why would I want to withdraw? I have yet to lose a match myself,' Sayrid retorted, giving him a furious glare. She was fighting for her home and her family, he was only fighting for glory.

Sayrid sank down on a bench while pandemonium raged around her and everyone began laying bets on who would win. The enormity of what she had done sunk in. She was going to fight a sea king, someone who had carved his legend with his sword, not some youthful farmer who had never been in battle or a drunken warrior well past his prime.

And she had to win or else she'd lose everything.

Chapter Three

The full moon lit the space where her bout against Hrolf would be held in the morning with a ghostly silver hue. Sayrid shivered slightly and tried to concentrate on how she wanted the bout to go. She paced the area, imagining what her first few moves would be. Everything would hinge on those first crucial blows. If she could get Hrolf on the back foot from the beginning, she would stand a very good chance of winning.

'Sayrid! Here I find you!' Her sister's voice rang out from the shadows.

'Sleep evaded me,' Sayrid admitted, turning towards where Auda stood. 'It seemed best to come out here and practise before the crowds started gathering.'

'Blodvin is crying her eyes out, convinced we are all doomed as you are bound to lose.' Auda pressed her hands to her eyes. 'No one can sleep when Blodvin weeps.'

'What would she have me do? Back down? Give our land away? Lose my reputation?' Sayrid gritted her teeth. 'She should have more faith. We have everything to gain. Finally I will have the ships and men to make our fortune. Hrolf is overly proud. He will make the first mistake.'

'Regin told her that. He wanted to wager, but Blodvin clawed at his face and told him not to be more a fool than usual.'

'Hopefully they are not regretting their match after all the trouble it has caused.' She shed her cloak and grabbed her favourite sword, the one that had belonged to her father, and a light shield.

'Did you have to accept? Don't we have enough gold? Enough honour? We get by, Sayrid.'

'There is a world out there, waiting to be explored. Hrolf's defeat will mean I can realize my dreams.' Sayrid tried to stretch a sudden kink out of her back, the one that always came before she battled. Didn't Auda understand what would have happened if she had refused? How much they would have lost? 'And why should I give him anything?'

'You could have tried to reach an agreement.'

Auda grabbed her arm. 'Found out what he really wanted. We have gold.'

Sayrid tried to banish the memory of how they had nearly kissed. It was fantasy and folly on her part. In the second challenge, he'd never mentioned marriage.

'If I hadn't accepted the challenge, I would have lost my reputation and any hope of retaining such valuable and strategic lands until Regin proves himself.' Sayrid shook her sister's hand off. 'I'm not going to lose everything I have sweated to build.'

'But…do you really think you can defeat a warrior with his reputation?'

'My own sister thinks I'll lose.'

Auda pulled her shawl tighter about her body. 'Someone has to be practical and both you and Regin are the dreamers in the family.'

'I make my dreams happen.'

Auda shook her head. 'You're fighting for your pride. You can't stand the thought of not being the Shield Maiden and being an ordinary woman again.'

'You talk a lot of nonsense, Auda. What shall I bring you from the East? Enough silk to make seven gowns?'

'I think you ought to have an alternative plan… just in case…'

Sayrid adjusted Auda's shawl. In moments like these, she found it hard to believe how quickly her half-sister had grown up. Auda was old enough for the truth. 'I'm going to win, Auda. I have to. If I'd refused, Kettil would never have trusted me with a ship again. And he would have stripped the lands from me. From us. Unlike men, I have to win and keep on winning. Luckily I find it easy to do.'

'Look after these for me, Bragi,' Hrolf said, handing his friend his arm rings as he finished his preparations for the bout with Sayrid. 'I don't want to get them damaged in the fight.'

Bragi accepted the rings, sliding them on his forearm. 'Can you accept a woman as an overlord for a year? I don't know if I could. You are worse than me when it comes to having only one use for a woman. Even with Anya, who bore your child, you barely had any time for her.'

'Where else but in my my bed should a woman I desire be?' Hrolf laughed. He followed his uncle's path and kept the two parts of his life separate. He had seen from his father what happened when a man hid behind a woman's skirts.

Sayrid was the key to gaining control of the headland, but he would also prove once and for all time that he was the best warrior to hold it.

He was going to win. Sayrid might enjoy a certain reputation, but it had not been forged in battle. She had not fought for everything as he had.

'That does not answer my question.'

'I hold your pledge. You follow me, not the other way around.' Hrolf gave Bragi a hard look. His second-in-command was doubting his ability? Kettil might think Sayrid Avildottar could fight, but had she ever come up against real opposition? 'Do you wish to become an oath breaker because of something which might not happen? You are worse than an old woman.'

'But do you think you will win?'

Hrolf did a few squats to loosen his legs up. 'My sword arm forged my reputation. Every man or woman has a weakness. The question is how to exploit it.' He thought about how Sayrid had trembled when she stood next to him. She felt the attraction as well. She would end up in his bed. By Freya's cats, she probably hated the front of toughness she had to put up. She needed a real warrior in her life. 'And I know her weakness. She will concede with me barely breaking a sweat.'

Bragi clapped him on the back. 'And you haven't forgotten the land you owe me.'

'I pay my debts, Bragi. Always.' Hrolf did several practice swipes with his sword. It would be easy to tame this shield maiden. Kettil had cleverly talked up her prowess in order to keep rivals from claiming the bay. But he looked forward to exposing the lie and gaining the woman.

'Where is this land of hers that you covet?'

'The headland which first attracted me here and the land round to the next bay.' Hrolf clenched his fist as he considered his rival sea king, Lavrans, and the trouble he had caused over the years. The alliance with Kettil would bring him from his hiding place to attack. 'It will be enough to force Lavrans to act if he truly intends to cause mischief. I agree with Kettil. Someone here is alerting Lavrans to the movements of the ships and until we discover his identity, we have little hope of stopping it except by stationing our ships where they can exercise control of the bay.'

'After you have dealt with Lavrans? What happens then? Will we be forced to make the trip east once again? You know how many men we lost on our last trip to Constantinople.'

'We will do well here, Bragi—no more Desolation Pass or Heartbreak Rapids for us. Time for Sayrid to learn there is more to being a warrior than a scowl, swagger and a gleaming sword.'

Bragi's face cleared. 'Ah, I see you are thinking with your head.'

Hrolf turned his unflinching gaze on his second-in-command. 'Since when do I think with any other part of me?'

The cleared area looked very different in the early-morning sunlight from the way it had last night—larger and more open with less chance to hide. Her stomach clenched. She'd forgotten how much she hated being the centre of attention.

Despite the hour, a great crowd thronged around the perimeter. It seemed as though the entire village plus a good portion of the countryside were here to watch her fight. Sayrid elbowed her way through to the empty arena. She ground her teeth. She'd deliberately arrived late to put pressure on Hrolf, only to find he was even later.

'Where is Hrolf Eymundsson?' She shaded her

eyes and surveyed the crowd. 'Perhaps the great sea king has thought better of his challenge?'

A hush fell over the crowd and they fell back, parting like waves on the shore.

Her breath stopped in her throat. Hrolf had not only shed his cloak. He had also shed his tunic. His muscular chest and broad shoulders gleamed in the early-morning sun.

'I wanted to make sure you knew what you might be getting,' he said.

Sayrid pressed her lips together. Arrogant in the extreme. 'You'll have to forgive me if I don't do the same.'

His eyes roamed over her figure. 'I look forward to having the pleasure of unwrapping you later.'

She deepened her scowl and banished the bubbly feeling to a far corner of her brain. 'That depends on the outcome of this bout.'

'That outcome is not in doubt.' A faint smile touched his lips. 'But if I should lose, I shall be at *your* service…one year. Think about that. I will be bound to do whatever service you require without question or hesitation for an entire year.'

Her face flamed like it was on fire. He was talking about their joining, not about who would win this contest. She concentrated on the ground and attempted to restore some measure of calm. She had never before had any trouble focusing on the match, but now she was intensely aware of the man. 'Why would you say that?'

'You made me a promise the other night. I intend to see it is fulfilled.'

'What promise?' She made the mistake of glancing at his face and was catapulted headlong into the fierceness of his gaze.

Her entire body tingled, but then she recalled his reputation with women and thought of the number of women he must have bedded. The man knew what he was doing.

Angrily, she made a swipe with her sword. 'Stop trying to twist things to your advantage.'

His smile widened.

'My mistake. Your body must have made the promise without informing your head.' He leant towards her and lowered his voice. 'We will be good together, Sayrid. Think about that as we fight.'

Sayrid glowered at him. 'I know your game, Hrolf, and choose not to play it. Think about that as we fight. I am indifferent to you.'

Her heart beat far too fast, giving lie to her

words. But he couldn't have guessed. Sayrid tightened her grip on her sword. He must never know of her attraction.

'You know nothing about me.' He gave a mock blow to his chest. 'I'll never break your heart, fair lady.'

'That's because my heart will never be yours to break. I intend on teaching you a lesson. Shall we get on with it?' She shrugged. 'It will be a shame to mark your skin, but then maybe the next time you will not treat a woman opponent with such contempt.'

He snapped his fingers and one of his men brought his shirt. 'The maiden has accused me of distracting her. And here I thought you and your unbreakable heart impervious to my charms!'

Sayrid saluted him with her sword. 'Your future ladies will thank me one day.'

'What makes you think I want any other woman?'

He returned the salute as the noise from the crowd grew louder. Sayrid took three breaths and focused on his sword. The first few clashes would be to assess his strength and identify his weakness. Warriors always had a weakness. Once she found his, she could exploit it. His arrogance would assist her, but she'd need something more to make him overreach. She could almost taste the power she'd command once she'd won.

Their swords clashed as he blocked her move and countered with a move that she easily blocked.

'You're not trying very hard.'

A wide smile split his face. 'I've *no* wish to mark your skin, Valkyrie.'

'That is my concern.'

'Mine as well. I need to look after my bed partner-to-be.'

Sayrid ground her teeth. She didn't know which was worse—talking about marring her skin as if that mattered or proclaiming it was a foregone conclusion that they'd share a bed whatever the outcome.

She redoubled her efforts to focus and the battle began in earnest. Sword meeting shield and sword meeting sword. Each time she tried something, he had a counter for it.

She had to admit that Hrolf was highly skilled, a far better opponent than she had faced before. His strength matched his agility. This was no drunken sot trying his luck or an ageing farmer, but a seasoned warrior.

Rivulets of sweat snaked down her face, nearly blinding her. With an impatient arm, she wiped them away. Surely he would make a mistake soon. Her light shield grew heavier and it took more effort to move it into place. But she forced her body to continue and to wait. Round and round the ring they went. One probing and then the other. Always searching for an opening, but not finding one. The cries of the crowd grew louder.

Despite her screaming back muscles she tried for a downward stroke. He blocked it with ease, but his eyes took on a triumphal gleam.

Sayrid swallowed hard. She summoned all her remaining energy. One more burst and she knew she'd break him.

He went for a deceptively simple move, but Sayrid was ready with the counter-attack and managed to land a blow on his arm. She pressed her advantage and forced him on the back foot. He stumbled and fell. His sword landed a few inches from him.

A wild exhilaration went through her. She had done it! He had made the first mistake. She was going to win. After this, no one would doubt her prowess. She'd be safe and her dreams would all come true. Her family would be provided for and she could stop waking up at night with worry clawing at her gut.

His lips turned up. 'Definitely a Valkyrie. The last move proved it. You do Odin proud.'

'Will you yield?' she asked, standing over him with her sword point towards his neck. 'You have lost your sword. I could drive my sword into your throat. Yield, Hrolf Sea-Rider, and I may spare your life.'

'Overconfidence will be your downfall, Valkyrie.'

His foot snaked out and caught her calf, sending her tumbling to the ground. Her cheek bumped against a rock and sent a pain ricocheting through her. The air went from her lungs with the unexpectedness of it. One instant she was on her feet and the next, staring up at the sky. Her shield slipped from her grasp.

He made a downward stroke which she raised her sword to block. To her horror, she mistimed the move and her sword arched through the air, landing quivering in the dirt several feet from her.

'Will you yield, Valkyrie?' he asked with his

sword a breath away from her neck. 'Will you concede to a man?'

Sayrid collapsed back against the ground, utterly spent. Above her the clouds skittered across the sky and all about her was silence from the stunned crowd.

'I can't rise without aid,' she whispered into the quiet.

Summoning the remaining bits of his energy, Hrolf reached down with his hand and clasped hers. He pulled her to standing. Sayrid, with rivulets of sweat running down her face and her hair plastered to her skull, looked every bit as exhausted as he felt. But she was his now.

'It is over,' he said. 'You've lost your sword. Would you lose your life as well?'

A solitary unheeded tear hovered in the corner of her eye. 'Yes, it is over.'

Hrolf glanced towards where Kettil stood, stony-faced. He gave a slight nod, acknowledging the outcome.

'Sayrid Avildottar conceded!' He raised their clasped hands. 'I claim victory. I claim Sayrid Avildottar and her lands.'

The entire throng hushed.

'What does the Shield Maiden say?' someone called out. 'Has she given way?'

'Go on,' he commanded. 'Say it so they can hear.'

'Hrolf is correct. He has won.' Sayrid's shoulders slumped as she bowed her head. 'I'll honour my oath. My lands will be his.'

'I claim everything, including your body!'

At his words, the crowd burst into loud laughter and cheers. Hrolf's shoulders relaxed, but he kept hold of Sayrid's wrist. Her expression of absolute horror intensified.

In all his years of fighting, he had never met a better opponent and he had begun to despair of winning, something he'd never experienced before.

Sayrid's instant of hesitation had happened just after he'd sent a prayer towards any god who might be listening. Obviously Freya, the goddess of love and marriage, had been following the proceedings because he suddenly had known what to do and his strength had returned. He would honour the goddess today—by claiming Sayrid as his bride.

'Marriage is not a death sentence,' he murmured, hating the bruised patch just under her eye. He had tried to be careful, but obviously there had been moments when his fighting instinct had taken over.

Silently he vowed that it would never happen again. He would ensure that his wife was properly looked after, not left to fend for herself in a hostile world. He would make it right. His wife should be dressed in furs and silks, not battling for her life.

'Set the date,' she growled, twisting slightly to free herself from his grasp.

Hrolf concentrated and clung on to his prize— half to keep her next to him and half because if he let go, he knew he'd collapse in a heap of spent muscle.

'When would you have this marriage of ours?' she ground out. 'A month? Two months? How long will you give me to prepare?'

A fury swept over him. Like most women, she delighted in treachery and deception. She might have escaped him the other night by diving into the river and swimming, but he knew what she was capable of now. And he wasn't minded to chase halfway around the world after her.

This marriage would take place now while he could bind the loyalty of those she commanded to him. She would learn her place in his household. He had no need of women warriors—what he required was a wife.

'The cooks had best get busy. Another feast is required.' He gave a triumphant smile which took in all the onlookers. 'The marriage takes place today!'

The crowd broke out in loud cheers.

All colour drained from her face. 'Today? Impossible. A wedding requires arrangements. The proper alignment of the stars, the reading of portents and your father's sword...'

He slowly lowered their arms before letting her go. She staggered back a step. 'Nothing is impossible to a determined man. And my determination has never been in doubt.'

'Why the speed?' She licked her lips and her eyes darted about the arena. She gave every impression of a cornered animal searching for the nearest bolthole.

'I would not put it past you to decide to go on a long voyage which you claim is vital for everyone in the village or, worse, disappear into the world, dressed as a man.' He forced his mouth to smile as he cupped her cheek.

Her entire being bristled with anger and she

turned her face away. 'Having just returned from a long voyage, I wanted some months at home.'

'These words are supposed to act as your guarantee?' He inclined his head. 'Forgive me if I require more.'

'Snaking out your foot to trip me was unworthy.' Her mouth turned mulish, but he could see the latent hint of passion in it.

'There was nothing in the rules, my lady, against tripping. I saw an opportunity and took it.'

'The only reason you challenged me was to prove a point. You are the better warrior than I am. Well, you've proved that. You can have the land you require.'

Hrolf watched her mouth. The exertion of the fight had turned it strawberry ripe and her tunic now clung to her body. His fingers itched to unwrap her. But he refused to give any woman power over him. He'd seen what gibbering wrecks men could become. When he discovered his father's frozen body on his mother's grave, Hrolf had vowed never to allow a woman to touch his heart, a sentiment that his uncle had encouraged.

'Why do you attempt to put words in my mouth?' he asked in a cold tone. 'I know what we bargained for. I always claim what is mine by right and I do it in my fashion.'

Her eyes became a blue flame and she pulled her shoulders back. 'My honour is without question. Do not suggest I would dishonour my oaths again.'

'Sayrid, I marry a woman, not a man. Find a dress.'

Sayrid stared at him uncomprehending. 'A dress?'

'You do own a dress...don't you?'

Sayrid released a breath and offered a prayer up to all goddesses in the Aesir and Vanir. At last, a way to postpone the evil day with dignity. Hrolf wanted to marry a properly dressed bride. His request made sense given the finery he wore. She could use it, buy time and find a solution to the mess. Somehow she'd discover what he truly wanted before she started believing that he wanted her. It wasn't over until the ceremony was done.

'My best dress is at home. What a pity. We will have to name another day when I can be attired in the sort of clothes fit for a sea king's bride.'

'Borrow one.' A glint showed in his eye as he

raked her form. 'Or come naked. But I marry a woman. Today.'

Renewed anger flooded through her. Why in the name of Freya did he want to marry her? And why did it have to be today?

'Every other woman is smaller than me by at least a full head.'

His smile became positively merciless. 'That is not my problem. You do as I command.'

She stood toe to toe with him. 'Or what?'

'Or I will have you and anyone who helps declared outlaw and all their lands forfeit as well as yours.' He bowed low. 'Your choice, Sayrid Avildottar. Time to decide. Do you actually care about your family and the people who work the land? Or do you just care about yourself?'

Chapter Four

'How could he do this? Wasn't it enough to win and take my land? Why does he have to humiliate me further?'

Sayrid stomped around the narrow hut where she had retired after Hrolf had delivered his ultimatum. Regin had attempted to console her, telling her to look for the positives but she had growled at him. She wanted to wallow, instead of being falsely cheerful or coming up with impossible plans of escape. Regin beat a hasty retreat.

'Come dressed as a woman or naked,' she said, swinging her arms back and forth. 'Marry today or forfeit everything you hold most dear in this life. He is a sea king through and through, completely full of treachery.'

'Can you blame him?' her sister asked with a laugh. 'You've escaped from tighter situations before. Or were they simply stories for after supper?'

'It wasn't an empty threat, Auda. Hrolf Eymundsson would have taken great pleasure in stripping all my clothing from me in front of everyone.'

'Then your clothing had better be disposed of, in case you get ideas,' Blodvin said.

'And what do you propose I wear? This?' Sayrid gestured to the apron dress she now wore. Blodvin's dress would have been too small on a normal-sized woman but on Sayrid it barely reached her calves.

'It is one of my favourites,' Blodvin protested.

'It is just as well Blodvin brought another dress in case her first choice clashed with the tapestry at the feast,' Auda said in placating tone.

'I can barely breathe, even with the bodice being let out. And yellow makes me look sallow. My stepmother always said that and it is the absolute truth.'

'Hold still, sister, while we fix your hair. You might not have a crown, but Blodvin found some flowers.' Auda held up a mixture of yellow and white daisies. 'They will go well in your hair.'

'Going bareheaded is as bad as going naked,'

Blodvin argued. 'Have some pride in your appearance.'

Sayrid clenched her fists and longed to hit something. Very hard.

Auda's eyes welled up. 'Please, be good and do this for me. I have longed to see my big sister as a bride. The wedding will be wonderful and Hrolf is a very lucky man to have won you as a bride. But people will think it odd if you fail to wear a crown. The flowers are the best I can do.'

Sayrid stared up at the ceiling. Refusing either of her siblings was impossible. She had to do this for the honour of their house. 'Oh, very well. I don't want you upset, but I warn you—the words "gigantic flower-topped beanpole" will not be far from people's lips.'

She crouched down and allowed the other two women to twine the flowers in her hair. They both exclaimed loudly how lovely she looked.

'Everyone will laugh at me.' Sayrid bit her lip. For once in her life she wanted to look normal, instead of being the person she was—overgrown with less grace than a cow on a bad day.

'No one will dare to laugh and you're only in a bad mood because you lost,' Auda remarked. 'Admit it. You expected to win. You expected to grind him into the dirt and he wriggled free at the final instant.'

Sayrid grasped her sister's hand. 'I tasted victory, Auda, but I lost focus for a single heartbeat and he took advantage of it.'

'Don't blame yourself. You always tell Regin to keep his focus until the end of the fight and he never does.'

'I feel…I feel terrible. I have let you and Regin down,' Sayrid admitted.

Auda squeezed her hand. 'You haven't let anyone down. Get that idea from your head immediately. You have done so much for us. More than we ever thought possible.'

Sayrid swallowed hard. Auda was taking this much better than she had expected. She could have been filled with great wailing and recriminations. They at least would have given her something to fight against.

'I won't be a shield maiden any more,' she whispered into the silence.

'I can't see why you wanted to be a warrior in the first place.' Blodvin gave a distinct sniff. 'All the blood and gore of the battlefield. How could anyone find it attractive? And sailing one of those ships? My stomach is quite unsettled thinking about it.'

'I, for one, am very proud of my sister's accomplishments,' Auda said. 'The marriage means I will be able to see you more often. I miss you dreadfully when you are away on your voyages, Say. The hall never feels right without you and your sword arm there to protect me. You will still do that?'

'Of course.' Sayrid pressed her lips together and held back the scream. Neither Auda nor Blodvin understood. She liked being a shield maiden. She enjoyed the tactics and the thrill of competing to get the best price for her goods. While battlefields were scary, they were also intensely exciting and she always felt alive on the sea, battling the wind and the currents.

She was no good at woman's work. She had found her place in the world: being a shield maiden. But with one slight hesitation, all that was gone. She didn't even have time to mourn her lost life. She had to be married by sundown or see everything she had worked and bled for destroyed. Somehow she was going to carve a bit of her old life back. She wasn't going to become like Blodvin, content with sewing and batting her eyelashes, she silently promised.

'I made mistakes today, but it's not finished,' she said finally. 'There will be a way around this problem. I simply need to discover what Hrolf Eymundsson truly wants, get it for him and he'll depart. Sea kings seldom remain in one place for long. Then we can go back to the way we were.'

'Any man would be proud to have such a beautiful bride,' Blodvin said, clapping, but the pucker between her eyebrows told a different story. 'Quite transformed. Honestly, Sayrid, you would have men breaking down your door long before now if you had worn dresses instead of... what you wore. You have far more curves than I thought.'

Sayrid gave her new sister-in-law one of her severest looks. 'Any man who breaks down my door will get the sort of reception he deserves— the point of my sword in his belly.'

Blodvin retreated a few steps. 'I was merely trying to be helpful. My mother always told me to find the good in any situation. But I will admit that I'm struggling here. Sayrid, you're just so... so obstinate. You don't want to listen to any of my compliments.'

'I will take you to the pond so you can see that Blodvin is telling the truth,' Auda said, grabbing Sayrid's elbow and restraining her from tearing off the flowers. 'If you wipe that scowl off, you will look pretty.'

Sayrid forced a smile. 'Better?'

Blodvin gave a delicate shudder. 'You should be grateful Hrolf Eymundsson has made it so you won't have to fight again. You just need to manage your household. You can do that, can't you?'

'The pond. Now.' Sayrid slowly clenched and unclenched her fist. One of the first things she would do when they returned home would be insist that Regin and his new wife move to a hall of their own.

Sayrid concentrated on keeping her head still as the flower crown threatened to slip off. The autumn sunshine warmed her back. Being outside made it easier to breathe, but she still struggled behind the pair who were busy gossiping.

'Slow down. My body aches and these flowers won't stay still,' Sayrid called out. 'I only hope Hrolf is suffering as much as I am.'

'No, you don't. You want him up to tonight's task.' Blodvin gave a little laugh which bordered on the dirty.

'I suspect he will be good in bed,' Auda added, with a speculative gleam in her eye. 'His torso was impossible to miss before the fight. He has huge shoulders and feet. You know what they say about feet...'

Blodvin giggled. 'It's true. Regin—'

'You're unmarried, Auda,' Sayrid said, using her I-expect-to-be-obeyed voice. When had her sister grown up? And she most definitely did not want to hear about her brother's anatomy from his wife. There were certain things which should remain...well...private.

'Do I need to explain what passes between a man and a woman in secret to my older sister?' Auda adopted an innocent face.

Sayrid's cheeks overheated. She knew precisely what went on. Or the theory at least. And the thought that Hrolf might do that to her made her insides do funny things. 'I can really do without this sort of conversation right now. I declare you two are worse than the men for tittle-tattle and pointless gossip.'

Auda ran back to her and gave her a quick hug. 'He is a man and you're a woman. You'll work it out.'

'I know very well what I am!' Sayrid attempted

to loosen her overly tight back muscles and knocked the crown sideways.

She made an annoyed noise and crouched down to look in the pond. Despite their now bedraggled appearance, the flowers did soften the harsh planes of her face and her eyes appeared larger.

There was an unfortunate bruise on her right cheek where she'd taken a blow, but little could be done about that. Sayrid touched it gingerly.

'I could put some paint on the bruise before we go to the ceremony,' Auda offered.

Sayrid shook her head. 'Hrolf is marrying me for the land and the loyalty of my people. Without it, he'd never have looked at me twice. I doubt he will even notice a little thing like that.'

'Try to make the marriage work, Sayrid. For all our sakes,' Auda said. 'He is not the sort of man I'd wish you to have as an enemy. They say he is more ruthless than Lavrans and you know what he did to the north of here.'

'I will try, but I can't make any promises,' Sayrid replied, carefully schooling her features as she gave her reflection once last glance. She had spent her early life hiding her emotions from her father and stepmother. No one would ever guess how scared she was, especially not Hrolf.

Auda and Blodvin exchanged glances as she fought against the urge to break down and cry for her lost life. She loved having the wind in her hair and pitting her wits against the sea. 'I can make sure that everyone is kept safe…I suppose. I'm afraid I don't trust your father, Blodvin. He accepted everything too readily.'

'Surely anything like that is a matter for Hrolf,' Blodvin said. 'An attack against your family would be a direct insult to him. Leave it to your new husband to sort out.'

'*I* have always looked after my family without help.'

Hrolf stood next to the priest and solemnly said his vows. He hadn't planned for this at the start of the day, but sailing with fortune's wind had always brought him good things.

Sayrid's dress showed that he'd been right to marry her. The shortness revealed a shapely calf and the bodice clung, revealing the hidden curves he had encountered the other night. The flowers in the crown had slipped to one side and were all wrong for her colouring. But he was touched that she had tried.

He dreaded to think what she must have gone

through for all those years—having to deny her sex and behave like a man. And it appeared that her younger brother had not taken on his role as head of the house, preferring instead to allow his sister to risk her life on the wild sea. It ceased now, Hrolf silently vowed. Sayrid would have the chance to be a woman.

At the priest's final words, he cupped her face. A bruise showed under her eye. He brushed it with his finger. She flinched.

'Does it hurt?'

She started to shake her head.

'The truth, Sayrid Avildottar. I want honesty between us. Always.'

Her tongue flicked out, wetting her lips and turning them strawberry red.

'I've endured worse,' she whispered finally.

'There should never again be any reason for you to suffer an injury in battle.'

Her blue eyes swam. 'But…all I know how to do is fight.'

'Learn how to be a woman.'

He gave into temptation and tasted her mouth before she could utter another word. Her lips trembled briefly under his, softened and parted. A sigh emerged from her throat.

Hrolf allowed his mouth one more heartbeat of pleasure and then lifted it. Her eyes were dilated and her lips full.

Ribald jests rang out. Instantly she stiffened and began to scrub her mouth. 'What was that for?'

'Your first lesson in being a woman—brides kiss their husbands after the ceremony. Tradition,' he replied smoothly, seeking to cover his body's intense reaction to her closeness.

'Lesson?' She froze in mid-scrub.

'I would hardly want anyone else trying *my* wife's mouth before me.'

Her cheeks glowed bright pink and her brow lowered. 'I doubt you will have any cause to be concerned. I've managed thus far without a teacher.'

He ran a hand down her back. She jumped like a startled animal. Silently he cursed whoever had made her like this and he was willing to wager that her family had something to do with it. But he'd never been one to shrink from a challenge. He wanted to unlock the passion he'd briefly glimpsed in her eyes the night they first met.

'But you have one now.' He captured her hand and raised it to his lips. 'You're my wife and will be afforded all the privileges that title brings, but I expect loyalty from you.'

His wife. Lessons? Privileges? Sayrid's entire body thrummed from his casual touch. Her mouth tingled from the earlier kiss. She dampened the feelings down. His words had another meaning.

'Loyalty must be earned.'

A flame flickered in his eyes. 'My sentiments entirely.'

Sayrid forced her shoulders back. She might be attracted to him, but he touched her like this only to make his public mark on her. If she forgot that, she was doomed. Both her father and stepmother had hammered the idea into her brain that no man could desire a woman like her. She hated that suddenly she wanted to believe differently. 'You wrong me if you think I don't know why you married me and it wasn't for any hidden charms. You wouldn't have looked twice at me if I hadn't held the land you coveted.'

His thumb traced a lazy pattern on her skin. 'When we first met, I had no idea that you owned land and I'd have kissed you then.'

She snatched her hand away. 'When we first met, you wanted to marry someone else.'

'I married you. And you possess land which I desire. Sometimes the gods smile on mortals like me.' The light in his eyes did strange things to her insides, pinning her to the ground, making her want to sway towards him and try his mouth again.

Standing there, staring at him for the rest of her life was an impossibility.

'Shall we go to the feast? Hopefully the *skald* will be on better form today. Maybe he will recite something other than the Tryfling saga,' she said, and tried to get her numb legs moving. 'I have had my fill of shield maidens and their exploits.'

He blinked and she wondered what he'd been thinking about. 'Yes, yes, of course. The *skald* will sing something different.'

'Thank you.'

'Far! Far! Is that your new wife? My new mother?' A young girl, about six years old, dashed forward and wrapped her arms about Hrolf's legs.

Sayrid stared at the girl in astonishment. Her new mother? There was something otherworldly in her beauty with honey-golden hair and dark eyes tipped up like a cat's. Something tightened in her gut. The girl had called Hrolf father and she was about the same age as Sayrid had been when her own father remarried.

Sayrid scowled. How many times had she promised her heart that she'd never marry a man with a child, particularly a little girl? She'd be useless as a mother of girls. What did she know about weaving, sewing and cooking? How many times had her stepmother told her the simple truth of her unnatural destiny? She had decided never to put it to the test, never to allow her stepmother a chance to proclaim that she had told her so.

Her greed for gold and ships had blinded her to the truth. She had never thought to question why Hrolf was desperate for marriage. It made so much sense. Blodvin with her honeyed manner would have seemed a natural choice for someone who needed a mother for their girl.

She plucked at the overly tight bodice of her apron dress and tried to concentrate on Hrolf instead of on the golden-haired child hugging his legs. Sayrid knew that she'd never have dared do that to her father at that age.

'We…we…ought to talk,' she began, wondering how to explain about her stepmother and why she never wanted to be one. 'Hrolf…I'm many things, but a mother to a little girl isn't one of them. Your daughter will require a very different sort of mother.'

The words came out as a hoarse whisper. However Hrolf gave no indication he'd heard. Instead he knelt down to get his head level with the girl's.

'Yes, Inga. Sayrid has married me and you are going to live in her home. It will be your home now. Forever and ever.'

'Truly? I have a mother again? And no more ships which make me sick to my stomach?' The little girl looked solemnly up at Hrolf. 'I hate it when the waves crash over the ship's side and my tummy pains me.'

'I know, sweetling.' Hrolf absently brushed the girl's hair. 'I did promise. This was your last big sea voyage.'

'And you always keep your promises.'

'That's right.' Hrolf's gaze caught Sayrid's. 'I always keep my promises. Sayrid is your new mother. Sayrid, my daughter Inga, who is six.'

Sayrid swallowed. Turning her back on the child was an impossibility, particularly when she sounded so hopeful about having a mother. She could remember being like that and it all going wrong when she spilt a beaker of wine on her new stepmother.

'I'm pleased to meet you, Inga Hrolfdottar.' Sayrid crouched down. 'I hope we can become friends.'

The little girl backed away, her eyes as wide as porridge bowls.

'What do you say, Inga?' Hrolf asked with underlying steel in his voice. 'How do you properly greet your new mother?'

'But she is an ugly giantess!' Inga held out pleading hands to her father. 'She can't be my new mother. She just can't be. She'll eat me up like in the stories my nurse tells. My new mother is supposed to be beautiful and be able to sew a fine seam, cook brilliantly and weave pretty patterns.'

'I'm not a giantess,' Sayrid said between clenched teeth. Inga's remark cut deeper than she'd have liked. She knew her limited charms and they weren't sewing linen, weaving and cooking. If Hrolf had to have a child, why couldn't the child have been a boy? She could have trained a boy.

'Your face is marked!' Inga's screams reverberated in Sayrid's ears. 'Giantesses always have that sort of mark. It is in all the stories!'

'Be quiet!' Hrolf gave her a little shake. 'Who

put you up to this? You know how to behave! Sayrid's face is bruised from the battle I won. I explained how I won my wife and our land.'

The little girl gave a hiccup as she hid her face in Hrolf's knee. 'I decided myself. Magda said it was a matter for me and the gods. Should I have decided differently?'

'You should decide to support me.' Hrolf knelt by his daughter. 'Now tell Sayrid Avildottar you're sorry.'

Inga shook her head.

'Where is your nurse?' Hrolf asked in an annoyed tone. 'Why were you allowed to run out on your own?'

'I 'scaped.' Inga pointed towards an elderly woman who was advancing at speed.

The woman came up and started loudly apologising as she caught Inga about the waist. Her words were heavily accented, but Sayrid understood that her knees were far from good and she found it hard to run.

Hrolf's face settled into imperious planes. 'I know what Inga is like. She is excited to meet her new mother properly, but this is unacceptable. Keep better control of her or else.'

'Just so.' The woman bobbed a curtsy. 'She longs for a mother.'

'Excited or not, she waits until after the festivities are concluded. Hopefully by then she'll have learnt some manners.'

Sayrid gulped hard. Excited was not the word she would have used. The poor girl looked petrified. And there was nothing she could do about her height. She hunched her shoulders.

The nurse flushed and said something unintelligible in a foreign language.

'Inga was very rude,' Hrolf said, drawing his brows together. 'I will have no more tales of giants eating children. And you are to speak my language now, Magda. We are in Svear, not Rus. Take her away now!'

Magda said something sharply to Inga and the child gave a reluctant nod.

Sayrid's instinct told her to bend down and speak to the girl in a reassuring tone, but Hrolf had given an order. Defying him in front of everyone would be a poor way to start the marriage.

The nurse led the protesting girl away.

'I'm sorry you witnessed that,' Hrolf said into the silence. 'Magda obviously put Inga up to it. She thinks I have been bewitched and no good will come of this union. She is a superstitious old woman.'

'Your daughter?' she asked, taking a step away from him and wrapping her arms about her waist. She wished she was wearing her trousers and tunic instead of this thin gown. Her entire being seemed to be made from ice. 'You never said you had a child.'

'Her mother claimed I was the father. I saw no good reason to doubt her word.' A muscle jumped in his jaw. 'I took the responsibility.'

Sayrid firmed her lips. Hrolf was taking care of the child out of duty. And he didn't fully believe the girl was his daughter. Despite everything, her heart panged for the little girl. She, too, knew what it was like to long for love from your father.

'And your daughter is one of the reasons you are in Svear.'

'I wish her to be brought up properly amongst my people.' He tilted his head to one side. 'Why else would I return here? It is no secret. Surely you must have asked about me.'

'Obviously not.'

He shrugged. 'You were the one who encouraged me to listen to gossip. I assumed you had found out everything there was to know about me.'

'Is the mother…?' Sayrid choked out.

'She died while I was away on my last voyage to Constantinople. Inga was left to run wild.' Hrolf stood up straighter. 'Magda knows what is expected of her if she wishes to continue as her nurse.'

Sayrid shivered in the light breeze. She had married a complete stranger because her desire for glory had outshone common sense. 'You should have said something earlier.'

'Does it make a difference? You lost. I won. What has my daughter done to you?'

Sayrid gathered the tattered remnants of pride about her. 'You never said anything about a child. I'm to be her stepmother. I wasn't prepared. I frightened her. She thinks me a giantess.'

'Inga has a vivid imagination and enjoys attention. But she has a loving heart.' He lightly grasped her elbow. The impersonal touch sent a flame coursing through her body. 'It is her nurse's doing. I've warned her about stories that keep Inga awake at night, but she delights in telling them. When I returned to the village after her mother's death, Inga thought I was a troll come to eat her up as I shouted so loudly.'

'Indeed.'

Sayrid firmed her mouth and silently vowed that she'd find a way to explain about her lack of womanly skills before things became too complicated. Panic seldom solved anything. 'You intend to leave your daughter with me when you depart? How soon are you planning to go east? I need to make plans.'

'Shall we greet the well-wishers?' Hrolf cupped her elbow and prised one of her arms away from her waist. 'A smile wins more friends than a scowl—something my mother used to say and it has proved true more times than I can count.'

'Save me from pithy wisdom.' She forced her mouth up into a smile. 'Is this better?'

'It will have to do.' His fingers tightened on her arm, sending a warm pulse throughout her body. To onlookers it had to appear that he was being the attentive bridegroom, but Sayrid knew he was just keeping her next to him. He thought she was going to run.

Sayrid moved as if she was in a waking dream, barely hearing anyone's words of congratulations as everyone crowded around her and Hrolf, blocking and confining her.

A violent shiver rocked her. And another one. Her entire being felt as if she had been encased in ice. The world started to go black at the edges. She churned her arms, trying to keep her balance.

'My lady is cold,' Hrolf said, lifting his brow. He gathered her hands between his, but she pulled away.

'Very.' Sayrid wrapped her arms about her middle and seized the excuse. 'The dress is far thinner than I'm used to. It will pass once we get to the hall. It is nothing really. I shall ignore it.'

'I'd be a poor excuse for a husband if I allowed that.' He undid his cloak and put it around her shoulders. 'I need to make sure my wife is well looked after. I take my responsibilities seriously.'

'Another lesson?'

'A demonstration.'

'You have such a way with words.' Sayrid glared at him and somehow the anger kept the blackness at bay. 'Is this how you treat your men? Like little children?'

'I want to know if you are unwell or injured.' Something glinted in his eyes. 'I say the same to all my men when they start serving under me. A *felag* is only as good as its weakest member.'

'And you consider our marriage a *felag*?'

He shrugged. 'It works for me.'

She pinched the bridge of her nose and tried to concentrate. The lingering warmth from his body sunk into her bones, clouding her mind. She knew she should be grateful, but Hrolf wanted everyone to see that she now belonged to him. It was nothing to do with her personal discomfort. All for show, like her father had been. In public her father and stepmother had pretended to be concerned, but in private, she rapidly learnt not to talk about her own discomfort and to never ask for help.

Change a habit of a lifetime? That was something she refused to do.

She forced her lips to turn up in the imitation of a smile. 'I will walk to the feast. Without assistance.'

He laughed.

She took a step and the ground seemed to wobble beneath her feet. Hrolf's face went in and out of focus.

'I need air.' She put her hands on her knees

and tried to gulp a breath. The tight bodice of the dress prevented her and the world started to go black at the edges. 'Help me.'

Chapter Five

'Sayrid? Can you breathe? Where are you hurt?'

At Sayrid's faint cry, Hrolf turned back towards her. In the space of a heartbeat, all colour drained from her face. She made a wild grab for support as her knees began to buckle.

Before she fully crumpled to the ground, Hrolf captured her about her middle and hoisted her on to his shoulder to general approval. Silently he kicked himself. He should have known she'd stubbornly refuse to admit any injury and would carry on regardless. She was like him in that way, but it stopped now.

'Next time tell me before you faint,' he murmured. 'I have you.'

The movement seemed to revive her. Hrolf breathed a sigh of relief.

'I walk on my own,' she said, striking his muscular back. One fist landed straight on a bruise, but Hrolf paid it little attention. 'There is no need for this pretence. I'm far too big to be carried like a normal bride.'

He shook his head at her stubbornness. The woman had practically fainted away and then insisted she was fine. She was his responsibility now and he refused to lose everything he'd won simply because Sayrid Avildottar didn't look after herself properly. He tightened his grip on her kicking legs and strode away from the hall where the feast was prepared.

She hit her fist against his back, harder this time. The pain ratcheted through him. 'You're going the wrong way!'

'You are my bride and you go where I go.' Hrolf drew his sword. 'And I will fight any man or woman who says differently.'

She stopped squirming. 'Where are we going?'

'I wish to enjoy my bride. Alone!' he thundered.

The crowd parted in front of him.

He carried her to the deserted street and carefully lowered her down. Her front slid along his. Her breasts touched his chest, making his flesh ache with desire. It was wrong. He knew she wasn't well and he still wanted her. He had never felt this way about a woman before.

'You can walk if you wish.' His voice rasped with banked passion.

'I do wish.'

Sayrid hated that she had enjoyed how her curves moulded to his hard muscles for that all-too-brief instant when he lowered her down. She stepped hurriedly back and made a show of straightening the pleats in the skirts so it concealed more of her legs.

'Why did you feel the need to carry me?' she asked, studying the ground with great intensity.

'You asked for help. I obliged. You may thank me properly later.'

She risked a glance upwards and saw something in his eyes which made her draw her breath in, but it vanished so quickly she couldn't be sure. Her mind kept remembering how his tongue had darted into her mouth during the kiss after the ceremony. Was that the sort of thanking he wanted? She curled her fists, tensing her body as she imagined how he'd laugh if she gave in to the impulse.

'That wasn't the help I meant...the crowd was far too close...I just needed air.'

'You fainted.' His face became full of uncompromising planes. 'Kettil will understand that my first duty is to my bride. I've no wish for her to drop dead on our wedding night.'

'You're overreacting.'

'How badly injured were you in our battle? The truth.'

Sayrid drew on her years of experience and jutted her jaw forward. Her touch-me-and-I-break-your-arm face, as Auda once called it. 'I'll live. Two years ago on the way to Birka, the mast broke in a storm and landed squarely on my shoulder. I kept going then and steered the boat to safety. I can certainly keep going now.'

He captured her chin, forcing her to look into his eyes. 'This is not about the safety of your men or anyone else but you. I will not have my bride keeping secrets about her health. I know how quickly people can die.'

'Bruises, nothing more.' She wrenched her chin away. Keeping secrets indeed! He was the one who hadn't informed her about his daughter. If she had known... Sayrid curled her fists. 'The crowd hemmed me in. And the gown is far too tight. But fainting was a mistake. I should have been stronger. I will do better next time.'

Sayrid concentrated on a spot above his right shoulder and carefully composed her face. How could she begin to explain the sheer terror which had washed over her when she encountered his daughter? How all the memories of her stepmother flooded back?

'Can we go to the feast? People will be disappointed if the bride and groom leave before the feast starts. They might whisper that it shows disrespect.' She forced her feet to move.

'Either I carry you over my shoulder again, which will aggravate the injury you inflicted on my back, or you walk to where I am staying.' He reached out and plucked a wilted flower from her hair. 'We aren't going to the feast because you look as exhausted as I feel.'

Looking at the flower, she knew how she must appear—not radiant, but bruised and battered, a parody of a bride. Her insides twisted. So much for hoping he might desire her. 'You have such a way with words.'

'And you, Valkyrie, have a tendency to want your own way. I know what you are like for disappearing.'

A flash of understanding went through her. He actually thought she had planned on vanishing during the feast! She gritted her teeth. As if she'd play a shabby trick like that. Too many people depended on her.

'Where are we going?'

'Kettil has loaned me a house to use for as long as I wish.'

'Am I to have more lessons in being a woman?'

A flame flickered in his eyes. 'Only if you require them. But not all lessons are painful.'

Sayrid pressed her lips together. Lessons were generally painful in her experience. 'I'll take your word for it.'

'Do.'

Sayrid tried to peer around Hrolf's bulk. All seemed quiet, but the back of her neck prickled, just like it always did before an attack. It was nonsense. Who would attack them?

Her breath stopped. She hadn't seen Regin since she ordered him out of the hut before the wedding.

'Even now, your attention wanders.' He put an arm about her waist and started to draw her close.

Sayrid tore her eyes away from the shadows as her heart started to beat double time. 'I was thinking of something…'

'We have company.' Hrolf adopted a wary pose. 'Friends of yours?'

A group of men had gathered in the street. Sayrid recognised her brother's outline. Sayrid's stomach plummeted. He'd been busy gathering men to rescue her, when she thought he'd been sulking because of her earlier sharpness. Why did her brother specialize in futile gestures? Particularly when she had everything under control.

'You left before the feast began, Hrolf Sea-Rider,' her brother said, stepping forward. 'And I spy the tracks of tears on my sister's cheeks.'

Sayrid furiously scrubbed her cheeks. She knew her brother used the ritual words, but even so!

'If there are any tears, they are tears of joy.' Hrolf used the ritual reply.

'We want to know that Sayrid goes willingly. She is not one to insult our *jaarl* in this fashion—leaving before a feast has begun,' one of the men shouted.

'What does Kettil say? Is he insulted?' Sayrid asked.

'He sends his regards to the winner of the bout.'

'No one held a sword to her back when she made her vows,' Hrolf answered, keeping one hand on her shoulder and preventing her from moving. Sayrid attempted to shrug him off, but his grip tightened. 'Wedding feasts are for the enjoyment of friends and relations, not for the couple! It is the wedding night they long for.'

One or two guffaws rang out from the crowd. The muscles in Sayrid's neck relaxed. No blood would be spilt. She would just have to survive the wedding night.

'You were arguing just now,' her brother protested, silencing the laughter and the mood instantly turned ugly. 'The sound of raised voices echoed around the harbour. You will hand my sister over to me. We can protect you, Sayrid, like you protected me all those years ago. I have a debt to repay. I am ready to be the warrior you proclaimed I could be.'

'I go willingly with Hrolf,' Sayrid shouted and stamped her foot heavily on the ground to punctuate the point. Her brother was taking idiocy to a new height. She wished he'd consulted her instead of acting. 'Allow us to pass, brother. You have done your duty as Svear custom requires.'

Regin motioned to his friends and they blocked the street. 'For your own good, Sayrid. You will thank me later.'

'We should all return to the feast,' one of her men said. 'And lift our horns of mead together.'

Sayrid glanced at Hrolf. Put in those terms, he had to refuse. Her brother had threatened him beyond the bounds of wedding custom. 'But I've no wish to return. Like Hrolf Sea-Rider, I wanted to leave...' Her cheeks burnt fire. There was no need for Regin to know about her fainting. He'd be even more mother hen–like.

'I, too, was eager for the night to begin,' she choked out, wishing the ground would open up and swallow her. 'I demanded to leave and start our private celebrations.'

'I suggest you heed your lady's request and treat her with respect,' Hrolf thundered. 'I for one wouldn't like to get on the wrong side of her.'

Regin stuck his chest out and his face took on a stubborn cast. 'Sayrid would never raise her sword against me. She is only saying these things because she doesn't want to see me injured in a fight.'

Sayrid winced, knowing what Regin said was true. She might bluster, but she could never attack Regin or for that matter the men who stood behind him. They had served her family for too long and too well.

The men beat their swords against their shields in agreement with Regin and shouted 'Sayrid! Sayrid!'

Regin circled his arms, encouraging them.

'The numbers may be on your side.' Hrolf stroked his chin. 'What about a contest between you and me? Here and now? Settle the matter once and for all. I fought your sister for the right to marry her. But I will fight you as well.'

Her brother's hand twitched over his sword.

'Think about Blodvin and your child, Regin,' she whispered, staring at him hard and speaking to him like she used to when he was a boy and their father had just asked him to do something impossible. 'Let me take care of it. In my way and in my fashion. Trust me.'

Sweat trickled down her back and each heartbeat took longer. Silently she willed Regin to see sense and leave his sword in its hilt.

'You think I'm a useless warrior, Sayrid. Is that it? Deep down, you believe the same as our father?' Regin drew out his sword and swayed. The stench of sour ale wafted over Sayrid. 'You will see, Sayrid, I can fight. Your little brother is better than you think. I challenge you, Hrolf Eymundsson!'

'Regin! Respect my wishes! It is my wedding day.' Sayrid turned towards her new husband. Hrolf stood completely still, but his stance remained one of a warrior about to go into battle. 'My brother reeks of drink. Where is the glory in fighting a drunkard?'

A muscle jumped in Hrolf's jaw. 'He is old enough to know when it is appropriate to issue such a challenge.'

'It would be an ill omen to start the marriage with a feud.' She concentrated on Hrolf's face. 'Allow him to sober up. He will apologize then. Today is about celebrating the joining of two families.'

'He drops his sword first. At my feet.'

'Go, Regin, leave,' she whispered into the silence which followed.

Instead there was a sharp hiss as Regin drew his sword. Giving into instinct, Sayrid put her hand out and blocked his wrist. The fragile dress material gave way under her arm and across her back with a loud rip. Regin froze.

Sayrid clutched the remaining bit together, grateful for Hrolf's cloak which would hide any scars or flesh.

'Just bother,' she muttered.

Hrolf turned around with a glower. At the sight of her difficulties, he lifted his brow. 'Problems, Valkyrie?'

'What were you going to do with that?' she asked her brother, wrenching the sword away from him. It was far easier to concentrate on her brother's misdemeanours than to worry about her ruined dress or how she looked. Righteous anger filled her. 'Since when are you that sort of warrior? Since when have you become like a sea king? We agreed peace. Ironfist's children never dishonour oaths.'

Regin hung his head. 'I wanted to do something for you, Say... What was done to you was wrong and it is all my fault. I wish I'd never fallen in love with Blodvin, then everyone could have been happy.'

A huge great tide of misery rose in Sayrid's breast. Some day her brother would go too far. 'I know you did, but this was the wrong way to go about it. Just as it was wrong to bed Blodvin before you wedded her.'

'I've no wish to start a blood feud, Avilson.' Hrolf plucked the sword from Sayrid's grip. He balanced it lightly on his hand before returning it to her brother, hilt first. 'What is past remains in the past. You have a wife and child on the way. Enjoy them. But allow me the bride I won in peace and friendship.'

Her brother gulped twice. 'You return my sword? Unbroken?'

'I am in a good mood. Wedding days are a time of celebration. It is your sister's wish that we be joined in matrimony. No one forced her. Respect her and do not seek to dishonour her again.'

Regin's mouth took a bitter twist. 'I was willing to die for you, Sayrid.'

'Then be willing to live for me as well. You have a new wife and a baby on the way. Consider their future before you attempt to avenge imagined slights.' Sayrid nodded towards some of her more loyal men. 'Sober him up before he sees his wife.'

The men grabbed Regin's arms and hustled him away.

Sayrid adjusted the cloak more firmly about her shoulders. 'Shall we go, husband?'

Hrolf glowered at her as the men dispersed, leaving them once again alone. 'What else must I endure before our wedding night? Or is that the extent of your escape preparations?'

Sayrid raised her chin and met his furious gaze

head-on. 'A simple thank you would have been pleasant in the circumstances.'

His brow furrowed and he seemed genuinely perplexed. 'Why?'

'I—I—I prevented things from escalating,' she stammered. 'You were outnumbered. My brother may not be a brilliant warrior, but he can hold his own.'

'Did I ask for your assessment of the situation?' His voice was as cold as ice.

She shook her head slowly. 'I used my own judgement.'

He put his hand under her elbow. 'I gave my pledge to look after you. I married to gain a wife, not a warrior or an advisor.'

'But you married me,' she whispered. 'And I don't know how to be anything but a warrior.'

'Are you ready for the next lesson...in pleasure?'

Chapter Six

Hrolf heaved a sigh of relief as they rounded the corner towards where he was staying. The show of bravado by Sayrid's brother had been the only difficulty.

Two of his men stood guard ten paces outside the house. Had they been closer to the door, Hrolf would have known the house was a trap. He wanted to rid himself of the notion that she had fainted on purpose, but his brain kept circling back to it. Could he really trust the woman he'd won as a bride?

'Who are the guards who stand at the door? My gaolers to ensure cooperation?' Sayrid asked in a crisp tone. 'Is this the next lesson I should learn?'

'My bodyguards. From Rus. They are Magda's kin and have no part in my lessons.' He paused and gave her a hard look. She was a warrior. She had to have seen the men and weighed up how well armed they were and what threat they posed. 'You waited long enough to ask.'

She gave a quick laugh. 'Maybe I feared the answer.'

'And here I thought you were afraid of nothing except the marriage bed.'

'I find it best to keep my fears private. Exposing them makes you seem weak and helpless.' Her eyes flashed. 'And I take pride in my strength.'

His heart unexpectedly twisted. He hated to think what she had been through on her various sea voyages. It had been hard for him during the first years—the testing and the proving able in battle. It must have been far worse for her.

He pushed it aside. Sayrid was born a woman, not a warrior. She had fought for her life.

'The last thing you are is weak or helpless. You have nothing to fear from me or my men. They know you are my bride and will treat you with respect.'

'I want to believe that. Truly I do.'

Hrolf weighed up the risks of being attacked before he nodded to his bodyguards. 'You may join the feast now. I have no more need of you tonight.'

They each in turn bowed low and wished the couple good fortune before leaving.

'You did that for me?' Her cheeks became stained pink. 'Most unexpected.'

He clenched his fist. It was a little thing, not important and yet Sayrid's eyes shone. Had anyone ever done anything for her? Ever?

'We won't be disturbed further tonight,' he said, opening the door with far more force than he intended. 'There will be no reason to fear and no one but you is keeping you here. But I'm pleased you are here with me. I want to give you pleasure. Shall we go in?'

The room had been prepared as he requested. The coal smouldered in the fire pit, sweet wine and a light supper stood on the table next to a *tafl* board and finally a profusion of furs were heaped on the bed. A scene designed for seduction, but not tonight. Tonight was for finding out more and taming his wild bride. Lessons leading up to a pleasurable seduction for the both of them.

She tilted her head to one side, revealing the sweep of her long neck, but making no move to enter. His body thrummed with desire, but with difficulty he reined it in. Her eyes kept darting about as though she was searching for an exit as she waited on the threshold. 'You are not going to carry me?'

'I will allow you to walk as you wanted to.' He stretched out his back. His muscles protested at the simple movement. The fight had taken more out of him than he realized.

'I did warn you.' She gave a throaty laugh, which caused his groin to tighten and made him forget the aches in his body. 'You should never have attempted it earlier.'

'Are you challenging me to do it again?'

'I like the night air.' She balanced on the threshold. 'Allow me to stay outside a little longer.'

'My mother used to like the night air as well.' Hrolf frowned. He rarely spoke of the distant past, before he became a sea king and when he had to fight for even a morsel of bread. He might have stayed at his uncle's hall, but his uncle did play favourites. He doubted that Sayrid would understand.

She might have chosen an unconventional life, but she had never had to fight for survival in the same way he had.

'Should any come past, I will carry you in. Enjoy the air, but know that I will protect you.'

'The night air has never held terror. Outside has always represented freedom.' Her white teeth nibbled her bottom lip, turning it the colour of summer raspberries, but she stayed on the threshold.

Hrolf reined in his temper. Did her finding peace outside have anything to do with her becoming a warrior? 'I look after my women. I don't keep them prisoner.'

'Inga's mother died and Inga was left alone.'

'And what of it? She had accepted another man's protection.'

Anya's death had hardly been his fault. She was the mother of his child, but she had found other lovers after they parted. She'd wanted more than he'd been prepared to offer.

He wasn't about to become like his father—unhinged with worry when his woman was out of his sight.

Her blue eyes met his in a refreshingly direct manner. 'I depend on my sword arm to keep me safe.'

'And when it fails?'

'I take the consequences.' She lifted her chin slightly. 'Just like I'm doing now.'

Hrolf tapped his finger against the table. Something stirred in his heart at the proud defiance he glimpsed in her eyes. He ruthlessly suppressed it. Once he had bedded her and made good the promise in her kiss, then she would be his wife, but that was to ensure the loyalty of her people. He would follow his uncle's example and guard his heart.

'What are the consequences precisely?'

Her eyes became troubled. 'Marriage wasn't supposed to be part of the destiny that the Norns spun for me. My stepmother told me that often enough.'

Naked vulnerability flitted across her face, giving him a glimpse of the woman behind her scowling mask. Could this stepmother be part of the reason for Sayrid's reaction to Inga? He dismissed the idea. Worrying about reasons changed nothing. 'It doesn't do to second-guess the Norns.'

'I lost focus for an instant.'

The curve of her upper lip positively cried out to be sampled. He reined in his increasingly rampant desire. He had to think with his head instead of with another part of him. Cool logic. Until he was established and the people saw the sense in having him as their overlord, he needed her good will.

'I saw my chance and took it. Do you blame me?'

She swallowed hard and the corner of her mouth trembled. 'I made my choice before we picked our swords. Had I won, would you expect me to offer you your freedom? Do you treat me differently because I am a woman?'

Hrolf concentrated on breathing. Something deep inside him panged. He had never thought to feel pity or any emotion beyond momentary desire for a woman. But this woman stirred up long-forgotten feelings. His father had been moved by pity when his mother had begged for one last chance to end the quarrel and he had ended up dead.

'If you are unwilling, say the words. But you have this one chance only,' he said, banishing the emotions to where they belonged. 'Was your brother right to attempt a rescue?'

When she finally spoke, she spoke pointedly to the embers in the fire. 'My legs would not have carried me far. And I can barely lift a sword with the way my shoulders ache.'

'No answer, Sayrid. I deserve better. Denying your sex doesn't change that you are a woman.'

She spun around. Her gown gaped at the neck where she'd torn it, but her eyes flashed. 'Will I keep my property if the marriage fails? Will I be able to be a shield maiden with a blameless reputation again? Will I be able to live with my honour intact? Answer those questions truthfully and you will have my answer. Now, what is the next lesson I am supposed to learn?'

'Sayrid…' He willed her to take his outstretched arm. Once he held her, he could concentrate on giving her pleasure and these uncomfortable thoughts about the past would vanish.

She pointedly ignored his gesture and he allowed his arm to drop. Against his better judgement, he admired her spirit. She had gambled and lost, but there was dignity in her bearing and she wasn't complaining about how unfair life was. Every other woman he had known would have been in tears. Tears never moved him, but there was something about her stoic silence which opened up long-forgotten places in his heart.

'The truth, Hrolf. Can you undo any of this?

Can you restore my honour?' She gave a wry smile. 'I thought not. Then I will do my duty. You may take me now.'

She closed her eyes, puckered up her mouth and opened her arms, more sacrifice than hot-blooded bed partner.

He shook his head. Sayrid made it seem like he was asking her to violate sacred oaths. But he wanted her too much to argue. He wanted to unwrap her layers and discover the passionate woman underneath the mask, the one who had returned his kiss earlier.

'Kettil is now my overlord and we share mutual interests. The only way you will have any influence over those lands is to remain married to me,' he said, taking a draught of the sweet wine. It burnt his throat, but the blood pumping through his veins was hotter still.

She blinked rapidly. 'That was uncommonly quick.'

'Kettil worries about Lavrans's intentions towards these lands. It is why he and I became allies. What happened today cements our alliance. I will hold the headland for him against all raiders. He wanted a strong warrior there. Your brother will never be strong. Kettil understands this now.'

'My opposition to Lavrans is well known.' Her teeth worried her bottom lip, turning it a glossy red. 'Why would Kettil doubt that?'

'How often are you there?'

'When I can be, but we need gold. There is no one else.'

'Regin is grown, long past the age where men show promise as a warrior or not. Can you honestly say he is ready to lead a *felag*?'

She ducked her head. 'You are the first man to challenge for the right to marry me in many years.'

'It is a comforting thought in many ways that the men are so weak-livered in this country. I shall have no trouble holding those lands.'

Her laugh echoed feebly in the chamber. 'Perhaps they worried I took my sword to bed.'

'And do you sleep with a weapon?'

'When I have to.'

He flinched at her words. What she had done had been out of necessity. Her brother had been far too weak and her father? 'There will be no weapons in our bed. I'll keep you safe.'

Her lips parted before firming. Hrolf silently willed her to stay with him, but also to confide her fears. What had made her so wary of pleasure? Why had she become a shield maiden?

'It is cold outside and there is a warm fire and a bed waiting,' he said into the silence. 'The proper place for such a thing. You are my wife, not some farm maid fit for tumbling in the hay.'

Her tongue wet her lips, turning them the colour of autumn berries which he remembered from his childhood. He wondered if they would taste as sweet. The trouble with kissing her at the ceremony was that he wanted more, but he was greedy. He wanted her participating fully.

'You're right. I will come in.'

He contemplated suggesting she strip, but instead he reached out and plucked the listing flower crown from her head. 'There is no need for that here. The flowers are fading fast, but the night remains young for us.'

He waited for her to melt in his arms. She continued to stand stiffly, making no attempt to brush the final petals from her hair. He placed the wilted crown down on the table.

This was going to prove harder than he had anticipated. He'd planned on the next lesson being her undressing, but she was far too tense.

He had never backed away from a challenge and the thought of tasting her lips again filled him with anticipation, but he was no unblooded warrior, facing his first woman. He needed to take his time and not rush her.

'Have something to drink.'

'The *jaarl*'s sweet wine is always excellent,' she said, moving away from him. 'You're right about your daughter. In time, we will become friends. I will make it happen. It won't be…it will be fine.'

Hrolf narrowed his eyes. There was a wealth of information in those words. Had Sayrid's stepmother been cruel?

'Pour the wine for the both of us. Time to drink to our new life.'

As Sayrid attempted to pour the wine, her body trembled and she spilt a little on the floor. She gave a cry. He took the flask from her, filled a horn and handed it to her.

'What do you have to be nervous about? Why do you fear me?' he asked softly. 'I mean you no harm. I'm your husband, not a sorcerer. Your mind is closed to me.'

Sayrid stopped in mid-crouch and stared at him wide-eyed. The steady sound of trickling wine resounded in her ears.

What did she have to be nervous about? Everything!

She had everything to be nervous about. She had never played the woman's part before. Her stepmother had always told her that she was far too clumsy to be trusted. She had no idea what Hrolf's expectations were—both as a mother to his little girl and as a woman or rather wife to him.

Would he be like her father and be quick with his fists once she was less than perfect? Her back still bore the scars from the beatings she had taken for Regin. The only thing she excelled at was fighting. Her spilling the wine tonight was just another example that proved her stepmother's long-ago words.

Every other woman she'd ever seen could pour wine with grace and skill. When her father brought her stepmother home, she'd watched as this beautiful creature had poured the wine with a dainty gesture and held it out to her. She'd hung back, but her father had pushed her forward and in taking the wine she'd poured it all down her stepmother's silk gown.

'Drink. It will give you courage.' He held out a fresh horn of wine.

'Do I need courage tonight?'

'It has helped some.'

The fiery liquid burnt her throat and she spluttered. He tapped her back. Even that simple touch made her intensely aware of him and what was supposed to be happening here tonight. Her stomach knotted tighter than the ropes on the mainsail in a gale.

'Went down the wrong way,' she said, ducking her head and moving away from him. 'My father would have his head in his hands with shame. A child of his should be able to drink wine without coughing.'

He watched her with unfathomable eyes. 'I know about your father's reputation as a warrior, but not as a man. Was he a good father?'

Sayrid instinctively wrapped her arms about her waist. Of course he knew her father's reputation. He had obviously been talking to Kettil about her, whereas she knew very little about him beyond the rumours. 'How much do you know? A man's public reputation is not necessarily how he acts in private.'

'I know enough. He was a highly regarded warrior and amassed a great deal of land. Had a witch not cursed him, he and Kettil planned to go east.' Hrolf's mouth took on a bitter twist. 'He fought in the same *felag* as my father and uncle for several years.'

'He served Kettil well and he never dishonoured a member of any *felag* in which he served.' The sweat started to pool on the back of her neck like it always did when she spoke about her father.

He took a long considering draught of his wine. 'But you rather less well.'

'Why would you say that?'

'You were forced to become a shield maiden and had control of your family's land until your brother becomes a good enough warrior.'

'He will do,' Sayrid said much too quickly.

'Your father made you fight for your honour, instead of defending it with his final breath as I would do for Inga,' he continued on relentlessly. 'Your brother compounded the error.'

Sayrid clenched the horn so tightly that her knuckles shone white. He knew nothing of what she'd been through or the reasons for her behaviour. Blaming Regin was wrong. She was the eldest. 'Becoming a warrior was something I fought for. Swordplay and tactics were my meat and drink. And I ate well.'

Hrolf raised a maddening brow. 'My body bears bruises because of your skill, but you will have time now to develop other skills and talents, perhaps some more suited to being the wife of a sea king.'

'I must warn you that I have little talent for the needle and thread. And I've no intention of meekly allowing myself to be protected. Or my family dishonoured.'

Hrolf made a cutting motion. 'I will never permit my wife to be dishonoured.'

'Sometimes things happen which you are powerless to prevent.' Sayrid tilted her chin upwards. 'I claim the right to defend myself.'

A muscle twitched in his jaw and he appeared to grow several inches. 'You deliberately insult me.'

She stood her ground, matching his glare. Sayrid ground her teeth. The anger felt good. Anything to stop thinking about what was supposed to happen in this room tonight. 'I speak the truth. You sail off and who will protect me then?'

'I will make arrangements.'

'And if the arrangements prove inadequate?' Sayrid straightened her shoulders and stared directly at her husband. 'The only way you can ensure my safety is to take me with you on any voyage.'

His jaw dropped before he recovered to let out a loud roar of laughter. 'You are good, Sayrid. I can see why you prospered.'

'Then you will take me with you if you go to the East?'

'Should I go there, I will,' he agreed. 'But you must turn your mind to other more womanly occupations before that day. Will you accept that bargain?'

She drained the horn in a single gulp. She forced a belch to show him that she was truly uncouth. It came out as a small hiccup instead of the hoped-for rude noise. She pressed her lips together. How could she be incapable of a simple thing like that?

'Truly, I'm not domesticated. Ask anyone. Ask my stepmother. My sister...'

He took the now-empty horn from her nerveless fingers. 'Do we have a bargain?'

'Yes.' Sayrid took a step backwards, knocking over the *tafl* pieces. She bent down and started to gather them up. He might think she was the correct bride, but how could she be? Her father's words of scorn filled her ears. She screwed up her eyes and tried to block out the words pounding through her brain.

He wanted her for reasons that had nothing to do with her person or her mind and everything to do with her land. She knew the way the world worked and it was no good her heart whispering that he might be interested in her. Thinking that way was an excellent means of getting hurt.

He covered her hand. 'Leave it. Leave everything. You need to be in bed.'

'But…but…' She withdrew her hand. Blunt nails and calloused palms from years of practising with a sword and piloting her ship. A great lady's hand should be delicate with no discernible blemish, her stepmother used to declare, stretching out her fine-boned fingers. How could he be attracted to one such as her? She'd no wish to become an object of pity, lusting after her husband. Too many women like that littered the markets where she visited. She'd heard the laughter and obscene jokes about them at the docks and on the ships. 'I like to clear up the messes I make.'

He didn't move away from her as she expected, but continued to look at her with a hooded glance which sent her heart racing and made her knees weak.

'Truly I do.' She hated how her breath caught and made her voice sound as if she'd just negotiated a particularly difficult section of the blockade. 'Allow me to show you that I can do something besides fight.'

Capturing her wrists, he lightly held her arms above her head. He searched her face before rubbing his other thumb along her lips. Heat radiated outwards from her mouth.

'Go to bed,' he commanded. 'They will not disappear in the night.'

Her glance shot towards the mountain of furs, the thing she had been avoiding looking at. She had to hope that it would be over quickly and wouldn't hurt too much. Her stepmother had taken great delight in detailing how much men could hurt a woman and how she must lie back and take it. And how disgusted he would be at the scars on her back. It had been one of the reasons she fought so hard in the early days. 'Bed? With you? Is that an order?'

He shook his head. 'I'll sleep on the floor.'

'On the floor?' Her heart leapt and then plummeted. Both Auda and Blodvin were certain to ask about the wedding night. They would want the intimate details. She'd have to confess that her groom preferred the hard floor to sharing a bed with her. She regarded the mound of furs, rather than look in his pitying eyes. Silently she cursed her wayward mind. 'Why?'

'My muscles ache from our fight, Shield Maiden. Yours must as well.' He gave a husky laugh. 'I want to ensure you are properly welcomed into this marriage of ours. And while my mind might be willing, my flesh most decidedly isn't. It is that simple. The ground feels softer than a feather bed when you are exhausted.'

Sayrid tucked her chin into her neck and pretended to examine the *tafl* pieces. Of course his body ached. He had fought just as hard as she had.

'I'll take the floor. You won the bout. You should have the pleasant sleep. I've slept on rough ground before,' she said decisively. 'I'm used to it. As you said—I'm so tired I won't notice the difference.'

A muscle jumped in his cheek. 'My bride's comfort comes before mine. What sort of arrogant men did your family produce?'

'What does that have to do with anything? You take the bed if your muscles are in agony.' She attempted a back stretch. Her muscles screamed. A small groan escaped her lips.

'You are in pain as well.'

Her lips parted to deny it, but he grabbed her elbow.

'You will find me a tolerant husband, Sayrid, but never lie to me, not about something as important as your health.'

She wrenched her arm away. 'You are guessing.'

'You move like a warrior who has fought too many battles. Do I have to strip the remains of that dress from you to discover where you are hurt?'

Sayrid blinked twice, trying to rid her mind of the image of him running his hands down her body. All would be well until he discovered her scars. She had to keep her undershift on. 'You noticed? Nobody ever notices. The *skalds* have it that I'm impervious to pain.'

'Sagas seldom tell the truth.'

She gave a half smile. 'The only real bruising is to my pride.'

'And to your face.'

'That has ceased to hurt.' She carefully fingered it and tried not to wince at the pain. 'I'm sorry it frightened Inga. I know what it is like to want someone important to like you.'

His laughter filled the room, warming her. 'Sayrid, Sayrid, what am I going to do with you? Take the bed and be done with it. There will be plenty of time to consummate our marriage. If you are worried about old women gossiping, a chicken can be killed and your thighs rubbed with blood.'

Sayrid wanted the ground to open and swallow her. Of course everyone knew she had never had a man. They would be looking for blood on the sheets. 'I wasn't worried about that.'

'Cease your arguing.' He started to take the furs off the bed, but a groan escaped his lips as he lifted the first one.

'We share the bed and end this,' she said without allowing herself anytime to consider. It was the right thing to do. From the awkward way he held his shoulders, she knew the aches had to be setting in. The thought gave her a moment of satisfaction—Hrolf wasn't as godlike as everyone considered.

He stilled. 'Is that what you want?'

'There is more than room enough for two. The consummation can happen when we desire.' She gave a weak laugh which sounded false to her ears. 'Custom never dictates what I do, as you well know.'

His back remained turned towards her. 'Never let it be said that I refused a beautiful woman's warm bed.'

'A bed at least.'

He made a low bow. 'After you. You look ready to drop.'

The tiny flower of hope which had grown at his first words withered. She looked ready to drop could only mean that she looked hideous. Whatever faint hope she had about him finding her attractive vanished. She curled her fist, hating that for once she wanted a man to desire her body instead of envying her fighting skills.

She straightened her shoulders and gave him a crushing look. 'I shall sleep in my clothes.'

A dimple played in the corner of his mouth. 'Do you normally?'

Hope flickered in her breast. She could hide her scars…a little while longer. 'It depends on the circumstance.'

He caught her elbow. The tiny touch sent a lick of fire down her arm. 'You must do as you see fit, but I will sleep how I always sleep—without clothes.'

'If you must...'

'Have you considered what the gown will look like tomorrow? You must find another.'

'I won't be wearing it.' She stuck her chin in the air. 'You only specified a dress for the wedding. I have done that. I will wear what I please from now on.'

'And what will that be?' He glanced about the room. 'Forgive me, but I don't see any clothes' trunks in this room.'

'My trousers and tunic!'

He gave her a look. Her stomach knotted and she retreated a step. 'You haven't had them destroyed, have you?'

'Not yet,' he replied smoothly. 'But I prefer my bride to dress like a woman. You are no longer a shield maiden. Your dress reflects on me and my status. Fighting people who mock you is not the best use of my time.'

'I fight my own battles. And I've learnt to ignore whispers.'

He gave her a hooded look. 'I always look after my women.'

She swallowed hard. His woman! As if she was

little more than a possession. 'I will endeavour to find suitable clothes, but I can't promise.'

'With the gown, it depends on how much you wish to expose of your body to my men. But I will cut off any trousers you wear. You will have to expose your thighs to my men.'

Sayrid stared at him horrified. She might have been a shield maiden, but she had always dressed modestly, never flaunting her body. 'You wouldn't dare!'

'Do you want to take that risk?'

Sayrid undid the belt and pulled it over her head. She dropped all her garments on the floor before diving under the covers and pulling them up to her chin. She breathed easier. She had kept her scarred back to him. After tonight she doubted that he'd grace her bed and he would never need to know of her shame.

Hrolf took rather longer in divesting his garments. The firelight played on his skin, turning it a golden hue. When their gazes locked as his fingers went to his trousers, his lips went up in a knowing smile. She hastily screwed up her eyes and gave several loud snores for good measure.

Sayrid wished she hadn't offered him a place in the bed. She could hardly go back on it now, having invited him. She hugged her knees to her chest and made herself as small as possible.

The bed dipped slightly as he climbed in. She clung to the edge of the mattress to prevent her body from rolling towards him. The bed was suddenly much smaller than she had thought and appeared to be shrinking with each breath she took. There was going to be no way that she could sleep.

'Pleasant dreams, Sayrid. To protect your modesty, I have kept my trousers on. You will see that I am a man of my word if you care to look.'

She gave an imitation of a snore and his soft chuckle tickled the back of her neck. She tightened her grip on the edge of the mattress. If it was the last thing she did, she would keep to her side of the bed.

Chapter Seven

Sayrid woke with a start, half-convinced her memories of last night were a fanciful dream. But a heavy arm lay across her middle and curled against her naked back was a warm body. In her ear she heard the enticing sound of steady rhythmic breathing. Her entire being thrummed for a heartbeat.

She wanted to lie there forever, savouring the sensation and sinking into it. In the dappled morning light he might be able to see her back, something her stepmother had vowed would be sure to turn any man's stomach.

Instinctively, she moved her elbow back, jabbing him in the stomach.

The arm tightened about her middle, hauling her back against him. Sayrid wriggled slightly as her bottom connected with his groin, leaving her in no doubt of his morning arousal despite the soft leather of his trousers. 'You won't escape that easily, sweetling. Our marriage will be a real one. Time for the next lesson.'

She instantly went still and concentrated on taking deep breaths. Time to consummate the marriage. Time for her to make more mistakes and prove her stepmother's prediction true. She wanted it to be otherwise, but how could it be? She started to edge away from temptation.

'I was quite enjoying the movement,' he said as his breath caressed her ear, tickling her. 'Let your instinct guide you.'

Strange sensations warred within her body. She wanted to keep moving, but equally the burgeoning warmth terrified her. It was far worse than piloting her ship during a storm.

'I didn't mean to… That is…' Sayrid struggled to think of a polite way of rectifying her mistake. 'I meant to keep to my side, not sleep in your arms. We made a bargain. You and I.'

'Did you hear any complaints from me?' His hand slowly ran down her flank. Her flesh quivered under his touch and her breasts began to ache. 'I still wear my trousers. We will go at your pace. Slowly, step by step.'

Sayrid struggled to keep her mind clear. Safety was a matter of opinion. Right now, she felt anything but safe with him, particularly as his hand skimmed her thighs, first one way and then the other. Each time his fingers strayed closer to the apex of her thighs. She wanted them to continue but... She wrenched her mind away.

'When I give my word, I prefer to keep it.'

His fingers instantly ceased their quest.

Firmly but gently he turned her so she was facing him. In the dull light, she could clearly see the shadow of his stubble and the faint beginnings of crows' feet in the corners of his eyes.

'It was far from taking a liberty.' He cupped her face, drawing feather-light lines along her jaw which sent tingles racing throughout her body. 'Who made you wary?'

'I'll try to remember that...for when I next find myself in this situation.' Silently she vowed that she'd find a reason not to share a bed with him again. The longer she could keep him from finding out about how marked she was, the better chance she had of making this marriage work. And to her surprise, she wanted it to work.

He held her palm against the silken skin of his

chest. For a heartbeat she savoured how the muscles rose and fell with each breath he took.

'I intend for it to happen again,' he said in a low husky voice. 'We will share a bed. I positively insist. Next time we will do more than sleep.'

Their breath interlaced and her lips went incredibly dry. She flicked her tongue over them and watched as his eyes became lit with fire. *He is going to kiss me. He wants to. He desires me—* thudded through her brain. Her stomach knotted. She wanted him to do more than kiss her. Truly kiss her, long and slow. But also to show her that her stepmother and father were wrong. A real man could desire her...at least for a little while.

He wound a tendril of her hair about his forefinger. 'Do you want to know what I am thinking?'

Helplessly caught in his gaze, she nodded.

He cupped her face with gentle fingers. His mouth lowered. 'This.'

The kiss was tenderer than she had expected, teasing and persuading, not plundering and all-conquering. Delicate and yet calling to that wild fire deep within her. Giving into instinct, she parted her lips and tasted him. Fresh and clean, which made her hungry for more. She opened her mouth further and drew him in.

The kiss instantly deepened and his tongue toyed with hers, probing and then retreating, enticing her to follow.

He rolled them over so he was on top and the whole length of him pressed down on her. She arched her back to feel more of him as his mouth moved ever more deeply over hers.

A pounding at the door and distressed cries startled her and called her back to reality, the place where she ought to be. She tore her lips from his.

'Someone shouts.'

'Ignore them.' He traced her lips with his forefinger. 'They will go away. You have your customs. My people have theirs. It is a game we play.'

'Game?'

'Bothering a man after he has spent a night with a woman. I regret even starting it.'

'Have you slept a whole night with a woman before?'

'Not the full night.' He moved his lips down her neck, taking little nibbles. 'You are the first.'

'And this is how you honour your wife?' she whispered.

'In part.' His tongue circled the hollow of her throat.

The pounding was incessant, enough to wake the dead. He rolled off her and lay there, breathing heavily.

'Yes?' he shouted out. 'Who dares disturb me on my wedding morning?'

'Trouble at the harbour, Hrolf. Bragi sent us.'

Sayrid started to slide out of the bed, but Hrolf's hand pressed her back against the pillow.

'Let someone else deal with it. Bragi is more than capable.' His hand trailed down her shoulder, drawing an intricate pattern which made her breathless. 'I refuse to be distracted just when it has become interesting.'

'Unbolt the door or we will smash it in.'

Sayrid's stomach clenched. Something was truly wrong. Her mind raced with the possibilities—a raid, or a sail spotted or even a fight between her men and his. 'Can you take the chance? We should both go.'

Hrolf sighed and rolled back on to his side. 'It is the morning after my wedding night. I know the tricks my men can play. By Freyr's grove, I've played them often enough myself.'

'Do you dare take the risk?'

He shook his head. 'Thank you for understanding. Not many women would.'

Sayrid swallowed the sudden feeling of disappointment which intermingled with relief. If things had continued, he'd soon discover how hopeless she was. She'd actually jabbed him in the stomach earlier. And thank every goddess he hadn't seen her back or he'd have turned away from her. All her stepmother's warnings crowded back and she wondered that she'd forgotten even for an instant.

'Waiting could prove fatal. In my experience, problems only grow.' She reached for her discarded gown. 'I'm sure it won't take long. Then you can return here. We still have to…well…the marriage needs to begin properly.'

He dropped a swift impersonal kiss on her forehead. 'My bride is a goddess among women.'

'There will be other times.'

'Anticipation is an excellent thing.' He reached over and retrieved his shirt. In a heartbeat his magnificent chest was covered. 'You will see… in time.'

Sayrid held her body very still and hoped he would miss the burn in her cheeks. 'Ships come before everything.'

'Stay there so that I can think of you waiting for me.' A flash of fire shone in his eyes. 'I won't be long and we can enjoy the morning as I planned.'

He left the room before she had a chance to protest. She dug her fist into the fur and fell backwards. This was not how her life was supposed to go. One kiss, a few caresses and she lacked all willpower to make her own decisions? She thought not. Mealy-mouthed women who deferred constantly to their men, even when they were capable of sorting out the trouble, were creatures to be despised.

She'd been a complete idiot. She should have demanded she go with him or at least not given him the option of saying no.

'I may be a wife, but I'm not suddenly a doormat,' she muttered, pulling the gown on and ripping it in another place. She rooted around and found a needle and some thread. She pulled off the gown and did a few more basic alterations. When she had finished, she examined the gown. It was shorter than ever but at least she wouldn't burst out of it again.

'Marriage doesn't mean I've stopped being me. I want to know what is going on. Sitting around, waiting for my husband to take care of everything is something I've always rejected.'

'Your reason for calling me out had better be a good one,' Hrolf said, approaching Bragi where he stood beside the ship's hull with his tattoos glistening and a smug smile playing on his misbegotten face. 'Particularly as I don't see Kettil. It will bode ill for you if you seek to anger me today of all days.'

'And how was your night?' Bragi asked, revealing his filed teeth. 'Was she every bit as passionate in bed as she was on the battlefield? By the gods, she fights well.'

'I warned you yesterday, Bragi. You are my sworn man. You disobeyed a direct order. I've killed men for less.'

'Tetchy, are we?' Bragi stroked his chin. 'I reckon last night did not go precisely as you planned.'

Hrolf fastened his gaze on several pennants blowing in the breeze. There was no point in explaining his strategy to Bragi, who had little idea of the subtlety. He wanted a willing participant in his bed, not a woman who had been forced. He wanted the passionate woman who he was sure lurked behind the mask of toughness she wore. It frightened him how much he wanted it. He clenched his fists. He was never going to be weak like his father.

'None of your business,' he ground out. 'I'm not here to discuss my wife's charms. What's the problem with the ship? Absolutely urgent or did the messenger get it wrong? I will have him whipped.'

Bragi blinked twice. 'Merely trying to pass the time, old friend, before Kettil arrives.'

'Start talking if you wish to keep your thick head attached to your body.' Hrolf banged his fist against his open palm. 'What is this all about? What is the emergency? Where is the threat to our fleet? Why did I have to leave my bed with my *bride*?'

'Kettil has been summoned,' Bragi explained rapidly, all bravado vanished. 'I thought it wise to ensure you arrived first. We need to decide what action is appropriate and measured. And I didn't want to alert your new wife...just in case she is involved. But you need to see the *Sea Bird* for yourself. If the damage had not been spotted, she could have sunk quickly in deep water.'

A cold chill went down Hrolf's back. Bragi suspected sabotage. 'Continue...'

'Her brother last night...at the feast...well, he had too much to drink. He has a reputation for doing daft things. I've asked around quiet like. He stays out of trouble only because no one wants to provoke Sayrid. She protects him and the little sister. But he will never be of the right calibre to hold somewhere as important as that headland and harbour.'

'Tell me something new. I hold the headland now by virtue of my marriage and Kettil's good grace.' Hrolf schooled his features. That the brother was drunk at the feast was utterly predictable. Presumably he had had a few choice words after being bested. Silently he vowed that the brother would take a long voyage in the very near future.

'I'd have knocked sense into his smug face, but you gave your orders—no violence on your wedding day.'

'I've no wish to make Sayrid choose between her family and us. Not yet at any rate.' Hrolf concentrated on the ship, trying to discern how the sabotage had been carried out, instead of pondering the sinking sensation in his gut. His father had forced his mother to choose over a pointless quarrel and had regretted it for the rest of his life. 'We've waited long enough for Kettil and his entourage. What has happened to my ship?'

'This.' Bragi gestured towards the hull. 'A few loosened boards, just above the water line. If I hadn't spotted them, we could have had trouble once we put out to sea. You know what happened in Ribe. It goes beyond simple wedding-night mischief, Hrolf.'

Minor damage and easily fixed, but potentially lethal if the boards came loose while they were out at sea. Hrolf ran his hands over the sun-warmed boards. He had helped to make this ship, designing the hull, choosing the trees to be felled and finally working with the wood so that it rode over the waves at great speed. It pained him that anyone would behave in this fashion towards this ship.

Hrolf tapped a finger against the hull. It was a cheap trick, but the question was who had done this. He disliked pointing an accusatory finger at Regin unless he had solid proof.

He clapped Bragi on the back. 'You were right

to call me down to the harbour. I forgive you. You can keep your life.'

'Still, the look on your face was worth it!' Bragi laughed. 'I do hope what I interrupted will improve your temper when finally completed.'

'Bragi!' Hrolf reached for his sword.

'You forget I've a death wish.'

'And I've no wish to see you gracing Odin's hall just yet.'

Bragi's face eased. 'What do you want me to do?'

'Quietly check the other ships. See if anyone saw anything. See if you can learn the whereabouts of Sayrid's brother while you are at it. Report back as soon as you can. I'll wait here for Kettil.'

'Say! Say! Wait up! You are walking far too fast.'

Sayrid halted. The tattered gown had hampered her progress. First the harbour to find out about the fuss and then back to her old house to retrieve her clothes. Hrolf might wish her to wear gowns, but until she had one which fitted her properly, she intended to be comfortable—she glanced ruefully down at her bare calves—and decent. 'I'd expected to find you back at the house.'

Auda picked up her skirts and ran. 'Regin and Blodvin have left.'

Sayrid's mouth went dry. Trouble at the harbour and then Regin mysteriously departs. It sounded very much like something Regin had done had gone badly wrong and he wanted to hide away, leaving her to clean up the mess. 'Left when?'

'Sometime before dawn. I found the rune this morning when I woke.' Auda held out a scrap of wood. 'Blodvin wrote it, I think, rather than Regin. He knows how to spell.'

Sayrid took it. Blodvin had scratched the briefest of messages. They'd departed to visit Regin's mother in Götaland. Her stepmother had left before the ashes on her father's funeral pyre were cold, leaving her children much as a cuckoo leaves her eggs for other birds to rear. In the last four years, Regin had visited her once and then only because Sayrid had insisted.

'Why did they go there? I've a bad feeling about this. You know what Regin swore the last time I tackled him on the necessity of visiting her.'

Auda's cheeks flamed. 'Blodvin wanted to make sure that our mother received the news of the marriages first from a family member. She went on and on to me about it. We argued about it last night after Regin disgraced himself at the feast.'

Sayrid lifted her brow. 'What did he do? Fight with Hrolf's men? Tell me the worst.'

Auda shrugged. 'He was a bit vocal at the feast, but when he sobers up, he will apologize.'

'He tried to provoke Hrolf into a battle last night.' Sayrid attempted to move her stiff shoulder and heard the gown rip some more under her arm. 'Since when do I need anyone to rescue me?'

Auda looked her up and down. 'Did Hrolf tear your gown? Was he a brute? You know the reputation Lavrans has. Hrolf Eymundsson could be cut from the same cloth. Regin proclaimed he was.'

'My own stupid fault and the fact that the dress was designed to fit Blodvin's form.' Sayrid shrugged and kept her gaze carefully on the ground. 'There's a reason I prefer tunic and trousers. Once I know what is going on at the harbour, I'm putting my tunic and trousers back on.'

'You can't.'

'I refuse to shame our family by appearing

naked and my legs are far too exposed.' Sayrid glanced at the gown, which was now several inches shorter. 'This apron dress borders on the indecent.'

'Blodvin tossed all your clothes in the fire. She claimed she was being helpful.' Auda balled her fists. 'Perhaps you could borrow something from Hrolf? He is a little taller than you.'

Sayrid tried to ease the sudden tension in her neck. Her mind must have been made of porridge this morning. Hrolf appeared to have a larger wardrobe than many women. 'We are talking about the man who insisted on a dress for the wedding or me going naked. I doubt he would be impressed if I stole his clothes.'

'When we return to the hall, I'll get that length of blue cloth I've been saving for my wedding and will fashion you a dress which fits and flows to the ground.' Auda began to tick off items of on her fingers. 'I will also teach you how to weave properly. You will get the hang of it in next to no time. If Blodvin can weave, so can you, regardless of what my mother used to say.'

Sayrid blinked hard. Her siblings never ceased to amaze her. They made all her sacrifices worth it. They had always been there for her. She could remember how Auda had held the bowl and Regin had sponged her back after her stepmother had rubbed salt and sand into her wounds. Without them she'd have died and it was a debt she could never repay.

'You're the best sister.'

'I'm your only sister.' Auda wrinkled her nose. 'Blodvin doesn't count.'

'What else did she do? It has to be more than burning my clothes.'

Auda made a little deprecating gesture and Sayrid knew Blodvin's tongue was every bit as poisonous as Auda's mother's. She wished she'd never rescued the young woman.

Her heart lurched. But then she'd never have known Hrolf's touch this morning. Sayrid angrily dampened down the feeling.

'Blodvin will learn mocking anyone in our family is a very bad idea.'

'Where are you going?' Auda asked, quite clearly changing the subject away from her problems with Blodvin. 'I'd expected you to stay in bed far longer.'

Sayrid winced as the heat in her cheeks increased. 'You're unmarried, Auda.'

'What does that have to do with anything?'

Auda rolled her eyes upwards. 'You'd have to be blind, deaf or daft not to know what passes between a man and woman. And I'm none of those things. The way you two kissed at the wedding… made me think…that's all.'

'The interrogation about my wedding night will wait until I've finished at the harbour. Hrolf was called away because of some trouble.' Sayrid silently vowed that there would never be a good time to discuss it. Some things remained private.

'Do you think Regin had anything to do with it?'

Sayrid looked over Auda's shoulder towards the harbour. She could just see the dragon prows bobbing gently in the oncoming tide. Ships were sacred. They ensured the community could survive through trade. Harming one of them would cause the gods to be angry. 'He gave me his word last night.'

Auda's shoulders sagged. 'That is good. If Regin gives his word, he does keep it.'

'The trouble is making everyone else believe it.' Sayrid watched the sunlight play on the waves. 'Particularly if Regin was unwise in his choice of words before he so hastily departed.'

'I will do what I can to help.' Auda reached

out a quivering hand. Sayrid took it and noticed that it was as cold as ice. 'I'd feel happier if he had stayed.'

'I would as well,' Sayrid admitted. 'But tell anyone I said that and I will deny it.'

'Do you have any idea of who might have done this?' Kettil asked when Hrolf showed him the damage to the hull.

'Unfortunately I was in bed with my bride and the culprit did not leave any clues behind.' Hrolf fixed the *jaarl* with a stare. 'But enough people knew I wanted to depart for my new hall as soon as possible.'

He wanted to tear whoever had endangered their lives apart with his bare hands, but until he had solid proof Hrolf contented himself with flexing his fingers.

'There was the trouble with Regin Avilson at the feast,' Bragi said. 'He was drunk and made threats.'

The *jaarl* bristled. 'Regin Avilson might be a fool, but he'd never harm his sister. He owes her too much. Ironfist despised the boy, but he was secretly proud of Sayrid.'

Hrolf frowned. Ironfist was probably not an

ironic name. It would explain a great deal if he had beaten his children. Silently he promised to learn more about Sayrid's past. And then he gave a wry smile. How his uncle would have laughed and repeated his oft-quoted phrase—women were for pleasure only. Caring was the start of the end for his father. It had dulled his edge, according to his uncle.

'Kettil! Kettil!' Sayrid strode towards them. She was taking too-big steps and the dress was plastered against her legs, revealing rather more curve of her calf than before. A deep primitive urge to murder any man who looked at her filled Hrolf. He struggled to contain his annoyance at himself. Lovesick was certainly something that he refused to become. He did not possess a jealous bone in his body.

'If your wife had looked like that when she was a shield maiden, I would have been too busy noticing her curves to listen to her counsel,' Kettil said in a low voice.

Hrolf dragged his eyes away from the way the wind whipped the skirt about Sayrid's calves. The memory of their silken length tangled with his this morning was seared deep on his soul.

And it bothered him that all the other men were now staring at her.

His plan of teaching Sayrid a lesson had rebounded on him. She'd warned that she didn't possess any other dresses. After this, he'd be magnanimous and allow her to change into her trousers and tunic—at least they would cover up her assets. There would be no reason to explain the true reason behind his change of heart.

'Here I find you.' Sayrid hurried towards where Hrolf stood talking to Kettil.

'Why are you here, Sayrid?' Hrolf drew his brows together, every inch the terrifying sea king of legend.

Sayrid set her jaw. Looks never cowed her.

'You were longer than I thought you would be, husband.' She waved an airy hand, which caused her cloak to open. At his darker look, she clutched it shut. The gown was far worse now than when she had started out. The barest thread kept it up. She was going to need Auda's needle soon. With Hrolf in this mood, there was no way she could ask about another set of clothes or confess about Blodvin's bonfire of her old ones. 'It is our wedding morning after all.'

The sweetness of her voice made her stomach

churn worse than ever, particularly as his brows drew even closer together. She studiously ignored the grins of the other men.

She wondered briefly if she should kiss his cheek, but decided that it would be pushing things too far. She simply stood close enough to him to feel the heat of his body.

'I know what day it is.' A muscle twitched in his cheek.

'Then you can have no objections to me being here.'

She started to pull away, but his arm snaked around her middle and hauled her against his muscular body. The breath left her lungs.

'It is refreshing how my bride desires my company. And dressed like that.'

She forced a smile and silently damned Blodvin. The gown made her feel as if men were looking at her figure rather than paying attention to her words. 'Why else would I be here but to please my husband?'

His low voice tickled her ear as his hand slid possessively down her back. 'You brought your sister, but not your brother. Where is he?'

Sayrid wriggled free and concentrated on the ship's hull in front of her until her heartbeat went back to normal. 'My brother has left to visit my stepmother.'

She crossed her arms over her aching breasts and prayed that the stitching would not give way. He was deliberately using her attraction to him.

'Did you know about the intended trip?' Hrolf asked Kettil, who shook his head, mystified.

'A son must honour his mother.' Sayrid fixed Kettil with her gaze. 'You spoke of the necessity the other day, Jaarl, when I returned from my voyage. Regin has a possibility of inheriting land, now that her current husband's only child has died from a fever.'

Kettil had the grace to look uncomfortable. Inwardly Sayrid fumed. He'd conveniently forgotten the conversation. At the time she had privately doubted Regin would go.

Sayrid forced her feet to move to beside the hull. To her surprise, the hull used wooden nails instead of the more usual iron ones. But she quickly spotted the trouble. It was easy to fix. However, if it had not been discovered, it could have posed a problem when they next put to sea. 'When do you think they struck?'

'Who?'

'Lavrans or one of his men. This goes beyond

simple wedding-night mischief.' Sayrid tapped her forefinger against the wood. 'It must be them or another enemy of the Svear. You can't believe anyone from Svear would do such a thing. It would go against all the laws of hospitality.'

'I can see why you listened to my wife's counsel, Kettil, and it wasn't just because of her good legs.'

Sayrid ignored the tiny fluttering in her stomach. Hrolf thought she had good legs.

'Lavrans is far from stupid,' she said, adopting a no-nonsense tone. 'There will be people who are in secret alliance with him. Men who have benefited for years from not being attacked and who stand to lose everything if this alliance between you and Kettil continues.'

'Do you have the names of these traitors?'

Slowly she shook her head. 'If I'd known the names, I'd have told Kettil many months ago. But I'm sure someone must be tipping Lavrans off. There have been far too many times that our ships have been attacked and others haven't. Someone must be selling information. Either here or in Ribe.'

'Speculation serves no useful purpose. We need

solid proof, Sayrid Avildottar,' Kettil said with a frown.

She crossed her arms over her breasts and wished she had worn a different cloak, one which did not carry Hrolf's scent. Right now she had to put what had nearly happened in that room behind her. She had to fight for her brother and not allow him to be condemned. Her attraction to her husband, the man most likely to condemn her brother, was far from welcome and she refused to let it stop her from doing what was right. 'I merely state the obvious. But one thing is certain: my family have never been traitors.'

Hrolf's gaze narrowed. 'No one has accused your brother. We merely want to talk to him, but you say he has departed to visit his mother whom he has ignored for months despite Kettil's request.'

Kettil's lined face settled into its more familiar serenity. 'Auda, my wife had a question about embroidery. If you could attend to her while we wait for the inspection to be completed. I personally think it is wedding-night mischief gone wrong.'

Auda gave her a panicked look. 'I'm honoured of course...that is...'

Sayrid motioned to Auda to agree as she silently cursed Regin's overly hasty departure. It was obvious that Kettil wanted leverage over the family. 'My sister will be delighted to accept your kind invitation. She does love talking about needlework.'

Auda gulped hard, bobbed a curtsy, agreeing to the request. Sayrid curled her fists. Somehow she'd unmask the true culprit and prove Regin's innocence.

Kettil nodded to Hrolf. 'When you've finished your inspections and if it is simple wedding-night mischief, send word. Until then, my wife will enjoy Auda's company. Sayrid, it is your choice if you wish to stay here or not.'

Kettil strode off with cloak flapping in the breeze as Auda hurried alongside him. He still walked with purpose, but Sayrid could see a stiffness in his gait.

The *jaarl* was at least her father's age and had no children. She glanced at Hrolf. Was he the heir apparent? Was that part of the tribute the *jaarl* had agreed to when they exchanged peace rings?

A shiver ran down her spine. Why had she missed this earlier? It made sense why he had made an alliance with Hrolf against Lavrans. She had been blind before.

Sayrid hung her head. How many other little things had she missed because she was so intent on improving her family's fortune? But she could start again now, making sure nothing was overlooked.

Hrolf waited ten heartbeats after Kettil and his entourage disappeared. His uncle's words about how a woman would always choose her family resonated.

'Shall I help with the inspection?' Sayrid cleared her throat. 'I made a practice of it after Birka. My method takes less time than some of the others.'

She started towards the nearest ship, but Hrolf grabbed her arm.

'My men know what they are about,' he ground out.

He deliberately smoothed a strand of hair from her forehead. Her flesh quivered under his fingertips. She was far from immune. A surge of desire went through him, but he hardened his heart. Desire belonged to bedrooms and the night. Out here in the sunlit harbour, he had to concentrate on what was best for his ships and his men, the important constants in his life. 'Why won't you act like a woman? And why do you have to wear that dress? It is little better than rags.'

Sayrid drew on all her experience with her father and stepmother and kept her face blank, but inside she seethed. How stinging to be dismissed with such a very few words. As if all her experience counted for nothing. Act like a woman indeed! Next he'd have her chained to a loom.

'You believe I will try to deflect your men away from any evidence that might implicate my brother. As if I would do such a thing! It is in my family's best interest to have the real culprit found.'

'And if he is your brother?'

She crossed her arms, bristling. 'If my brother took leave of his senses, then I want to know. I will not hesitate in administering the punishment. But he will be found innocent.'

'Why wouldn't your brother make common cause with Lavrans? Other men have. Lavrans specializes in treachery and corruption.'

'My father killed Lavrans's father in a fight over a woman.'

'Which woman?'

'My stepmother.' Sayrid choked back the words

to stop herself saying that life would have been much easier if her father had never laid eyes on her stepmother. 'Lavrans swore eternal hatred and vowed to pour salt on our lands. There were rumours that Regin wasn't my father's because he was born early.'

'Lavrans is pragmatic. That must have been years ago.'

'Not about Ironfist or his children.' Sayrid stood up straighter. 'It is why no one expected me to return from my first voyage and why I have learnt to guard my plans and listen to gossip. Give me a chance to prove what I'm capable of. You will be well rewarded.' She hated the pleading note in her voice. 'I want to find the culprit and clear my family's name. Regin left because he regretted his words at the feast. My brother is like that.'

'Keeping away will ensure my men trust the outcome,' he murmured against her ear. She tried to hold her body stiff, but the warmth of his arm enticed her to lean towards him. The gleam deepened in his eyes. 'You may change into your old clothes if it will make you feel more comfortable.'

She pulled away from him, annoyed at her reaction to his nearness and that he was using her attraction to him against her. 'Impossible. Blodvin burnt them. Blodvin and I will have words.'

'All the more reason not to remain here.'

'I could go and see your daughter, get to know her. It went badly after the wedding. The last thing I want is for her to be frightened of me.'

Hrolf went very still. 'You want to do that? Truly? After the way my daughter behaved yesterday?'

'You sound surprised.' Sayrid threw back her shoulders. Displaying confidence was easy. Men, particularly warriors, only noticed the surface. She'd learnt that lesson time and again in her trips—a scowl and a swagger made her seem tough even though her insides quaked. 'I'm determined to make this marriage work. In time, she will see that she has no cause to fear me.'

Sayrid gave the ground a little kick. She wished she knew the proper procedure for taking leave of one's husband. Just turning her back on him didn't seem right. Her foot connected with a metal object and sent it sailing through the air. A finely wrought animal-head brooch landed a few feet from her. 'Where did this come from?'

Hrolf reached her in a single stride. 'What have you found?'

'A brooch, half-buried in the mud.'

'Deliberately dropped?'

Sayrid turned the brooch over. 'The clasp is broken. Perhaps it fell off without the owner realizing.'

He nodded. 'Have you seen it before?'

Sayrid shook her head. 'It is not a design I recognise. Most of the women wear oval brooches, rather than animal-head ones. In Götaland, it is different. There every second woman seemed to be wearing a pair of animal heads.'

'What makes you so certain it is a woman's brooch?'

'The design and the size.' Sayrid pressed her lips together. She refused to argue with Hrolf, but this made her feel that somehow a woman was involved. 'We should show this to Kettil. It proves my brother had nothing to do with it. He has never owned a brooch like this. I don't recognize the craftsmanship.' She rubbed the back to see if there were any runes to provide a clue. The faint scratches initially made her heart leap, but then it sank. 'And the runes make no sense unless they are a sort of code.'

'And you know everything your brother owns?'

'He tends to show things to me. A silversmith

cheated him once in Birka and I had a quiet conversation with the man in question, and Regin's money was returned.'

Sayrid kept silent about how precisely the conversation was conducted. Her sword and various hangings in the man's forge did feature prominently. She doubted that the man would try to disguise poor-quality swords again.

'You have done a lot for your brother. Would he do as much for you?'

She peered at the scratches on the finely wrought gold of the brooch, trying to puzzle out the code. 'Find the person this belongs to and you will find the culprit.'

'Why?'

'If it had been dropped before last night, someone would have picked it up or it would have been washed away by the tide.'

Hrolf raised her chin so that she stared into his eyes. His mouth dropped down on hers and she tasted his mouth. A warm pulse went through her, turning her legs to jelly. She clung to his tunic and drank in his scent. His arms went around her and hauled her close to his body.

Then abruptly it was over and he had to let her

go. She touched her faintly swollen lips. 'Another of your lessons?'

'It was either kiss you or shake you. I chose the more pleasurable option for the both of us.' He pocketed the brooch.

He openly caressed the curve of her flank. Her body quivered and he gave a knowing smile. All behind her, a loud clapping erupted. The warmth inside her shrivelled. His touch had been for public consumption, possibly to hide the discovery of the brooch.

She pulled away as her stomach knotted tighter. 'You need to oversee the inspection. There isn't time for this sort of thing.'

His thumb rubbed her swollen bottom lip. 'See my daughter. I will find you. Know that I will always find you.'

'Is that a threat or a promise?'

He tilted his head. 'Both.'

She straightened her back. He was using her naked attraction to him to manipulate her. Her loyalties lay with her family and she would find a way to prove Regin's innocence and rescue Auda as well as teaching this sea king a lesson in humility and having respect for others. 'You married me, you didn't enslave me.'

Chapter Eight

Sayrid discovered Inga and her nurse sat on a bench, heads bent, stitching. The embroidered cloth was far finer than anything she could produce. Inga's needle positively flew.

A wave of inadequacy washed over Sayrid. She was totally wrong for this delicate creature's mother. Inga needed a mother who was…well… more womanly. All the cruel jibes her stepmother used to throw at her came racing back, preventing her from breathing properly.

She shook her head. This was nonsense. She who had faced far fiercer foes was tempted to retreat and find something else to do? However, she'd given Hrolf her word that it was where she'd be. She hardly wanted him accusing her of colluding with whoever had done that to the ship.

She set her shoulders and strode towards the

pair as if she were going into battle. They stopped mid-laugh. Inga pricked her finger. A drop of blood fell on the snow-white cloth. Sayrid stared at it in horror, remembering how her stepmother used to berate her for spoiling fine linen.

'Is there some reason you are here, my lady?' The nurse's face was hostile and her manner bordered on the insolent. 'Inga always spends her mornings sewing. She is learning to be a fine lady who will make her father proud.'

'That is an admirable occupation, but on a day like today the last thing I would want to do is sit still. Maybe we could go for a walk? I could show you the different shields my men use.'

Inga clung tighter to the nurse and buried her face in the nurse's ample bosom.

'You must go for your walk. Inga is trying to finish her tapestry for her father.' The nurse frowned. 'He is determined that she will be a great needlewoman like his mother was.'

'I'm here to visit my new daughter,' Sayrid said, looking the nurse in the eye and ignoring the stain on the cloth. Of course Inga idolized her father. Little girls did at six. She had done. But sewing took concentration and she had hated sitting still. 'The needlework is superb. Is the pattern from your country? I've never seen it before. Can I take a closer look?'

Inga shrank back against the nurse, giving an urgent whisper.

'Did the master say you might?' the nurse asked, hugging the cloth to her chest.

Sayrid reined in her temper. Shouting at the woman would do more harm than good. Instead she knelt beside the little girl. Silently she vowed that the nurse would learn—Hrolf didn't order her about. She had no master. And she deserved respect. 'I wanted to meet my new daughter. Properly, without people around. Hrolf is busy at the harbour with his ship. How can needlework be a secret?'

The nurse gave a loud sniff.

'Is it because of the ghost?' Inga asked in a trembling voice, finally lifting her head.

'What ghost?'

'The lady ghost I saw last night. She stood next to Far's ship.'

Every nerve in Sayrid's body came alive. She knew it! A woman had done the damage. Hrolf had dismissed the notion, but with Inga's evidence, he'd have to listen. 'How do you know it was a ghost? What did she look like? Can you describe her?'

The girl stared at her with feline eyes. Sayrid tried not to wonder what her mother must have looked like. 'You're very tall. Your dress is very ugly and doesn't fit you properly. Ghosts look like ghosts. Everyone knows that.'

Sayrid hurriedly hunched her shoulders. 'Until yesterday, I rarely wore gowns, but your father insisted. I've never seen a ghost. Are you sure it wasn't a real person?'

'Did my father send you?'

The hopeful note in the girl's voice tugged at Sayrid's heart. She could easily remember how she once longed for her own father to pay her attention. And now it would appear Hrolf was behaving precisely as Ironfist had. Silently she vowed that Inga would not be forgotten again.

'He'll come along as soon as he has finished. And he will want to hear about the person you saw.'

'Ghost. He'll believe me about the ghost.' Inga tilted her chin up. Unshed tears swam in her eyes. 'He always believes me.'

'Inga is easily upset.' The nurse moved between Sayrid and the girl. 'She says things and thinks later.' The nurse turned towards Inga. 'What did I say about not provoking the giantess?'

Inga immediately hung her head. 'I don't want to be eaten. I want to grow up.'

'I'm not…' Sayrid gritted her teeth. Somehow she'd have to win both of them over. 'Did you see the ghost as well or only Inga?'

The nurse's eyes widened. 'My lady?'

'It is a simple enough question. Did you see this ghost? Or were you too busy with your needlework?'

The woman rapidly pulled the needle in and out of the cloth. 'Nobody pays attention to what an old woman like me sees. It makes no difference what I say. You will send me away because it is what new wives do.'

Sayrid clenched her jaw. Losing her temper was not going to help the situation, but she was certain Inga and her nurse had seen a real person. They could be the key to clearing Regin and allowing Auda her freedom.

'You look after Inga,' she said sharply. 'Inga must have been out of bed to see this lady by her father's ship. It stands to reason.'

The woman went pale. 'All I want is for Inga to please her father.'

Sayrid knelt down beside the nurse. 'I wanted to know if you saw it as well. It is a simple enough request. I'm not looking to get you in trouble or send you away, simply to solve a mystery.'

'Inga escaped when I went to get a drink. I was a few steps behind and the ghost had gone,' the woman admitted. 'Ghosts have a way of doing that.'

Sayrid clung on to her temper. It was wrong of the nurse to allow Inga to go down to the harbour, but it was also the best lead they had. 'Did Inga say anything more about the ghost at the time?'

'She said that the ghost was dressed in white with long blonde hair.' The nurse glanced at Inga. 'To my mind it sounded like Inga's mother come to warn us.'

'I lost my mother when I was about your age. Seeing her ghost would have been wonderful but frightening all at the same time. Was it like that for you?'

'Your mother…died?'

'From a fever,' Sayrid confirmed.

Inga held out the cloth. 'Would you like to sew with us? My mother used to sew with me.'

Sayrid gulped hard. Surely sewing on fine cloth was no more difficult than sewing on coarse sail.

'I could sew with you for a while and maybe you will remember more. I do so love a good ghost story.'

The nurse and Inga exchanged glances. Inga whispered something and the nurse's mouth twitched. She quickly shook her head.

'Do you want to?' the nurse asked. 'The pattern is quite complex.'

Sayrid set her jaw. 'I can sew.'

Inga clapped her hands and whispered something else. The nurse's frown increased. 'If you are certain you want to.'

Sayrid settled herself next to the pair. How hard could putting a few stitches in a cloth be? 'I wish to get to know my new daughter better. For that I will sew.'

Inga gave her a shy smile, but there was a twinkling in her eye which Sayrid knew meant mischief. 'I would like that.'

Sayrid chose to focus on the smile. She would find a way to make friends with the girl. She would not repeat her stepmother's mistakes.

Hrolf stepped back from the final ship. The only one which showed any signs of tampering was his main ship. Either his flagship had been deliberately targeted or the saboteurs had been interrupted. Both options left him distinctly uncomfortable. The sooner he and his family were in his new hall, which could be properly defended, the better. Other than the brooch Sayrid had found, there had been no clues.

'You have a theory?' he asked Bragi.

Bragi shrugged. 'An unwelcome mystery, but this was no wedding-night mischief.'

'A warning perhaps. Or perhaps they were disturbed by revellers if Sayrid's theory is correct. It is hard to know.' Hrolf fingered the brooch. His new wife had a quick brain, something he'd rarely encountered in a woman. Following his uncle's creed, most of the women he'd intimately known were for bedding only. Even Inga's mother had bored him once she opened her mouth with all her talk of sewing and weaving.

The marriage was for a specific purpose—to provide land and ensure Inga was brought up in the right way. If he forgot that, he was doomed just as his father had been.

His father had quarrelled with his uncle over a piece of land one jul feast and the family had left abruptly. When they arrived home, his mother discovered she'd left her precious mirror behind.

His father refused to return for it and forbade her to go. But she went anyway, declaring that her brother was right about him. When she didn't return, his father refused to search for her. When her frozen body was discovered, she had the mirror with her and grief and guilt had unhinged his father's mind.

He'd already seen the tricks Sayrid was willing to play to get her own way.

'What do you make of this?' he asked, holding out the brooch. 'Man or woman's?'

Bragi examined the brooch with a frown. 'The working is very delicate, more like a woman would wear. But it would be good for trading purposes. I couldn't tell the identity of its last owner.'

'And you are certain it was a warrior who moved the boards?'

Bragi gave a laugh. 'The only woman capable of such a feat would be your lady wife.'

'A woman could have been a lookout.' Hrolf dislodged a bit of dirt from the back of the brooch and the meaning of the runes suddenly became clear. His blood ran cold. His old enemy Lavrans had used the simple code before and it would appear he had done so again. *Lavrans Sea*

King gave this to...but the final rune was badly scratched and unreadable.

Hrolf pursed his lips. Lavrans might have been his rival and fellow sea king, but there the comparison stopped. Hrolf had never betrayed a comrade or looted villages that were supposedly loyal or raped women for the sheer pleasure of hearing them scream. Hrolf prided himself on never having to force a woman. The bad blood between them had started when Inga's mother had preferred Hrolf to Lavrans and made no secret of her preference. Lavrans had tried to rape her, but Hrolf had intervened and taken the woman under his protection. But the affair had rapidly cooled and Hrolf had found excuses to stay away.

'These markings tell a very interesting tale.' He held out the brooch. 'They're the same trading code we use in the East. Lavrans's name is on it.'

'You can read them? They seem like gibberish to me.' Bragi scratched his head. 'But I'm not so good with runes.'

'It would appear Sayrid was correct when she swore that there must be a traitor.'

'We have been here weeks without incident.'

Hrolf stared at the sunlight playing on the waters of the harbour. Everything seemed at peace, but he refused to trust the calm. 'We need to take steps before Lavrans strikes. I won't squander this opportunity.'

'Sayrid and her family...what of them? Will they be involved? Could the brother be the elusive traitor?'

'No, Lavrans hated Ironfist with a passion.' Hrolf rapidly explained the story Sayrid had told him.

'What do you intend to do?'

'I intend to take control of my hall and its fabled harbour as soon as possible. Whoever controls that will be able to dictate terms.' Hrolf took the brooch back and pocketed it. If Lavrans hated Sayrid before for what her father had done, he would have even more cause for hatred now that she was married to Hrolf. 'No one will take it from me.'

The other warrior's face became troubled. 'The *jaarl* is certain to want to keep the sister. If, as you say, Lavrans hates the family...you know what he is capable of.'

'Developing a soft spot, Bragi?'

'I admired Sayrid's bravery earlier.' The warrior did not meet Hrolf's eye. 'It takes a certain amount of courage to speak up. And to wear a dress like that. Trousers were wasted on her. By Thor, she has spirit.'

A surge of blood went to Hrolf's head. 'Bragi!'

The other man laughed. 'I never thought to see the day when you'd react to a little teasing.'

'I'll speak to Kettil.' Hrolf tossed the brooch in the air and concentrated on catching it as he forcibly put the anger from his mind. 'Taking control of the headland becomes a priority, but our treaty with Kettil includes providing protection in case of attack. You remain here.'

The other warrior looked unhappy, but nodded his agreement. 'I gave you my oath to obey.'

'When you can, bring the girl to the hall. It is her home.'

'How will you keep Sayrid from fighting if he does attack the hall?'

Hrolf lifted a brow. 'My wife will obey me.'

'Good luck with that. I've rarely met a stronger-willed woman.'

'I will tame her, Bragi.'

Sayrid struggled with her needlework. Her silk kept tangling. She wanted to throw it down in disgust, but one glace at Inga and her perfect stitching showed her why she couldn't. She wanted to make friends with her stepdaughter, only perhaps she had made the wrong choice. Sayrid gave the thread a yank and it snapped. She muttered a curse under her breath.

'Perhaps my lady would rather be elsewhere,' the nurse said with an inscrutable face.

Sayrid silently agreed, but being elsewhere was not an option. She'd given Hrolf her word. Hopefully Inga now saw that she wasn't someone to be feared.

'There is something wrong,' she said with a frown. 'My bit bears little resemblance to yours.'

'It should be red there, not blue. We are embroidering my father's badge,' Inga remarked.

Sayrid struggled to control the scream welling up inside her. 'I thought you said it was blue.'

Inga gave a deceptively innocent smile. 'Oh dear. I made a mistake.'

'On purpose?'

Inga hung her head. 'Yes.'

'How would you like it if I had done that to you?'

Inga's startled gaze met hers. Sayrid returned it steadily. Inga was the first to look away.

'Not much,' she mumbled.

Playing tricks was progress of a sort. And she

could clearly remember the sort of tricks her men had played on her during that first voyage. The non-response always worked best.

'I will get this right now I know the correct pattern.' Sayrid gritted her teeth and unpicked the work for the third time.

'What is happening here?' Hrolf's voice called out. 'I never thought I'd see a former shield maiden contentedly sewing fine linen.'

'Appearances can be deceptive,' Sayrid muttered.

Inga jumped up, spilling the silks to the ground as she ran to her father. He picked her up and spun her around as she shrieked.

Sayrid leant down to pick the threads up, hoping it would give her time to have her heart rate return to normal. 'My lord. You will see that I can keep my promises.'

He set his daughter down and came over to where Sayrid stood. Nothing in his demeanour gave her a clue about what had happened at the harbour. She concentrated on breathing deeply. Demanding to know if he'd found the proof of Regin's innocence would only inflame the situation.

'Your daughter is an accomplished seamstress,' she said instead.

He held out a deep-red tunic and a pair of wool trousers. 'I believe you will find these more to your taste. When we get to the hall, you will have plenty of time to use your needle and thread.'

Sayrid stared at the tunic and trousers in shock. He was offering her clothes which would fit far better than the rags she currently wore. 'Yours?'

'I can only wear one set of clothes at a time.' He shook his head. 'That dress is all wrong. Go inside and put them on.'

'What made you change your mind?'

He shrugged. 'Call it a peace offering. Whoever attempted to sabotage the ship has nothing to do with us.'

Sayrid fingered the tunic. A peace offering. The unexpectedness of it made her heart turn over. She wanted to hate him, but he kept giving her reasons to be grateful to him. He had given her clothes she could feel comfortable in.

She caught her upper lip between her teeth. The fact that he had come on his own without warriors or his bodyguard was a good sign. 'I will be a moment.'

She went into the house and rapidly changed.

The gown's final threads gave way as she pulled it over her head. She was pleased no one else was in there so she could strip off her undergown as well. She slid the tunic over her bare shoulders.

Hrolf's clothes were well made and the material finer than she normally wore and it felt good to be in trousers once again...even if they were a little larger than she was used to. She tied the belt tightly about her waist.

'She makes far too big stitches,' Inga was saying with a giggle when Sayrid returned. 'It is very easy to fool her, but then she is a giantess. I mean, her gown...'

Hrolf's face instantly became stern. 'Who gave you permission to criticise your new mother?'

The girl gulped twice. 'I...I...thought it was best to speak the truth.'

'If I ever discover you had a hand in playing a trick on Sayrid or her being publically humiliated, there will be consequences. Do you remember what I said the last time you told tales?'

Inga appeared close to tears as she threw her arms about Hrolf's knees. 'You won't send me away, will you?'

'Inga speaks the truth,' Sayrid called out, acting on impulse as a warm spot grew within her. Hrolf was defending her.

They turned towards her. Inga's eyes widened. 'You're wearing men's clothes! My far's clothes.'

'They fitted me better than the gown.'

'I agree about the clothes, but continue,' Hrolf said. 'You intrigue me. Why does Inga speak the truth?'

'Every time I start to sew, I seem to get the colour wrong or the stitch in the wrong place. Inga might have tried to trick me, but truly, she needn't have bothered. I know my limitations. Ask Auda or, better still, ask my stepmother if you ever encounter her,' Sayrid admitted with a laugh. Long ago she'd learnt to laugh at herself before others did. It took some of the pain away. And now she was back in her usual uniform of tunic and trousers, it was easier. 'But I did warn you of that…before we married. I've little talent with such things.'

'Running a household takes more skills than sewing a fine seam,' Hrolf said to Inga, frowning. 'Sayrid will teach you. She is being falsely modest. Her estate is one of the best in all of Svear.'

Sayrid concentrated on the ground. Despite everything, he still believed she had something to offer and, unlike her stepmother or her father, he praised her. He was willing to give her the benefit of the doubt. It meant more than it should. Silently she promised that she would try, and not just for the promise of going east should he go again.

Inga gulped twice. 'I didn't want to make you angry, Far. I was playing a game, but it went too far.'

'I expect better from my daughter. Telling tales and playing tricks. You were supposed to leave such things behind in Rus. It is high time you were brought up in the Svear way! Perhaps Magda should go if she cannot control you.'

Both the nurse and Inga cowered.

'Did you find the culprit?' Sayrid asked to defuse the tension. She might not particularly like Inga's nurse, but getting rid of her would destroy any chance she had of developing a relationship with the girl. She would not lower herself to behave like her stepmother. 'Inga knows not to play tricks on me now. And I'm pleased to have such a clever stepdaughter. I wish I could sew like that.'

Inga positively glowed. 'See, Far. The giantess doesn't mind.'

'Do you have any more clues about who damaged the ship?' Sayrid asked.

'The only clue is the brooch you found,' Hrolf said gravely.

'Which doesn't belong to my brother.'

'I am rather inclined to believe you.'

'Maybe the ghost saw who did it,' Inga piped up.

Hrolf drew his brows together. 'What did I say about tales and tricks? Inga, your manners get worse and worse.'

'Hrolf, allow the child to speak,' Sayrid said. 'I used to hate it when my father dismissed me without a fair hearing.'

Inga screwed up her eyes. 'I know what I saw last night in the darkness. There was a ghost with long blonde hair.'

Hrolf knelt down. 'How could you see anything, Little One? You were in bed.' He looked over her head, directly at the nurse. 'Please tell me that my daughter was in bed where she was supposed to be.'

The nurse paled and took a step back. 'Your daughter had trouble sleeping. She wanted to go for a walk by the water.'

Hrolf's face contorted as he rose. In the space

of a heartbeat he'd gone from indulgent parent to fearsome warrior. 'What have I said about disobeying me?'

Inga gave a little squeak and hid her face while the nurse made little clucking noises.

Sayrid forced a smile. 'It can be hard to sleep when your father has just married and all are at the feast. A walk beside the harbour can be calming. And surely some goddess watched over Inga last night.'

'Why is Inga disobeying me a good thing?'

'There is a real possibility that Inga might have seen someone. As you are not planning on getting married again, the problem won't be repeated.'

The nurse started in surprise before giving her a grateful look. 'Just so. We went for a walk to get away from the loud shouting.'

'Oh, it hurt my ears,' Inga added. 'And I did see my mother's ghost, standing by your ship. All in white. Then I ran and ran back to my bed and didn't stop until I was lying next to Magda with the covers over my head.'

'I'm sure you did,' Sayrid replied and silently willed Hrolf to realize that ghosts did not drop brooches. For some reason a woman had stood there. Once they found the woman, they would discover the culprit. And that Inga's fright was more than enough to keep her from wandering again.

He knelt down beside Inga. 'Did you see anyone beside the ghost?'

Inga shook her head slowly. 'Does Magda have to go, because I escaped?'

'It depends on what Sayrid decides. It is the wife who decides such matters, not the husband in Svear.'

The little girl turned big eyes towards her. 'Please. I'm sorry if I did bad things. It was me, not Magda. I didn't want a new mother. I wanted my mother, but she isn't coming back. She's dead. Seeing the ghost showed me that. Please don't take Magda away from me.'

'Magda can stay...for now,' Sayrid said. 'Inga is obviously devoted to her. It can be hard to make a new life in an unfamiliar country.'

Magda blinked rapidly. 'You want me to stay? After I called you a giantess? After the sewing...'

Sayrid glanced towards where Inga stood, clutching her nurse's hand. It was Inga's wide-eyed stare that made her determined to do what was right for the child. It would be easy to dismiss the woman, but then she risked alienating

Inga forever. 'Yes, I do, but I want no more tales of frost giants or bewitching. Or tricks with sewing. Let us make peace.'

Hrolf spoke to the nurse very slowly, first in Norse and then in her own language. As he began to speak in the foreign tongue, the nurse fell down to her knees and raised her arms to the skies.

'She calls on all the spirits to bless your name and regrets she ever thought you an ogress who bewitched me.' A smile tugged at the corner of his mouth. 'I've explained that if it was up to me, she would have left on the next tide.'

Sayrid raised her brow. Men! Silently she resolved to find a way to earn this girl's trust. 'Then it is good that it's not to up you.'

'We leave on the turn of the tide.' His face allowed for no dissent. 'I want to inspect my new hall.'

'Just like that.'

'Do you have a problem with my order?'

Sayrid's heart thudded. Hrolf was up to something more than simply inspecting the hall. 'No, why would I?'

Hrolf turned towards Magda and told her to ensure Inga was ready to depart as he waited for no woman, large or small. The older woman hurried away with Inga in tow. Sayrid stared at him with growing frustration. He should have consulted her! She struggled to remember the last time she hadn't been consulted about something this major.

'Has Kettil agreed to our leaving? Will Auda be allowed to go with us?' she asked as he started to walk away.

He put an arm about her waist and drew her closer. 'I want to sail before any more damage can be done. Before the traitor has a chance to cause more mischief.'

His breath blew against her ear, making her remember the way they had lain together this morning before the interruption. She glanced over her shoulder to see who might watching, but they were alone. Her heart started beating far too fast, but her mind screamed not to trust him. What was good for Hrolf was not necessarily good for her or her family. Once he was at the hall, he would be able to hold it against everyone with very little manpower. Her father had begun the improvements to the harbour's defences, but she had strengthened them, creating a formidable blockade of sunken ships and other debris to narrow the entrance.

He began to caress her back, then his hand dipped ever lower, skimming her backside. She instantly stiffened. A couple of touches and she'd melt. She moved away from him.

'You believe Lavrans is about to attack and you plan to abandon Kettil?' she said, pouring scorn into her voice as she attempted to get her breathing under control. 'How like a sea king!'

'I'm leaving enough warriors for his needs, but neither of us wishes to lose your harbour.' He gazed at her with a puzzled expression. 'Lavrans needs a base to launch his raid.'

'I did not leave it unguarded.'

'And your men are loyal to whom, precisely? Forgive me, but after last night, I'm wary. Your brother could easily be headed there.'

'He is going to see my stepmother. He would never betray me in that fashion.' She stamped her feet in frustration. 'And Auda? Does she remain here? An innocent hostage?'

'Kettil's wife has taken a liking to her.'

A cold place developed in the pit of Sayrid's stomach. Auda was Kettil's hostage. No one paid the slightest heed to the implications of the brooch she'd discovered. It proved Regin's innocence. She knew it did.

She wanted to curl up in a ball and hide away from the world. But that option was not available to Ironfirst's eldest. She had to fight, particularly as this entire mess was the fault of her greed and arrogance.

'Unacceptable. I want my sister safe and that means at home with me. The brooch—'

'Your sister will be safe. I pledge my word. Kettil has pledged as well. He is satisfied that your sister knows nothing about the sabotage or your brother's future plans.'

'What do you expect? My brother is innocent.' She gazed directly at him and willed him to answer. 'What has changed?'

'You were right, Sayrid. I cleaned the brooch and another rune appeared—Lavrans's personal rune. Whoever sabotaged my boat wanted me to stay here. I'm in no mood to oblige.'

The knowledge rocked through her. 'Being right gives me no pleasure.'

A muscle jumped in his cheek. 'Nor should it.'

'And the urgency?' Sayrid tapped her foot on the ground and struggled to hold on to her temper. 'Why the next tide? Do I have to prise everything out of you? I can understand tactics, Hrolf. Better than most.'

He stopped and seemed to grow into the formidable sea king who commanded a fleet of long ships. Sayrid stood her ground.

'I am trying to protect you, Sayrid,' he said finally, his gaze softening. 'I can do that better if we are at my hall. I want to assess its strengths and weaknesses. If someone isn't there to prevent it, that harbour becomes the back door to this whole area. Lavrans wants a jaarldom at least.'

'Or potentially a trap to lure you out of the harbour. When the ships go around the headland, they will be exposed until they reach the bay.'

'In a sea fight, my men will win. I've beaten Lavrans before.'

'If there is a battle, I expect to fight.'

His hands rose as if he wanted to shake her, but he checked the movement. Instead he gave a placating smile. 'The women in my family are shielded so they don't have to lift a sword.'

'That has changed.'

'Why?'

'I've a tendency to fight first and ask questions after.'

He burst out in a loud laugh, breaking the tension which had sprung up between them. His lips lightly brushed her forehead. 'I'm anxious to continue our lessons. When we are at the hall, there'll be no interruptions, Sayrid. Far better for us. Think about that.'

Sayrid frowned as a warm tremor radiated out from his touch. 'I was being serious.'

He put his arm about her shoulders and pulled her close. 'We sail on the tide. We will begin our marriage properly on our lands.'

She stared up into his piercing blue gaze. A warm glow infused her being. She shook her head to clear it. His new lands were her home, the one she shared with her brother and sister. 'You need the secret to getting into the harbour.'

'And if I attempt it without a guide?'

'You would be dashed against the rocks.'

He raised a brow. 'Thus far I've avoided them.'

'There is always a first time.' Sayrid tilted her head to one side. She had to make sure that Auda was freed. 'I will tell you the secret to getting into the harbour if you allow Auda to travel with us.'

'You believe you can bargain?'

'Yes.' She tilted her chin upwards and met his gaze. 'The well-being of my family comes first.'

'Your sister will be safe with Kettil and his wife until we know the threat from Lavrans is gone.' Hrolf began to stride away. 'Bargaining with me won't work, Sayrid. You will tell me because you will want to save your life.'

'I can swim. Can you?'

He stared at her for a long while. 'We shall have to see who blinks first, but you will be coming with me and you will reveal all your secrets.'

The tunic rubbed across her scars. Not all her secrets if she wanted him to desire her.

Chapter Nine

The afternoon sun sparkled on the water and a small crowd gathered at the harbour to see them off. Auda stood next to the *jaarl*'s wife and watched with large reproachful eyes. Sayrid's heart sank. She hated failing either of her siblings. When Sayrid caught Auda's eye, Auda gave a brave wave, but it made things worse somehow.

'You will soon return home. I promise,' Sayrid mouthed.

Auda nodded as if she understood and linked arms with the *jaarl*'s wife.

Kettil came over to the pair and put his arm about his wife. She said something up to him and he looked down at her with love and devotion. Something within Sayrid melted.

For once in her life she wanted Hrolf to look

at her like that. She wanted to matter to her husband.

Annoyed at her thoughts, she adopted her fiercest face and put her shoulder against the boat, preparing to help push it out to the sea.

'What are you doing, Sayrid?' Hrolf thundered.

She braced her feet more firmly against the sandy shore. 'Helping to launch the boat.'

Strong hands lifted her up and carried her forward, before dumping her unceremoniously into the ship. The entire crew erupted into laughter.

She swiftly rose to her feet and glared at Hrolf. 'There was no call to do that!'

A smile played on his lips, but his eyes were deadly serious. 'My women do not do heavy work.'

'I'm your wife, not your woman.'

The laughter in the boat instantly died.

Hrolf leapt over the side and retook his place by the oar. He gave a maddening smile. 'All the more reason why you should be honoured instead of being made to work like a thrall.'

Sayrid squared her shoulders. 'Where should I sit, then? Do you expect me to row?'

'Where you like, but do not hinder the oarsmen,' Hrolf called from where he sat beside the steering oar. 'The tide favours us.'

Sayrid counted sixteen oarsmen and no other warriors. It was larger than the ship she normally used, but very well maintained and designed for skimming across the water. The oarsmen were placed in such a fashion that they would get maximum thrust from the oars. Sayrid had learnt to her cost on her second voyage that it mattered a great deal where the oarsmen were positioned.

Despite her determination not to be overawed, she couldn't help but be impressed. She could tell from the way it was built that it would glide over the water, unlike the sluggish pace her own ship used.

Inga and her nurse obviously had been assigned places near to where Hrolf manned the steering oar. Sayrid hesitated until the nurse gestured that she must sit with them.

'My father can walk the oars while the men are rowing,' Inga said, tilting her chin upwards. 'Can you do that?'

'I've never tried,' Sayrid said. 'My father used to boast of it, but it never made sense to my mind. What practical purpose does it serve?'

The girl shuffled over to make room on the

bench. 'Well, he can do it. He has very good balance. And it is ever so exciting to see. It means that the men can all row together or so Far says.'

'I hadn't thought about that,' Sayrid admitted.

Inga gave a pleased smile. 'Basic seamanship, or so my father says.'

'Walking the oars is not what is required now, Inga,' Hrolf called out from where he sat. 'Stop trying to make me seem better than I am. Allow Sayrid to judge my seamanship herself. She is an expert sailor.'

'Inga is rightfully proud of her father. Allow her to boast,' Sayrid called back. 'I used to think the same of my father when I was her age. And I can tell from the lines of the ship that the journey will take next to no time.'

Inga squeezed Sayrid's hand. 'I'm sorry I thought you were a giantess. You're far too friendly to be a frost giant in disguise. They're always cross. I should have remembered that. Maybe you're another sort of giantess, the friendly sort. And if I'm very lucky you will give me some magic potion and I'll grow big and strong like you. Then my father will have to notice me.'

Sayrid's heart did a little flip. She could well remember that feeling. In the end the only way her father had noticed her was when she challenged him with the point of a sword. There had to be a better way for Inga. 'What changed your mind?'

The little girl shrugged. 'You didn't get angry with me about the trick I played with the threads and sewing. A frost giantess would have turned me to ice.'

She gave a little pretend shiver.

'But it wasn't a very pleasant trick, particularly as I'm not very good at sewing.'

Inga's big eyes became solemn. 'I can teach you. Sewing is easy if you concentrate hard.'

'I'd like that.'

'Are we going to your house? Will I become big and strong like you? Will I be able to wear clothes like that?'

Sayrid blinked. Delicate Inga wanted to wear trousers like a man? 'Why would you want to?'

Inga glanced towards where Hrolf sat, making the final preparations. 'I want Far to be proud of me. He gave you his clothes and he has never done anything like that for me. Or any other lady.'

'I suspect it is because other women wear gowns.' The words hurt far more than she thought they would.

'Will you tell me the secret of the magical harbour?' Inga gave Sayrid's hand another squeeze. 'I overheard Magda's nephews talking.' She gestured towards where Hrolf's bodyguards sat. 'You cast a spell and the ships drown. You won't do that to us, will you?'

Sayrid knew in that instant what an empty threat it had been. She couldn't put Inga's life in jeopardy.

Sayrid opened her mouth to explain that it wasn't magic but sunken boats, but there was something akin to hope in Inga's eyes. Little girls should believe in such things, she decided. There was plenty of time for Inga to learn about the real world when she was older. 'When the time comes, I will see you safely through.'

The little girl nodded gravely.

'When he was a little boy, his father had a hall, but he lost it because when his wife died, he lost interest in everything,' Inga said after a short silence. 'My father had to fight, fight, fight and he gained more gold than anyone, but he has never allowed any woman to be close to him. You are the first woman he's married. Is it because you don't act like a woman?'

'No idea.' Sayrid forced her voice to sound light. She hated that even now her heart was busy dreaming dreams about Hrolf and what could never be. 'You will have to ask him.'

'We have to be quiet now,' Inga whispered when Hrolf gave her a dark look. 'Far needs to tell the oarsmen a story.'

Hrolf began to recite one of the sagas, putting an emphasis on the last word in each line. Each time he did, the men pulled their oars in unison. The method might be unorthodox but he appeared to have timed the strokes just right, taking full advantage of the turn in the tide to add extra speed.

Once they had cleared the harbour wall, he gave a nod and the oarsmen fell into a steady rhythm.

The spray as they left the harbour hit Sayrid in the face. She had forgotten how good it felt to be on the sea. Her clumsiness always seemed to vanish once she was out on the water. It just seemed strange to be sitting and doing nothing. For as long as she could remember, she had taken the steering oar, guiding the ship and calling out the time.

'I like it when we go fast,' Inga exclaimed, spluttering as another wave hit. 'Magda doesn't understand. We have to outrun the sea monsters. And the women on a boat have to sit still or they get in the way. Far's orders.'

'Funny, I've always found it difficult to obey such orders.' Sayrid crossed her arms. Hrolf might be an excellent navigator, but he was going to need her help to get through the blockade. She only hoped that he would listen. 'Does he allow anyone else to steer?'

'Never.' Inga gave a quick shake of her head. 'The boat only obeys him. It is how the magic works.'

Hrolf carefully steered the boat around the rocks of the headland, keeping the boat close enough to the shore to follow the contours, but far enough away not to run the risk of ending up on the rocks. The departure had gone smoothly. Kettil had made a good show of it and anyone who was watching would not suspect his real intentions of securing the headland so it could not be used against them.

The wind was strong, but not overly so. They would make Ironfist's hall before the sun fell.

His new life had begun, the one he'd sworn he'd have on his first battlefield, when he was covered with mud and gore, and one that he swore anew to have at the end of each voyage and battle. He had regained all that his father had lost and more.

And he was not about to make the same mistakes his father had. Not with ships and certainly not with women.

He adjusted the line of the boat. The pull he felt towards Sayrid would go once he had properly bedded her. It always did. He knew where the boundaries lay. He had followed his uncle's advice and made something of his life. Falling prey to the same folly as his father was not going to happen. Except Sayrid kept making him wish the boundaries were not as clear-cut.

He glanced towards where Inga and Sayrid sat. Inga had fallen asleep with her golden curls splayed out on Sayrid's lap. Sayrid's face wore a slightly panicked expression as she struggled to keep the little girl comfortable. When she thought no one was looking, she stroked Inga's head in a maternal way.

His groin tightened just looking at her and the way the sea breeze blew her hair from her face revealing the curve of her neck.

'Soon,' he whispered. 'Soon.'

'Hrolf!' Sayrid called out, shifting Inga on to Magda's lap and standing up. 'There is something on the starboard. Fast approaching.'

Hrolf quickly glanced towards where Sayrid pointed. A small movement against the blue sea, but all of his muscles tightened. He silently cursed his own inattention. He should have noticed it before Sayrid.

'Could be nothing. The wind playing on the waves.' Silently he prayed he was correct. Even Lavrans would not take the risk this far from a friendly harbour.

'It is moving far too purposefully.'

Hrolf shielded his eyes. Every sinew of his body strained. They were too far from the harbour to make it back and outrunning a fully armed boat would be difficult, but not impossible. Perhaps he should have heeded Kettil's advice and waited for Lavrans to make his move. But it was far too late for regrets. He would protect everyone on board ship.

A white spout of water caused his neck muscles to ease. His daughter was not going to be in the heat of battle. 'We have nothing to fear from a pod of whales. They are busy about their business.'

A tiny frown developed between Sayrid's brows. 'Whales? Really? At this time of year?'

He watched the magnificent creatures move before steering the boat closer towards the group. 'Whales can appear at any time.'

'Why are you doing this?' Sayrid grabbed his arm.

'To show you what they look like. Surely you don't consider them to be sea monsters like Magda?' He gave a half smile. 'I know how close I can go. I consider them to be part of my luck, a good omen. I have fought some of my best battles after seeing whales.'

'I know what whales look like. Occasionally a body washes up after a storm.' Her face took on a wistful expression, banishing the hardened-warrior face she often wore and giving him a glimpse of the woman she should have been. 'Once there was even one who was alive. My father said we shouldn't try to save it, but I had to.'

'What happened?' he asked softly, willing her to say more.

'I kept it wet and waited for the high tide, praying to any god who might be listening. It seemed such a shame to allow a magnificent creature to die without a fight.' Her eyes blazed defiance. 'It did go. My father said it was a waste as we could have used the whale for many things. And that the whale would just die out at sea and be good for no one.'

'But you did it anyway.'

The story told him a great deal about Sayrid's relationship with her father. He wished that he could have known the brave girl who dared defy one of the most fearsome warriors in Svear before she had developed her armour of indifference to femininity. He would unleash her from that armour, he silently promised. This morning her guard had been down and she had nearly yielded.

'I like to think it is out there swimming free,' she admitted with a shrug. 'I was younger then. I would probably be more inclined to my father's way of thinking these days.'

'Perhaps this pod has your whale.'

Her tongue flicked over her lips, turning them a kissable red. 'We still need to avoid them. One wave of the tail and this boat could be swamped.'

'I reckon I know what I'm doing.' Hrolf steered the boat closer. Concentrating on the boat and the whales would allow him time to control his reaction to her. His body ached with the need of her. He struggled to remember when a woman had last had this effect on him. He needed to bed her soon and get her out of his mind so he could concentrate on more important matters, like defeating Lavrans.

'Then I should get back to where Magda and Inga are.'

He captured her wrist and tugged. 'Stay. They are both sleeping. Magda would only panic about sea monsters. She is not a very good passenger and Inga often gets seasick. I've learnt to let them sleep.'

'Spoken with an experienced voice.'

'I've travelled a few times on the sea.' He stared at her, willing her to believe in him. 'Trust me with my boat. I won't put anyone in danger.'

She sank down beside him. Together they watched the progress of the whales. One surfaced near them and another went under the boat, but Hrolf gave quiet commands to his men who instantly obeyed them.

There was a final spout of water before the animals dived deep and disappeared. The entire boat sat in total silence with resting oars as the sunlight played on the water.

'Yes, I do believe you know how to handle a boat,' she said, breaking the almost reverent silence. 'The whales will bring luck.'

'High praise indeed.' Hrolf gave a command

and his men began to row in earnest. 'The whales are a good omen. Are you willing to admit that?'

'I'd forgotten how magnificent they could be,' Sayrid admitted with a half shrug. 'If I had been in charge of the steering oar, we wouldn't have seen that and it is something I will remember for a long time.'

Hrolf put his hand over hers. It trembled. 'The entrance to the fabled harbour is coming shortly. Kettil explained the landmarks so I wouldn't get lost. Will you share its secret, even though I was unable to bring your sister with us?'

'The entrance is blockaded.' She spoke to the oar. 'Even Kettil doesn't know the pathway through. I changed it before I left for the Assembly.'

Hrolf went completely still. She had confirmed what he suspected. 'I can pick my way through. It is why the boat rides high in the water. I've made my way through narrow passages before. I can post a man on the prow as a lookout.'

'There are only three people who know how to make it through—Regin, Auda and me. We have sworn never to utter the directions out loud or write them down.'

Hrolf closed his eyes. She was right. He might risk his men, but Inga? His uncle would not have hesitated, but Hrolf knew he couldn't do it. 'I suspect Lavrans will try to take the headland. And I think someone will betray the secret to him.'

He willed her to understand what he was saying and why they had to go ahead.

The breeze whipped her hair from her face, revealing her high cheekbones.

'The only way he could would be if Regin or Auda betrayed me and they won't,' she whispered.

'What is your price now?' he asked quietly and waited.

She wrinkled her nose. 'My price is steering your ship.'

Trust her with his ship? A day ago he'd have refused out of hand, but he'd seen Sayrid's intelligence and he knew her reputation for being a skilled oarsman. If anyone was capable of devising a secret way, it was her.

He had to do something he had sworn that he'd never do—he had to trust her with his beloved ship. He had no choice. He moved over on the bench. 'The *Sea Bird* would be honoured to have such a helmsman.'

Her throat worked up and down. 'Woman. Helmswoman.'

He put her fingers on the oar. 'The *Sea Bird* responds best to a light touch.'

She clasped the oar with an assurance that had to be from steering a hundred other voyages. 'I will show you that a woman can steer as well as a man.'

'When that woman is you, it will come as no surprise.' Hrolf put his hands behind his head, trying to give the impression of utter relaxation, but every sinew tensed until she brought the ship back to a steady course. His uncle had been wrong—women could have other skills than cooking, weaving and bed sport. But it was still his job to protect her.

The gabled hall rose up by the water. Its weathered roof gleamed grey in the afternoon sunlight. From where she sat, Sayrid could see its imperfections—the gables needed another coat of paint and the roof sagged badly at one end. But the birch and larch rose behind the house and the tuntreet spread its branches in front. Home.

She risked a glance at Hrolf, who had sat silent and tense during their progress through the blockade. Her shoulder ached from keeping the boat on the right course, but she had done it.

'The welcome party has gathered,' she said carefully, gesturing to where a group of farm-workers stood.

It was far too late for regrets, but she found it impossible to keep the faint hope down that he might actually fall in love with the hall and the surrounding farmland and give her time to prove her worth. She wanted… Sayrid forced her mind from it.

He was a sea king and they were always overly proud. The thought rang false to her. Hrolf might be proud, but he had reason to be. His seamanship was second to none.

'They appear hostile.' Hrolf's face darkened. 'What is going on, Sayrid? Have your people forgotten the basic laws of hospitality?'

'Watch and learn.'

Sayrid raised her right arm and made the boat give a hard wriggle to the right, to the left and to the right again before continuing straight. To her relief, the large ship obeyed her touch on the oar and did not overbalance.

'Is that strictly necessary?' Hrolf's face darkened.

'Yes.' Sayrid repeated the manoeuvre twice more, each time raising her right arm.

A ragged cry of welcome floated out over the water. Her pair of elkhounds started barking joyfully. The two dogs jumped into the water and started to guide the boat towards a good beaching spot.

'They know we are friendly before they can see my face.'

'Impressive. Just like the blockade. You have your people well trained…as long as someone doesn't betray you.'

She glanced at him. To explain about Regin and Auda would mean explaining about the scars on her back and she wasn't ready to see the revulsion on his face. She could still remember her stepmother's malicious pleasure as she rubbed the last of the sand in and how she crowed that even if a man married Sayrid, he would be revolted by what he found when he saw her naked and would never stay with her.

'And my dogs less so,' she said instead, pointing towards the pair of elkhounds that she had raised from puppies.

The elkhounds kept up a steady chorus of barks, waking Inga and Magda.

'They are pleased their mistress is home.'

Hrolf gave the order and the rowers did one more mighty heave before lifting the oars out of the water. Without stopping to think, Sayrid reacted as she always did and jumped into the water, getting ready to guide the boat to the best spot. She stopped just in time and contented herself with ducking her head under the water.

'I'm glad to be home,' she cried out to the sky and ducked her head a second time. As she did so, her borrowed tunic slid off her right shoulder.

When she surfaced, Hrolf was beside her. He put his arms about her waist. His eyes reflected the sun-sparkled water. On impulse she leant forward. His mouth tasted of salt, sea air and something indefinably him.

He lifted his mouth and gave her a searching look. There was a question in his eyes as his hand hovered by her neck. She tensed, waiting to see if he noticed her scarring.

He pulled her tunic up and retied the lace. 'Thank you.'

She blinked rapidly. Had he spotted her scars and pulled back? Silently she cursed that the tunic had slipped off one shoulder. 'Why?'

'For being you,' he murmured. 'You learn your lessons well. We are being watched.'

Sayrid bit her lip and held back the words explaining that the kiss had been impulsive. 'Why else would I have kissed you?'

'I can think of a few reasons.' His breath fanned her ear. 'I will tell you them later. Right now, we are on show.'

A tiny fluttering started in her stomach. He couldn't have seen her scars. She was fine. The trouble was that she wanted him to keep desiring her.

He cleared his throat and raised her arm above her head. 'Sayrid Avildottar is my bride. I won her.'

Stunned silence greeted the pronouncement. One of the women allowed her cup of ale to spill on the ground. Even the elkhounds sat on the shore with their heads tilted to one side as if waiting for Sayrid's confirmation.

'We want to hear it from Sayrid!' a voice shouted. 'Why isn't Regin or Auda with you?'

She started forward. 'Hrolf Eymundsson defeated me in a sword fight! Auda remains with Kettil and Regin and Blodvin have gone to see my stepmother. Who is going to greet their new lord?'

Various women hurried forward with cups of ale, offering the men a sip before they had advanced more than three paces from the boat.

'We should have wine, not ale,' Hrolf thundered.

Sayrid motioned to two of the women who hurried away.

'You should have allowed me to break the news gently,' she said in an undertone while they waited for the wine.

A twinkle shone his eyes. 'You were the one who kissed me in full view of the shore.'

Sayrid moved the tunic so that it was tighter about her neck. Had he seen the scars? The question stuck in her throat.

'An impulse,' she choked out.

'You should act on impulse more often.'

'There is no great love for sea kings here,' she said, pointedly changing the subject. 'It is one of the reasons why I made the elaborate defences.'

'Your system might not be orthodox, but it works. I doubt I could have found my way through. A magically protected harbour. I know Inga thinks so.'

Sayrid felt the heat on her cheeks increase. 'I wanted to take precautions. I had to go away from here to make a living, but I wanted to make sure that no one suffered for my absence. I've seen far too many holdings raided and seafarers returning to a pile of ash and all the sheep gone. And you can't always trust ships who go in with their shields hanging.'

'You did this? I thought your father...'

'He would have done it if he'd considered it,' she said far too quickly and instantly regretted it. She disliked criticising her father. Speaking ill of the dead never did anyone any good. She took a horn of wine from one of the serving women and held it out to him. 'He had other things on his mind. The might of his reputation kept most away in any case. May your reputation do the same. The people who work the land deserve to live in peace and not be harried by sea kings.'

'I see.' Hrolf drained it in a single gulp before mouthing the appropriate words accepting the hospitality. 'And your father is responsible for all this?'

'What do you mean?' Sayrid rubbed the back of her neck. A deep-within-the-bones tiredness swept over her now that she was home. She wanted to leave everything, find her bed and sleep. Her muscles ached from the fight. And she had no idea what tonight would bring. All she knew was that more than ever she wanted to protect the people who had served her so well.

'The farm and hall have prospered. After his death. Your sister is young and your brother's reputation inspires no confidence in his ability to successfully manage such an undertaking.'

'I have to be away. More often than I'd like, but someone must take our goods to market and I've been cheated before.' She watched the sunlight play on the waves, remembering how Bloodaxe and the others had laughed at her, offering her barely any gold for their timber and wool.

'And your brother wasn't capable? He is a grown warrior.'

She opened her mouth to protest and then shut it again. The less said about Regin the better. 'There were reasons.'

He looked as if he wanted to say more. She rapidly shook her head.

'There are people who will want to greet their new lord. It is well that I am here with you as they would never have believed this tale otherwise.'

'Will you give me a private tour after we get the introductions done?'

Her heart did a little flip. He must not have noticed the scarring. She was safe for a little while longer.

'There is sure to be a mass of things which require my attention. I'd barely come home before I had to leave for the Assembly.' She gestured to her clothes. 'I'm damp and should change.'

'But they can wait. Everything can wait until later. The sun is warm. Give them time to light the bath hut.' He brought her hand to his lips. 'Consider it an order if you must. But I want you as my tour guide and no false modesty about someone else having responsibility for this estate.'

Sayrid straightened her shoulders and tried to ignore the tingling sensation that coursed through her. 'You'd be better served by any number of people.'

He laced his fingers through hers. 'But I want *you.*'

Sayrid froze. Hrolf in this sort of mood was far more dangerous than when she had fought him for her life.

Chapter Ten

'This is the barn where we keep the hay,' Sayrid said, making her voice sound very matter-of-fact and practical rather than breathless and full of anticipation, which was how she kept feeling with Hrolf standing so close to her. As the tour progressed, his broad shoulders kept bumping her more and more frequently. With each touch, she found herself more reluctant to move away. 'We can go see the hiding places for the women in case of attack, but they are a little way from the main hall.'

'Another day. I assume they are a reasonable march.'

'Not too far. I wanted the women to be able to hide quickly. They are well stocked.'

'You have put a lot of thought into the defence of this place.'

'Someone had to.' She shrugged. 'Once my father died, we could no longer depend on his reputation as a warrior to keep the sea kings away.' She gave a strangled laugh. 'Did you pay much attention to reputations?'

'Some,' he admitted. 'Will you miss the voyages?'

'I always liked coming home the best,' she admitted, hugging her arms about her waist. Proof if she needed it that she wouldn't be travelling again. 'Seeing the gables rise up from the sea and knowing that everyone was safe. Some parts were exciting, but I did it for this place. Land gets into your blood. And you did promise that I could go with you to the East.'

'There were conditions to that promise. Have you fulfilled them?'

She crossed her arms and refused to allow her disappointment to show. He'd only given his word because he felt she wouldn't succeed. 'I'm trying.'

'Very trying.' His soft laugh rippled over her skin.

When she turned suddenly, he was there. Tall and unyielding. Masculine. She watched his mouth. She wanted to taste it again.

'Do you have much experience farming?' she asked in desperation. 'Do you know how to run an estate like this one? Or will more voyages be required to keep it functioning.'

'When I was a boy, I lived on a farm, but my father lost it and I was forced to seek my fortune. I always dreamt of owning somewhere like this.' He reached down, picked up a handful of grain and held it for a heartbeat before allowing it to trickle through his fingers. 'I will make it work. There is much that can be done. Walking around here, it continually amazes me that no one challenged you.'

'The reason is obvious to me.' Sayrid gave a careful shrug. 'My reputation as a warrior deterred many. A man wants to be a better warrior than his wife.'

'I've no worries on that score.' He took a step closer. 'Or maybe the way you scowl at everyone so they will think you tough when you are really scared. When are you going to let the true Sayrid come out from behind that mask you wear? The woman who kissed me down at the harbour? When are you going to stop hiding behind your sword arm?'

Sayrid bit her lip. There was no easy way to

answer that. She was proud of her skill, but she wasn't stupid. Her sword arm intimidated most men. Her stepmother had predicted it and she had been proved right. *Except for Hrolf,* whispered her heart. She quickly silenced it. Hrolf had married her for reasons which she still did not quite understand, but she was fairly certain had nothing to do with her as a person.

'I can teach your daughter. It is a way for me to keep my hand in, but I won't be fighting men.'

'My daughter knows enough. I've not left her defenceless.' He turned from her and picked up hay, which he gave to one of the horses. 'My seafaring days are over for the moment. I plan to farm. I won't have what happened to you happen to her.'

'What did happen to me?' Sayrid tapped her foot on the ground. 'I chose my path. I fought for it.'

'A shield maiden is not the life I would hope for her. No woman should have to endure it. Their menfolk should ensure it. A warrior's life is hard.'

Sayrid stared at the hay-strewn ground. The truth finally. It was as she feared. He disapproved of her and her lifestyle.

All that closeness on the boat had merely been

comradely. The bright shining hope she had had that she could continue to do the things she loved faded.

'I don't regret what I have done,' she said around the lump in her throat. 'I'm proud of it. I made sure my family survived and prospered. What is the harm in that?'

He lifted a brow. 'It is not something I'd wish for my daughter. Daughters should be kept safe.'

'I understand.' Sayrid turned away. She refused to show how much he'd hurt her. Underneath, he was like the others. He would never understand about her scars and would find them grotesque. Scars were expected on a warrior, but on a lady they repulsed, her stepmother had said with each swipe of the sand and seawater. The knowledge caused a great hollow to open in the pit of her stomach. 'You wish to forget what I was.'

In the dim light his eyes narrowed. 'When you have time, you may fashion gowns which fit you. You have to think about who you are now, not who you were. The sooner you embrace your new life, the sooner you get busy living it. My uncle once gave me that piece of advice and he was right. You have to stop being scared, Sayrid. I married to have a wife, not another warrior at my back.'

His voice had a certain finality about it.

She swallowed hard and started again. He didn't seem to understand how hopeless she was as a woman. She paused. If he cared anything for her, he would have understood that being a warrior was part of her.

'I hope you have found everything in order,' she said when she trusted her voice. 'Nothing is hidden. You may have the keys and inspect everything at your leisure, but you will want to get your men settled. We pride ourselves on our hospitality. They will be well entertained.'

'In good time.' His fingers brushed her elbow and his breath tickled the back of her neck. Her body tingled from his nearness. 'You seem to be in a hurry suddenly. Stay.'

Despite everything, her heart began to race, much faster than when she navigated her way through the blockade. 'You would not believe the list of things which requrie my attention. Because I had just returned from a voyage when the situation with Blodvin happened, there is even more to be done than usual. The land must be productive if another voyage is to be avoided.'

She finished, breathlessly aware of her frantic babbling. Hopefully he'd take her word and she could find reasons why they needed to be apart. In time they could settle for being companions and comrades.

She was the worst kind of idiot to think he wanted anything more. Her lands and the loyalty of her people were one thing. Her person was something else and she couldn't bear to be humiliated in the way her stepmother had predicted she would be.

'Those are excuses to run away.' His low voice penetrated her misery and pinned her to the ground, mid-flight. 'And you deliberately misunderstood me about my daughter. She enjoys womanly pursuits like sewing and weaving. I won't have her being forced into other activities.' He sighed. 'In Rus when I tried to get her interested in a sword, she could barely lift it and she cried.'

She spun around and nearly collided with him. She took a hurried step backwards, kicking over a bucket. She scrambled to right it, holding it in front of her like a shield. He stopped in midstoop, watching her every move.

'I'm merely trying to be efficient and I know

how a girl is supposed to be brought up,' she said, knowing she must seem anything but. And she wasn't trying to run away. It was simply if she stayed much longer, she'd do something stupid like kiss him again. And there were many reasons why she shouldn't, starting with her pride. 'There is nothing worse than prolonging an inspection when all the other person desires is a horn of sweet wine and a few songs from the *skald*. My father was very clear on that.'

His face turned speculative. 'Somehow I doubt you ever sit down with a horn of wine. And I'm not your father, not even remotely close.'

'You don't know me very well, then.' Sayrid snapped her fingers. 'I often sit down in the evening when I'm home. I know how to listen to the *skalds* and play *tafl*. I'm a very good *tafl* player.'

'What I know intrigues me.' He gave a half smile. 'I'm counting on you to be a good *tafl* player. All of my women before you have been poor *tafl* players.'

Her breath hitched. Intrigued him. Her body became infused with a light fizz, but just as quickly it vanished.

Damning with faint praise. In her mind she heard the echoes of her stepmother's cruel laugh to one of her father's more poisonous quips about her lack of femininity. She pinched the bridge of her nose. And Blodvin had already proclaimed that she thought *tafl* to be the sport of men when she first arrived. 'Will your daughter learn?'

'I'd never considered it. Perhaps when she is older.' He nodded. 'Yes, it would be a good thing. You will have to play me and we can see who is the most appropriate teacher.' He stroked his chin. 'We can consider a wager...unless you think your skill will be less than mine.'

'You haven't said what you think about the estate,' she said, forcing her voice to be bright as she firmly changed the subject.

'You prefer to speak of the estate.'

'A far better topic for conversation. You will soon see how I react to feasts and that I am more than capable of listening to music and drinking the appropriate number of healths.' She gave a small cough. 'I look forward to beating you at *tafl*, even though I probably shouldn't.'

'Why shouldn't you?' He appeared genuinely perplexed.

'My father hated being beaten at anything.'

'Little honour in winning if your opponent deliberately loses.' His eyes flashed. 'If you ever do that, you will know my anger.'

'The day I lose deliberately is the day I stop being true to myself.' She drew the cloak tighter about her. Her scars pained her slightly. 'I should go and change. You were right. I'm not a shield maiden any longer.'

His eyes darkened. 'Do you have clothes which fit? I do not want a repeat of earlier. My wife will be decently dressed in front of other men.'

'I do have a few old gowns. My stepmother used to insist that I dress like a woman when I was not training.'

Her throat closed about the words. She could so clearly remember coming home after her first voyage, all excited about her success and her stepmother refusing to acknowledge her until she had changed. She had come out to the barn and screamed her rage out.

'And you hated that.'

'How can you tell?'

He caught her chin between his fingers, holding her in place. 'I've been studying you. Intently.'

His thumb rubbed her lower lip. Off to one side, she heard the soft whoosh of the horses in their stalls. She hated that her body longed for his touch.

'What clues?' She barely recognised her voice.

'That would be telling.' He pushed her hair from her forehead. 'Stop being angry with me for wanting to enjoy my wife. Stop finding reasons to deny the woman you are.'

His mouth descended, claiming hers. Hot and heavy, but asking. Her traitorous lips parted as that rebellious part of her rejoiced that her mind had misread everything.

His tongue entered and stroked her, penetrating her inner recesses.

Her arm curled about his neck and held him there as she drank from his mouth, revelling in the faint taste of sweet wine.

She knew it was a madness to want more or to think that this was anything beyond his need for her land and wealth, but her heart no longer listened. No one was here in this dimly lit place. Her body had hungered for this ever since she woke to discover herself curled up next to him.

The small banked fire inside her sprang to life as the kiss intensified and grew, intoxicating her with its illicit invasion. Her heart soared and she arched her body forward, seeking intimate contact with the hard planes of his body.

His hands roamed her back, pulling her closer and she was left in no doubt of his arousal as it hit the apex of her thighs. Instead of frightening her, it called to something deep within her. She arched forward, seeking more, needing more.

His fingers came around and cupped her breasts, gently flicking her already erect nipples.

The belt she'd wrapped around her middle gave way under his gentle persuasion. And her too-large trousers fell to the ground, leaving her standing barelegged in the tunic.

The shock of the cool air hitting her skin made her pull back. What had she been doing? Pressing her body against him, practically begging like one of the serving girls. Anyone could have walked in.

She should have more dignity. Such things between husbands and wives happened at night, in the dark. She wanted him to treat her with the proper respect. Her stepmother had been clear on that—men needed to know where the boundaries lay. A man should respect his wife, not treat her as he would another woman.

She bent down to retrieve the trousers.

'Leave them.' He captured her wrist, preventing her from moving.

'But…but…'

Hrolf gave a very pleased male laugh as he ran a hand down her exposed flank. A shaft of sunlight caught his powerful throat. Her traitorous heart began to beat very fast as it whispered about the possibilities.

'What is so funny?' She narrowed her eyes and tried to concentrate on the large pile of hay.

'I never realized the possibilities of trousers before.'

'Do they have possibilities?' She crossed her arms over her aching breasts. Even in the dim light she was aware that he could see her body, full of hard lines and sinewy muscle instead of soft feminine curves.

'You really know very little about men. I keep forgetting that.'

'I know quite a lot about being a warrior,' she replied indignantly, clinging to the swift anger as a drowning man might cling to a wooden spar floating on a storm-tossed sea. 'It is enough. What more is there to know? I can compete with any man.'

'There is more to being a man than simply

fighting and competing.' A dimple shone in the corner of his mouth. 'You are very refreshing, Sayrid.'

Her entire body burnt. 'Refreshing?'

'You are ignorant of your charms. I look forward to showing you what can pass between a man and a woman.' He ran a finger down the side of her throat to where her shift caressed her skin.

'Here? Now?' She glanced over his shoulder.

'We are alone and alone is good. I've burnt for you long enough. I thought I would run my sword through Bragi earlier just for looking at you in that too-tight gown. Little did I realize how delectable you could be in just a tunic.'

'But I thought...'

He leant forward and nipped her nose. 'You thought wrong. In future, remember I'm a jealous husband.'

He took the bottom of the tunic and pulled it over her head, leaving her clad only in her short shift.

Her breasts became heavy and her nipples showed through the thin fabric. A primitive urge to be closer to him filled her. She moaned slightly in the back of her throat and grabbed on to his shoulders. The muscles rippled under her fingertips.

He cupped her breasts, gently rubbing and teasing them until her nipples ached. A delicious warmth radiated outwards. She held her body completely still, not daring to move in case he stopped.

He lowered his mouth to where the dusky rose showed faintly under the linen. His tongue lapped and a warm pulse went through her. Round and round. The material became damp, adding to the sensation as it slid over the now aching point.

Her legs became liquid and she clung to him, afraid he'd stop and afraid that he would continue. If he saw her back…

'Please.' The word was torn from her throat.

He lifted his head and smoothed the hair from her forehead. 'I need this. But if you need me to stop, say now. We can wait for darkness and our bed.'

She licked her swollen lips. The thought of him leaving her was unbearable. Just this once she wanted to hold all her demons at bay. She wanted the fantasy to be real. 'I need you. Keep going.'

He shrugged out of his tunic, revealing the gold of his chest before he laid it down and her discarded clothes on the pile of hay. He gently eased her back on to the makeshift bed.

The dusty scent of summer grass rose up around her, enveloping her in its sultry sweetness. He pushed her shift upwards and revealed her body. Her hands went automatically to hide her breasts, but he shook his head.

'No, never.' He moved them. 'I want to see. Never hide from me, Sayrid. You have nothing to be ashamed of.'

She gave the briefest of nods and concentrated on keeping her arms down. Her body wasn't womanly soft. She had worked far too long with a sword and shield for it to be anything but hard. And yet he made her feel as if it could be.

His gentle fingers brushed her skin, creating pools of fire. Her body twisted first one way and then the other.

'What are you doing?'

'Searching for bruises.' He kissed the one under her eye. 'I want to make them better.'

His mouth on her bare skin sent a fresh wave of heat coursing throughout her body and she forgot to think about how unwomanly she was. All she knew was that she craved this man's touch and nothing else mattered. Her body bucked upwards, seeking his fingers.

'Are they better?' He gave a husky laugh and his fingers moved inexorably lower until they reached her apex.

Her body twisted as fresh waves of heat went through her. All she knew was that she needed more.

She tugged at the waistband of his trousers, undoing them and releasing him. He sprang free. She gave into temptation and touched. Steely hard, but silken like the finest velvet.

He moaned in the back of his throat. His hips surged forward.

A knee parted her thighs and with one movement he impaled himself, driving deep.

The sharp pain drew a cry from the depths of her being, but just as quickly it was replaced by a powerful heat. His hips began to move and she struggled to keep the right rhythm, but then instinct took over. She began to move her hips, seeking relief. With each movement he went deeper inside and the intensity increased.

All too quickly a greater shuddering overtook him and he gave a great cry and drove so deep inside her that she was certain they were melded into one.

She slowly stroked his back, feeling his muscles move. And she knew her stepmother and father had been completely wrong. She was capable of being a woman, at least once in her life.

'I'm sorry.' His breath teased her earlobe. 'I didn't intend for this…well…I did, but not here and not like this. You should have soft furs and a down pillow for your first time. Not itchy straw.'

She pushed against him. Instantly he rolled off and lay looking up at the roof, breathing heavily but not saying a word.

'There is nothing to forgive.' She forced her voice to sound rough and matter-of-fact. 'We both know what happened here. I behaved little better than a kitchen maid. A roll in the hay.'

'A roll in the hay can be delightful with the right person.'

The hollow space inside her grew larger. What had she expected? Undying love? Romantic declarations? Theirs was a match of convenience. Their joining had had to take place. She supposed she should be grateful that it had happened without everyone knowing.

'We both knew it had to be sometime soon.

Best to get it out of the way. I can think of worse places.'

He reached out and put an arm about her shoulders. 'I wanted it to be different. I wanted it to be amazing.'

She blinked hard. 'It was. Thank you.'

Hrolf took his arm from around her shoulders, aware that he had made a complete mess of things.

He had not intended to bed her like that. He had known that she was a virgin and needed careful preparation, but he had behaved like a completely untried warrior, spilling his seed almost immediately and certainly before she was ready. What was worse, he wanted her again with a ravenous hunger.

He wanted to see if her eyes really did go dark with passion.

He sought to regain his legendary control.

His mouth twisted as he noticed the evidence of her virginity on her thighs. He had treated Sayrid like the lowest whore instead of the high-born lady that she undoubtedly was. He had to stop thinking about his base needs and start thinking about her and protecting her. He should behave like her husband, not her lover.

There was a difference. He should have treated her with the honour her status required.

'It is what you wanted to hear, isn't it?' she said with an earnest expression on her face.

'It seldom is amazing the first time,' he said as remorse swamped him. 'I want honesty between us, Sayrid. Saying a thing to please me won't make it so.'

The light went out of her eyes. She tucked her chin into her neck. 'I will take your word for it. I've nothing to compare it with.'

He hated that he'd hurt her, but she had to know the truth. And he did need honesty from her. He could count on the fingers of one hand the number of women who had been honest with him. He wanted more from Sayrid and it scared him.

He stood up and pulled on his trousers.

'We should go. I intend on feasting well in my hall tonight. By the hanged Odin, I've long dreamt of this moment.' He paused. 'Ever since I left my father's lands.'

'Did your father have much land?'

'A small farm, on the edge of Svear, near Götaland, but it was lost when he died.' Hrolf made a cutting motion. He had tried to forget his childhood and mostly he succeeded. He wished he'd never mentioned it, but it saved speaking about the mess he'd made of Sayrid's first bedding. 'It was then that I learnt the value of coin and land. My father had debts. There was nothing left. I was lucky to have his sword and shield.'

Sayrid stopped, holding the trousers up with one hand. 'And your mother?'

'She was the cause of it. She died before him. My maternal uncle took me in.' Stark words that did not tell the full tragedy of it. His mother had chosen her own family over Hrolf and her husband following the quarrel. She had abandoned them, only to be killed on the way back to her family's home in a snowstorm. His uncle had tried to say that she was returning to them, but Hrolf knew differently. He had overheard the fight his parents had had.

After her death, his father had been a changed man, eating very little and drinking more. He, too, eventually died in the snow.

'You left as soon as you were old enough to board a ship.'

Hrolf started. There had been little point in staying. His uncle had made it quite clear that his own sons would gain the land and the ships. All Hrolf had had was his sword arm and his wits.

'How did you know that?'

Sayrid fastened the belt about her waist. The transformation back to the forbidding warrior woman was complete and yet there was something new in her eyes. Hrolf wondered if he'd ever tire of looking into them.

'You left your uncle's and became a sea king,' she said. 'It takes years to build up the sort of following you have, particularly if you started from less than nothing.'

'He actively encouraged me to sail east and start afresh. I heard later that he had died and one of his offspring inherited.' Hrolf slammed his memory trunk shut. She'd no need to hear of his long-ago disappointments. 'It happened a long time ago and has no bearing on my life now.'

She tucked her chin into her neck and began to fiddle with her belt. 'I only wanted to know more about the man I married.'

'Do not ask for more than I can give.' He tried to dampen the sudden flaring of hope. She might come to care for him. She might choose him above her family, but how would he know for certain? He couldn't take the risk. His mother had chosen her family over her husband and young son. 'Have you told me everything about you?

Have you confided why you prefer training with men to sewing with the women?'

'Everyone will start to wonder where we are,' she said with a hiccupping laugh. 'The bathing hut is sure to be hot.'

'You should go first.' He plucked straw from her hair and noticed where his mouth had marred her skin. If he bathed with her, he'd be unable to resist temptation and would take her far too roughly once again. Silently he cursed his desire to know more about her and why she had felt the need to hide behind her warrior's mask. Such things were best left alone.

'Would you like me to send someone to help you? Anya used Magda as a maid as well as a nurse for Inga. Time you looked like a sea king's wife.'

'I will see to my own needs.' She brushed her trousers down. 'I've no need for any help. I'm perfectly capable of looking after myself.'

'Sayrid, tomorrow you take up your duties as the lady of this estate.'

'Leave me alone. You have done enough.'

She fled from the barn. He fought the impulse to go after her.

He silently cursed. He tried telling himself that

it was what he wanted. This marriage was about gaining land and fulfilling a dream, it had nothing to do with the woman he had married. He had to keep his eyes on what was important and learn from his father's mistakes. His uncle's advice had served him well in the past. But now he kept remembering how cold his uncle was and how lonely he had seemed.

Somehow it only compounded the heaviness in Hrolf's heart.

Chapter Eleven

'My lady Sayrid has been elusive.' Magda advanced towards where Sayrid stood sorting out the stores of weapons. The elderly nurse held out a bright blue gown which shimmered in the bright midmorning sunlight. 'Inga and I have searched for you. We have made the necessary alterations. You need not feel ashamed of attending any feast again. You will be properly clothed.'

'It is very kind of you, but...' Sayrid stopped, unable to continue. Hrolf had obviously given her lack of feminine clothing as the excuse for why she had missed the evening meal last night.

She had spent ages washing off the evidence of their joining. It bothered her more than it should have that someone might find out that they had waited until they arrived back here to consummate the marriage. And then she had taken to her bed and slept. She had watched the training this morning from behind a post, but had decided against directly confronting Hrolf. Instead she had gone to one of the storerooms and started sorting the weapons. Normally setting such things to rights calmed her, but today it made her feel uneasy and lost.

The blue cloth danced in front of her eyes. Deep in her soul, she wanted to wear it and have Hrolf look at her with appreciation in his eyes.

'Go on,' the older woman urged. 'See if we guessed your size correctly. You're a married woman now, my lady. You need to look like the wife of a sea king.'

Sayrid took the blue gown. The wife of a sea king with no womanly skills. The array of shields seemed to mock her. Lusting after this dress was not going to change what she was or how other people saw her.

She hated that she wanted Hrolf's eyes to light up when he saw her. A tiny ache started behind her brows. Wishing for things to be different was not going to change how they actually were.

'Do you like it, my lady?' the nurse asked.

'Where did you find the cloth?' she asked, holding the gown against her body.

'Inga and I looked in many chests in the ship. I found this half-made up. We noticed your gown was in a state yesterday before Hrolf brought you his trousers and tunic. We wish to make a present to the bride. We're sorry.'

'It is very kind of you, but unnecessary.' Sayrid put the gown to one side. 'As you can see, I do have other gowns. This one has served me well for years.' She kept quiet about the fact that every other gown she owned was in worse shape.

The older woman's gaze seemed to hone in on the patches and the faded cloth at the hem of Sayrid's gown. 'You cannot wear rags. You are the wife of a wealthy man. What is Hrolf thinking of? He has silks and gold-shot cloth. But this will do for now. His eyes will sparkle when he sees you, yes?'

Sayrid choked back the truth—it would take more than clothes to make her into the sort of wife Hrolf required.

'Silks are far too fine for every day. I will settle for good sturdy wool or perhaps linen in the high summer,' Sayrid said, giving the silk one last stroke. It rippled in the light. 'I will keep it for best.'

'Inga thought the blue would match your eyes. Summer eyes, she called them.'

'Inga has a way with words.'

'She would like to be a *skald*, but there are very few women *skalds*. I have explained this.' Magda shuffled her shoulders importantly. 'Hrolf wishes for his daughter to be a credit to him and marry well.'

'So she sews and tries to excel at women's work.' The words tasted bitter in her mouth. 'Did you see the cakes I burnt this morning? Thora, the cook, has banished me from the kitchen. I even toppled over the cat's milk on my way here.'

Silently she added that, at this rate, she'd never be able to travel again. Mastering even the simplest woman's task appeared to be beyond her. Every time she made the slightest error, she heard her stepmother's voice mocking her.

'You will make the right sort of wife for the Sea-Rider and the right sort of mother for my Inga. This is the third morning that I read the signs and they are good. The Norns approve.'

'There are precious few women warriors, but I was one.' Sayrid tapped a finger against her mouth. Silently she vowed that she'd help make

Inga's dream come true. 'I will see what can be done. Where is she?'

'Inga is too tired and has fallen asleep in her bed. But she made me promise to bring this to you as she wants to see your summer eyes sparkle.' The old woman smiled. 'I will wake her for the meal and perhaps she sees you in it, yes? Always this way with the travelling. The next day she sleeps.'

'Between you, Inga and my sister, my poor skill won't be missed.'

'If you try, you will succeed.' Magda thumped her chest. 'I teach you if you teach Inga to sail a boat and fight with a sword.'

'They are not occupations for a lady. Her father...'

The nurse tapped the side of her nose. 'But she wishes to learn. She speaks of nothing else as we stitch this dress this morning, but she fears asking the giantess.'

There was a way she could help Inga. Hrolf might object to her learning about swords, but there were other things she could teach, like *tafl* or the art of reciting poetry. Sayrid hugged the gown to her chest. 'I'll find a way to get Hrolf to agree.'

'You need to look like a woman, not wear the clothes of a man or a thrall when you ask for anything. He likes women in his bed, not boys.'

'To keep you happy, I will try it on.' Sayrid struggled out of her old gown.

'Shall I help?' Magda started to go around.

'I can do it,' Sayrid said quickly before Magda saw the scars. But the old woman had frozen and was staring. 'Is there a problem?'

'Did you get these from fighting?' Magda asked, pointing and making a little click in the back of her throat.

'Something like that. It happened a long time ago.' Sayrid scowled. 'Shall we get the dress on?'

Magda looked like she wanted to say more, but instead she pressed her lips together and lifted the new dress over Sayrid's head.

Unlike the one she had worn at the wedding, this one fitted, falling to a few inches above the floor. It swirled gently about her ankles as she turned. It made her feel soft and feminine. She stopped abruptly. She'd never expected to feel that way.

'Do you like?'

'You and Inga are geniuses with your needles. This is the best dress I have ever had.'

Magda smiled. 'Hrolf will only have eyes for his bride now.'

'What has my wife been doing now? Except for watching the men training from behind a wooden post?'

Sayrid's cheeks burnt. She rapidly went over the conversation. Surely there was nothing incriminating. And she had kept her scars covered for the most part. 'How long have you been standing there? What do you want? If you ask any of the servants, they will be happy to find it for you.'

'I've been standing here long enough. And the servants can't give me what I need.'

She pinched the bridge of her nose and attempted to breathe steadily. Her heart wanted there to be a wealth of hidden meaning in his words. 'The keys to all the cupboards are hanging up. Nothing is to be hidden. I gave orders. If you wish to inspect where the women hide during an attack, it can be arranged.'

He motioned to Magda and the nurse disappeared. 'You did not appear at supper last night. Or at breakfast. And despite my thinking the training would bring you out, you stayed away.'

'You don't want a wife who trains with the men.'

He raised his brow. 'Since when did my wishes have anything to do with your actions?'

'Isn't that what a wife is supposed to do?' she asked the floor.

'You're avoiding me.'

'I burnt the cakes.' She backed away slightly, knocking over a stack of shields. She gave a faint cry and started to pick them up, only to send the spears crashing in the other direction as the sleeve of her new dress caught them. 'I'll clean up this mess.'

'Did you hear me ask?' He took a spear from her and placed it back against the wall. 'I'd half expected that you would have gone to check the supplies at the safe houses—a necessary task, but one that would take you somewhere I couldn't find you. Yesterday…in the barn…'

'In future try the fish pond,' she said quickly before he could say what a mistake it had been.

She concentrated on piling the shields up. Keeping busy would stop her from looking at his fingers and thinking about the way they had played against her skin in the barn. 'Fishing relaxes me and with this amount of mouths to feed every effort helps. However, it is just as well that I'm not hungry as the trout proved elusive.'

Her stomach grumbled, giving voice to her lie.

He held out some bread and cheese. 'I suppose I'll have to eat this myself. Training makes me hungry.'

'You discovered my trail of destruction in the kitchen.'

He raised his brow. 'No, they were eager to sing your praises. Your people love you.'

'Why are you here, Hrolf?' she asked, keeping her gaze firmly on the shields and spears. 'I doubt you suddenly need another sparring partner.'

'No,' he admitted. 'But I missed arguing with you over it.' He placed the food on the bench beside her. 'Go on. A peace offering.'

'I've barely been home since I left in the spring.' Sayrid eyed the bread and cheese. Hunger gnawed at her stomach. It took all of her restraint not to grab the food and wolf it down. 'It is only natural I should be curious. With you and your warriors staying here, I'd hardly want to go short. I'm attempting to be a good wife. It is the only way I will get to travel.'

He tore off a chunk of bread and held it out to her. She grabbed it. The first bite tasted like ash, but the second was heaven. 'You need to look after yourself better.'

She wiped her mouth. 'I do well enough.'

'You slept somewhere else last night.'

'I went to where I always sleep.' Sayrid bit her lip. She could hardly confess about hearing the sounds of merriment and feeling utterly alone. 'Habit, and my eyes closed the instant I lay down.'

He raised an eyebrow. 'At least one of us slept.'

She waved an impatient hand. 'It seems ridiculous to pretend that you wanted anything more than to consummate the marriage. You must have been relieved I found somewhere else to sleep.'

He put an arm around her shoulder. 'I worried about you. I took you far too roughly.'

She shrugged him off. Her traitorous body thrummed from the touch. The evidence of his worry was less than convincing. She'd hardly hidden. 'I know how to be a warrior. I know the way warriors think and how they treat women once they are finished with them.'

He flinched as if she had struck him.

'But you know nothing about me.' He enfolded her in his arms, pulling her close so she could feel the hard planes of his body. 'A passion exists between us, Sayrid. What happened in the barns happened because we both wanted it, not because of some ill-conceived duty. My only regret is that I took you too quickly, before you were properly prepared. I wanted to apologize for that. If I'd stayed…it might have happened again and then…'

'Do I look like some wilting flower?' She twisted out of his arms. If she stayed there, she'd lose any capacity to think clearly. The trouble with Hrolf was that he always made her feel off balance. She was used to things being a certain way and now he had her wanting to believe that they could be different.

Her heart thumped in her ears. This was far worse than when she had faced him in the contest, but she kept her chin up. He dropped his eyes first.

'When I saw the evidence of your virginity something inside snapped and I realized what I'd done,' he said in a voice so low that she barely heard it. 'Say you will forgive me. Give me a chance to show you how good it can be.'

She crumbled the remaining bits of bread between her fingers. 'It hurt a little, but parts were exciting.'

His arms instantly came around her. 'You mean

I drank far too much last night and have nursed a bad head all morning for nothing. Next time, you will see.'

'You deserved the bad head for leaving me,' she mumbled, laying her head on his shoulder.

'I left you?' The blue in his eyes deepened. 'You were the one who fled.'

'You wanted me to go.'

Hrolf tightened his arms about Sayrid. Silently he thanked the gods that she had not completely turned from him. He treated her badly yesterday. Today he would make up for it. He had made himself all kinds of promises before he went looking for her—how he would be distant but kind, how he would explain that discord between a lord and his lady meant for an unhappy household…except by all the trees in Freyr's grove, he wanted her again and his body ached to be inside her once more. And when he couldn't find her, it had hurt.

'Maybe I did,' he said against her hair and breathed in her clean scent of sun-warmed hair.

Her direct gaze met his. 'You are admitting to a mistake?'

'I'm far from perfect.' He put her from him and tried to regain control of his body. He would not become like his father and allow a woman to have power over him. But equally he didn't want to be cold and remote. 'I want you to enjoy our time together.'

'Why?'

'Because your pleasure will increase mine.'

'You certainly know how to make a woman feel special.' Her eyes rolled. 'I understand that you're sorry it happened that way, but it did. Perhaps it is for the best. I won't tell anyone that you did not perform up to your usual standards. You may rest assured, your reputation as a peerless lover will remain intact.'

He stared at her. She was deliberately twisting his words.

'Don't provoke me.'

A blaze of passion flitted across her face, turning it from pleasant looking to totally irresistible. 'Why? What can you do to me that you haven't already done?'

'What have I done to you?' he rasped with the last vestiges of his legendary control.

'Do I have to make a list?' She tried to force her features into a scowl. 'You know as well as I and I don't have time!'

His final grip on his self-control slipped and

he grabbed her, roughly lowering his mouth to hers, stopping her words. His body shook with need for her.

She gave a small cry and her body became pliant against his. Her lips opened more fully and allowed him entrance.

He drank from it, plundering its depths. His hands crushed her body to him, trying to bend her will to his. He needed more. Last night's pent-up passion and frustration poured out of him.

She gave a little moan in the back of her throat, but it was enough to shock him back to where they were and what he'd been about to do. Outside the storeroom, he could hear the swords clanking as his men continued with the training. Silently he cursed. He'd nearly done it again. One taste of her and he behaved like the worst sort of raider, taking her as roughly as before.

'Tonight. My bed.'

Sayrid's fingers explored her mouth. Her lips ached, but the place deep inside her ached more. She wanted him to continue. Her mind raced with all the excuses. 'Excuse me?'

'The next time I take you, I intend for there to be a bed so that we can both enjoy it. And I've no wish to spoil your new dress.'

'The next time?' Her heart thudded in her chest. 'You mean there is to be more than once?'

'You didn't think I'd be content with only once?' He tilted his head to one side. 'Be in my bed tonight or suffer the consequences.'

Her heart soared. She had had it all wrong and her stepmother had been mistaken in her predictions. Her husband knew precisely what she had been and he wanted her for more than the legal consummation of the marriage. And her stepmother had been partly wrong about their joining. It had hurt, but not with the searing pain that she had predicted.

'And the consequences would be?' she asked in a husky whisper.

'Severe, but ultimately immensely pleasurable.' Hrolf regained a small measure of control. Taking Sayrid in this storeroom was not how he behaved. It had been bad enough that he had taken her so swiftly the first time, but he had needed to be inside her. Since then he'd been unable to get her and her response out of his mind. He kept coming up with new ways in which he wanted to enjoy her. He wanted to open her up to passion and have her an equal partner in bed sport. 'I was generous last night and allowed you time to recover. Losing your virginity can be painful. You would have been too sore to enjoy it properly.'

'You would say that.' Her tongue moistened her lips.

Inwardly he groaned. He wanted her, but it would have to wait. He had to put duty first. 'Do not seek to challenge me on this, Sayrid, but know I will find you wherever you choose to hide. And I will carry you to my bed. Naked if I have to.'

He turned on his heel and marched out of the storeroom.

Sayrid lay under the furs in the large bed, trying to breathe normally and not panic.

Waiting here seemed like a better option than being carried out of the hall. Naked, with her back exposed for all to see.

The torchlight highlighted the various tapestries which now hung in the room. Where her father had favoured gory battles, these tapestries had an altogether different subject. The tips of her ears burnt as she realized just how intimate the tapestries were.

Hrolf appeared in the entranceway with a set

face. The lines around his mouth relaxed slightly as he spotted her.

'I'm here as ordered.' Sayrid tore her gaze from the scene of a particularly close embrace.

'All ready, I see.'

She kept the furs pulled to her chin and hoped he'd douse the torch. She wanted her stepmother to be wrong about her back, but she also wanted one more night in his arms if she turned out to be right. 'I can't afford to have any more gowns ripped. Magda and Inga were already far too kind.'

His eyes crinkled at the corners, transforming his face. 'All for the sake of a gown?'

'Yes. A gown which your daughter made.'

Her voice faltered and she wondered if he expected her to invite him into the bed. Or if she should offer him a drink. She sank into the pillows, wishing she had considered this before.

'Do you like my improvements?' he asked, breaking the awkward silence which had sprung up.

'I wondered where they had come from.'

'Byzantium. A present.'

Sayrid nodded, hating the small curl of jealousy

at the woman who had given him the hangings. 'An expensive present.'

'I saved the man's life and family. He owed me.' He nodded towards them. 'It is the first time I've had them hung.'

'They look like they were made for this room.'

His smile became positively wolfish. 'It helps to set the mood, particularly when there is a naked woman in my bed.'

Her face burnt worse than before. 'After this afternoon, I didn't think you would require any assistance of that sort.'

'Sayrid!'

'What do you expect me to say?'

It was his turn to look uncomfortable. 'Not that.'

The bed sank under his weight. She struggled to keep her place and not tumble towards him. The ropes were far looser than they should have been. She made a mental note to get them seen to.

'Do you want to be here?' he asked in low voice, reaching towards her.

She put her fingers in his palm. He covered them.

'I'm trying to be understanding. I want what is best for everyone. Discord helps no one.'

'My men have been teasing me all day about my evident desire for you and my very bad temper.'

He raised her captured hand to his lips. The tiny touch made her feel like a precious piece of glass.

A flame flickered in her belly. If she hadn't loved him already, she'd fall for him now. She bit her knuckle. She couldn't love him, not so soon. And her love was doomed. She couldn't be the sort of woman he required. But she could have tonight, her heart argued.

'I'm trying to uphold my end of the bargain.'

'What, greeting your husband from bed?' He gave a bark of laughter. 'Who taught you that trick?'

'The new gown is far too pretty and delicate. Inga pointed out that I had already torn a shoulder seam.' Her cheeks burnt. 'I believe it happened in the storeroom.'

He shook his head. 'I'm going to show you what it is like to go slowly. I am going to treat you how you should have been treated yesterday.'

She opened her mouth to protest, but he laid a finger across her lips. 'Hush. I'm in charge and you will obey me for once.'

He followed his order with a kiss that took her breath away, gentle but persistently persuading. She opened her mouth and drew his tongue in.

One hand cupped the back of her head while the other trailed down her neck, making feather-light touches which did strange things to her insides.

He went ever lower until he reached her nipples. He rolled first one and then the other between his thumb and forefinger until they ached. She arched her back, wanting more as the heat began to rise in her middle.

He lazily moved his mouth down her body. He took each nipple in turn, drawing small circles, tugging at them and tracing their outline. With each touch, the heat inexorably rose. Her hips writhed under him, seeking relief.

She tugged at his tunic, needing to feel his skin against hers.

He nodded and slowly took it off. The torch-light turned his skin into gold. Her fingers traced the faint sprinkling of hair on his chest, accidentally brushing his nipples which hardened under her touch.

He groaned but allowed her a chance to explore. With each touch, her confidence grew. She grasped the waistband of his trousers. But he shook his head and captured her wrists, raising them above her, making her arch her back so that her breasts jutted out.

'Let me enjoy you,' he rasped out.

He sank down, trailing open-mouthed kisses down her body, teasing her. His tongue lapped at her navel, round and round before dipping lower.

She gasped as his head went to the apex of her thighs.

'Let me taste you. There. Please,' he said in a ragged voice.

Unable to speak beyond little moans, she nodded.

He wedged her thighs wider and his mouth touched her intimate core. Wave after wave of pleasure hit her as his tongue thrust slowly into her. When she thought she was about to die from the need of him, he divested his trousers, exposing his rampant erection.

He parted her thighs and drove deep. This time her body opened, taking the full length of him with ease. She wrapped her legs about him, urging him onwards. Their bodies moved like one. And she learnt what joining could really be like as the world exploded into a million potent points.

Later, she lay in his arms. Her muscles ached, but she felt complete.

The torch flickered and sent strange shadows over his skin. Languidly she traced them. 'Now I understand what you mean about beds being better.'

He ran his hand along her shoulder and stopped.

'Is there something wrong?' Her stomach dropped and she braced herself for his excuses of why he had to leave.

'How did you get the scars on your back? Kettil swore you were never wounded, not severely. Someone marked you, Sayrid.' He pinned her to the bed, preventing her from slipping off. 'I noticed them yesterday when the tunic you were wearing slipped from your shoulder in the water. They are not sword cuts and they are different colours, almost like runes.'

'They are from a long time ago.' Sayrid hugged her knees to her chest. She should have known he'd discover them. It had been too much to hope for. All the vile predictions her stepmother had poured in her ears would come to pass. 'They're unimportant.'

'From your father? Did he do this to you?'

She let out a breath. 'Yes. I took the beatings to

prove I was as strong as any man and that I had what it took to become a warrior.'

'These go far beyond mere beatings. And there is almost a runic pattern to them. They haven't healed like normal scars.'

'My stepmother rubbed salt and different-coloured sand into them.' Sayrid put a hand to her head. She'd stumbled half-blind with pain from the room after the beating, but had felt proud as her father hadn't managed to cow her as he had Regin, only to be confronted with her stepmother.

Afterwards the only person besides Auda who had helped her was Regin. She owed him her life.

'Can we speak of this later? I know what you will think of them. My stepmother used to make me repeat her words. She took great delight in saying them.'

'Let me see your scars. And I will tell you precisely what I think of them.' Gentle hands turned her over. She forced herself to lie still.

There was a sharp intake of breath and then silence.

'I understand if you wish to go. My stepmother warned me that men would find them repulsive and flee my bed. That even if a man should marry me, he would discover them and leave.'

She shrugged slightly and drew on all of her re-serves to keep her voice emotionless. 'Some-where in my tortured brain, I thought I could prolong our courtship and have a few days to look back on.'

She waited for him to go. He did not move, but continued to remain next to her.

'Hush now. Relax.'

Slowly he traced the network of the scars with his fingers. His lips swiftly followed. With each press of his mouth, it seemed like her stepmoth-er's voice faded from her mind until it signified nothing.

When he'd finished, he turned her over and raised her chin so she was forced to look directly into his eyes.

'These are honourable scars, Sayrid. You re-ceived them because you were defending people who were smaller and weaker than you. How anyone could be so twisted and perverted to think otherwise, I've no idea. And that is my hon-est opinion. I would like to run your stepmother through with my sword, but she isn't worth the effort.'

Her throat worked up and down, but no sound

came out. He thought them honourable. They did not repulse him.

'I see no shame in having been a shield maiden or protecting your family. Where there is shame is in forcing you to make the choice. In the branding of your back. Making you seem like you were little more than a thrall.'

'But…'

'Your stepmother is lucky that I do not make war against women or her life would be at an end. Your father is dead and it will be up to Odin to judge his actions. I know I wouldn't want a man like that to serve on one of my *felags*.'

Sayrid gave a little nod as she drew her knees into her chest.

'Why would I be put off by the scars? I have a network of my own. And having held you in my arms and sampled your mouth, why would I flee your bed?' He pressed another kiss against the nearest scar. 'You don't know men very well and you certainly don't know me.'

'I am a coward, Hrolf. My father always called me one and I've proved it,' Sayrid said, concentrating on the nearest tapestry. 'I should have confessed about my scars before. I used them as a reason why no man would ever want me. It made me fight harder, but truly I was scared.'

'Hush, you are one of the bravest people I have ever met.' He laced his fingers through hers. 'Trust me with your story. Explain to me why you did what you did. I want to know everything about you.'

Suddenly the words poured out of Sayrid. She explained about the beatings and the mockery. And after her back healed, she became determined to show them that she wasn't broken and she remained steadfast in her resolve to protect her younger siblings.

When she reached the shuddering end of her story, explaining how grateful her father had been when she had returned with gold from her first voyage, Hrolf said nothing. He reached for her and dragged her back against his chest.

She lay there, listening to the steady beat of his heart. She managed to stifle the words confessing her love for him. It was far too new and scary.

He brought her face to his. 'I will be the best husband I can be, Sayrid, but don't ask me to love you. I've vowed never to love a woman. My father died because he loved too much. I won't make his mistake.'

She gulped hard and swallowed her words, fiercely glad that she had not confessed her growing feelings for him. 'I understand.'

'I hope you do.' He dragged her mouth back to his. 'I hope you do.'

Chapter Twelve

The sound of a horn broke Sayrid's sleep a few mornings later. Hrolf was already up and pulling his tunic on.

'We have visitors...from the land,' she said, stretching. Her body ached in many places, but a strange feeling of peace infused her. There was something about waking up with Hrolf by her side. She was slowly coming to grips with the domestic arrangements. She'd even discovered that she enjoyed baking once she got the hang of it. There was something therapeutic about pounding bread and making cakes. 'They're friendly and known.'

Hrolf paused in his dressing. 'Are you sure?'

'The length of the horn blast. We've a little time yet.' Sayrid looped a strand of hair behind her ear. 'You'd hardly think I wouldn't have devised an early-warning system? Auda needed to know if she had to hide when I wasn't here to defend her. It works. Even my father was impressed. Of course he took the credit when Kettil asked.'

He gave a brief laugh. 'If Kettil had allowed you to lead a *felag*, who knows what markets you would have conquered?'

'I will take that as a compliment.' Her heart panged. If Kettil had put her in charge of a *felag* as she had begged, she'd never have met Hrolf and would never have known what it was like to feel like a woman in a man's arms. It went against everything she'd been taught—putting her needs and desires ahead of the needs of her family.

She hugged her knees to her chest. Less than a week married and she was already thinking like a woman with her heart instead with her head. Before when she woke, her mind whirled with all the things she had to get done to make every-one safe.

'It is important to be prepared. Common sense.'

She waited for him to wish her good morning or make some lover-like remark.

'Any idea who it could be? Does your warning system extend that far?' he asked, changing the subject as he buckled his sword about his waist.

'You are teasing now.'

'With you, I've discovered anything is possible.'

A great hollow opened within Sayrid. He might have lain in her arms all night. Their joining might have meant something to her, but it meant very little to him. He was doing what came naturally to a man, but his heart was not engaged.

'I'm no sorceress and don't possess the gift of second sight.'

'How long do we have? Can you tell me that much? Given the remoteness of the location on the peninsula, I can't believe the horn only sounds just before people arrive. You need time to assemble your men.'

'After the first horn sounds? A little while.' She hugged her knees to her chest and wished that Auda or Regin was here. Despite being in the hall where she grew up, she had no one to confide in. 'Whoever it is will be friendly. There has been no second or third blast.'

'I will make my men ready.'

'But they will be friendly.'

He lifted a brow. 'You have your system and I have mine.'

'If they're friendly towards me, they will be friendly to you.'

'One would hope so...'

She started to get up, but her muscles ached in places where she had never dreamt she had muscles before and she collapsed back with a groan. 'I feel worse than if I had been fighting!'

'You stay in bed.' His face had become like a mask again. She searched it, trying to find the man who had held her through the night and who had made her feel valued as a woman. In his arms, the voice that had mocked and haunted her for so many years fell silent. But that man had vanished, leaving behind a determined sea king who had no need of her.

'This shouldn't take long, particularly if your early-warning system is accurate.'

An ice-cold shiver went down her spine. He was expecting someone and expecting them to bring trouble. And what was more infuriating, he wanted her out of the way. As if she couldn't handle a sword! She fought better than most men.

She shook her head. 'You picked the wrong sort of woman. I want to see who has arrived. News travels fast, but I didn't expect it to travel this fast. It is sure to be innocent. I've no wish for pointless feuds if someone takes offence at not being properly greeted by the woman of the house.'

'As you wish...' He buckled his leather chest-protector on, before grabbing one of his velvet cloaks. Very much the lord of the hall, but prepared for war.

'Despite my words you dress for battle. Who do you think it could be?' Sayrid grabbed her clothes and began dressing.

'Your brother.' He gave a half smile. 'Here I was hoping to spend the morning in bed with you. All in all your brother seems to delight in making me do things I've no wish to do.'

She fastened her belt about her middle with furious fingers. 'Regin is on his way to see my stepmother, doing his duty finally. Why would he come here? It is at least a week overland to reach where she lives with her latest husband.'

'Your eyes flash adorably when you are angry.'

He tilted her chin upwards. His thumb lazily rubbed the bottom curve of her lip. The fire inside her roared into full flame. It was all she could do to stop from dragging his mouth to hers. 'And you are trying to get around my questioning.'

He let her go. Her traitorous body cried out in

protest. 'All my instincts scream that your brother is most likely to come here instead of visiting his mother. How often has he visited your stepmother in the past? Why does he want to mislead everyone? He was the only one to leave the village.'

'Never, but there were reasons. Something always came up.' Sayrid regarded the tapestries. Some of Regin's excuses had been pretty slender, but she had accepted them because she had no wish for a return visit. 'Once he was going to go, but turned around because he caught a fever. He didn't want to give it to my stepmother.'

'How noble of him.' He coughed. 'How will your stepmother feel about his marrying a woman without a dowry?'

'He still knows his duty.'

'And the damage to my ship, how do you explain that?'

'He is not in league with Lavrans. He just isn't.' A deep chill filled her bones. 'There must be another traitor.'

'If I were disaffected and had just lost my inheritance, who would I turn to? It has to be said, Sayrid.'

The words acted like ice water. He was doing

it deliberately. How little respect he had for her even to make that sort of suggestion.

'You're completely wrong. Auda swore that he had gone to see my stepmother and pay his respects now that he is properly married. Why would Regin lie to Auda?'

'And you are certain Auda told you the truth.'

'Auda is my sister.' She ticked off the points on her fingers, trying to piece the events together. 'Blodvin left a rune for her to find. It is possible I suppose that Regin changed his mind when he sobered up.'

'Nevertheless, would you care to wager?'

She stuck her chin in the air. Once these travellers arrived, she looked forward to hearing his abject apology. He might think he knew about people, but he didn't know her brother. 'Happily. You'll allow me the freedom to keep up my fighting skills, even though I haven't completely honed my housekeeping skills. I want to train with your men. And I want to train Inga with them as well.'

'She doesn't want to do such things.' Hrolf's eyes blazed. 'She prefers sewing and weaving.'

'She is trying to master *tafl*. We played ten

matches yesterday. You were busy when she wanted to play a game with you.'

'The last time you wagered with me, you lost.' He captured her chin. 'If I am right, you will stay with the women and not train at all. Is that high enough stakes for you or would you prefer something less important?' He nodded towards the bed. 'Maybe something where we both can win?'

She wrenched her chin away. He thought he could control her with sex!

'Then my luck is bound to change.' She stuck out her hand. 'I accept your wager.'

He grasped it and pulled her close. His lips plundered hers. 'This is how I seal a wager with you.'

She stumbled away from him, silently cursing that her body thrummed with desire. 'I will win. Marriage has made him realize his responsibilities.'

'That remains to be seen.' He gathered up his helm. 'My men will be ready to greet whoever comes.'

She tilted her head to one side. 'You should have told me that you expected my brother to arrive.'

He lifted his brow. 'Why? This has no bearing

on what passed between us and until it actually happened, I'd no wish to trouble you.'

'It is about trust. You should have said something. I could have allayed your fears. You must believe me. My brother is not like that.'

'Trusting you and trusting are two different matters.' He inclined his head. 'My lady.'

'I look forward to proving you wrong,' she taunted at his retreating back.

Sayrid retrieved a knife and slid it down her boot. Whatever happened she was not going to be unprotected. She raced out to the assembly area where they always gathered when visitors arrived.

Hrolf's men were already there, armed. Hrolf issued a number of low commands. The men obeyed him without question.

Sayrid shielded her eyes. She could make out a party on horseback. Her stomach triple-knotted. Regin was in the lead!

She blinked three times to make sure. But with each step the party took, the identity of the lead horseman became clearer.

Once again she had wagered with Hrolf and lost. She had been so sure that her brother was finally going to repay her faith in him. And if she'd misjudged him on this, what else had she misjudged him on?

'I owe you an apology,' she said, keeping her shoulders back, but her heart sank lower than her boots. 'My brother must have changed his mind. There will be a good explanation for it.'

'I look forward to discovering what it is.'

Hrolf struggled to contain his temper as Regin Avilson dismounted. His new bride, reasonably pregnant, rode behind him. Sayrid's face was now a frozen scowling mask, but her look of complete anguish when she first spied her brother cut him far more deeply than he'd like.

He tried to push the thought from his brain and focus. Worrying about Sayrid's feelings was not going to protect her or his lands. Until he knew for certain where Regin's loyalty lay, he had to treat him with caution, though it gave him no pleasure.

He moved squarely in the centre of his men with Sayrid on his right. He kept his hand firmly on her back, preventing her from moving and rushing towards her brother. She gave him a furious scowl, but he ignored it.

When Regin saw his sister, he blanched and

nearly fell off his horse. 'Sayrid! What are you doing here?'

'I could ask you the same question.' Sayrid's eyes blazed fury. 'I understood you were visiting your mother. Did you ask our sister to lie for you? Do you know the trouble you have caused? Auda is now a hostage.'

Hrolf dropped a casual arm about her shoulders. She stood stiff and unyielding. He tried to read her thoughts, but she'd closed down. Silently he cursed the wager and his arrogance.

Whatever Regin Avilson was up to, it did not involve his sister. Yet. And if Sayrid had to make a choice? His stomach knotted. He wanted to believe she'd choose him. He wanted to believe that she shared some of his feelings. It struck him then that he loved her in a way which took hold deep down inside and frightened him.

'It can't be.' Regin's eyes darted everywhere but on Sayrid's face.

'Well, it is, because of your actions!' Sayrid's body quivered with anger. 'Our baby sister!'

Hrolf silently ground his teeth.

'Easy,' he said in a low voice. 'Just because you lost our wager doesn't mean you need to take out your anger on your brother.'

She shrugged off the arm. 'How can you joke at a time like this?'

'I assure you, I am not joking.'

'Regin, what are you doing here with these men?' Sayrid advanced towards her brother.

Hrolf instinctively readied his body for a fight.

Regin went red and then white. 'That is… well…' He glanced back at Blodvin, who gave a confident nod. 'Blodvin knows why. She can explain it better than I can.'

Blodvin swiftly slid off the horse and curtsied low to Hrolf, totally ignoring the usual protocol and not even acknowledging Sayrid. Hrolf schooled his features. They might be Sayrid's relations, but he'd encourage them to depart as swiftly as they came. Then maybe Sayrid and he could continue to enjoy each other. And he could keep her from being hurt.

'I felt unwell and wished to return home.' Blodvin ran her fingers over her growing stomach. 'I worried about my precious babe.'

For good measure she batted her lashes as if she expected him to become a puddle at her feet. Hrolf silently thanked whichever god had been looking out for him when the proposed marriage to that ill-mannered witch had been interrupted and he'd encountered Sayrid instead. Sayrid with her good sense was what he needed, but he still had to wonder whose side she'd choose in a fight. His or her brother's.

'Indeed.'

'It is the truth,' Blodvin declared hotly. 'Tell him, Regin, tell your new brother. We had barely gone a few miles when I suddenly knew that I had to come here until the baby was born. My baby who will be born in his father's hall.'

Sayrid's brother stammered and looked everywhere but at Sayrid. 'It is like Blodvin says. I thought it best to return here. Our babe should be born in the hall of his fathers.'

'It is my hall now.'

Sayrid stepped forward. 'What Hrolf means is that you are welcome to rest here while one of the outlying farms is made ready for you.'

'I want one with a good aspect,' Blodvin declared. 'Tell them, Regin. Only the best for our child.'

Hrolf felt sorry for the man. He was under his wife's thumb and the marriage had barely begun. He was one of those who hid behind his wife's skirts.

'You expected Sayrid and me to remain with Kettil,' he stated flatly. 'Any particular reason?'

Regin scuffed his toe in the dirt. 'It crossed my mind that you might have duties there, but obviously I was wrong.'

'And your travelling companions?' Hrolf asked, keeping his voice smooth and ignoring Sayrid's sudden intake of breath. 'Were they on their way here?'

'Men we met on the road,' Blodvin answered, coming forward with a distinct sway to her hips. She allowed her cloak to gape open. Her blouse exposed a little more flesh than strictly necessary. 'They needed a place to rest. One must offer hospitality.'

'Naturally.'

'What is wrong with that?' Blodvin allowed her cloak to open a little more. 'Why are you trying to make out that we have done something wrong?'

Hrolf schooled his features. It irritated him that Blodvin considered he'd be distracted by such obvious measures. He glanced between his wife and the woman he had nearly married. There was no comparison. He had to wonder what he'd ever fleetingly seen in Blodvin and why he'd ever considered that she might be the correct sort of wife for him.

'Hrolf,' Sayrid said with a sharp edge to her voice. 'Do you have proof that these men mean to cause harm? And my brother?'

'While you rest under this roof, I will have your swords,' Hrolf replied, inclining his head towards the leader of the band. 'I will vouch for your protection while you are within my walls.'

He motioned to his men who formed a barrier behind him. 'I assume you mean us no harm.'

The men exchanged glances and with the briefest of hesitations began to lay down their wide variety of arms. Hrolf regarded each in turn. The second to the last reminded him of one of Lavrans's men, but he couldn't be sure. He wished Bragi was there as the man's memory for faces was unsurpassed.

The last one stood in front of the weapons pile and bared his teeth. He looked Sayrid up and down as if he were mentally undressing her. 'Your wife?'

Hrolf curled his fists. 'Is there a problem with that?'

The man gave a little swagger. 'No, no, I had heard the Shield Maiden had married. What does it feel like to be married to a Valkyrie? Or is she too wild for you?'

Hrolf heard the swift intake of breath echo around the yard. Sayrid went rigid next to him and her eyes were fastened on a distant point.

'You are a guest in this house. I suggest you behave like one.' Hrolf fixed the man with a deadly gaze. His fingers itched to draw his sword, but the man was unarmed. And right now he did not want to give anyone a pretext.

Silently he gave thanks that Sayrid had chosen not to react. Any other woman would have demanded his head, but Sayrid simply stood still. Hrolf's heart unexpectedly panged. She had clearly suffered this sort of behaviour many times before.

'A simple question.' The man raised his hands. 'Curiosity got the better of me.'

'Do not allow it to get the better of you again.' Hrolf inclined his head. 'The lady is my wife and will have your respect.'

The man blanched, clearly understanding the threat. 'I most humbly beg your pardon, Shield... my lady.'

'My husband is a more than able opponent as I discovered to my cost. Provoke him at your peril.' She tilted her head to one side. 'You have this warning because you are our guest. But these warnings are only given once.'

If possible the man went even paler and he stumbled away.

'Sayrid, if anyone makes any more remarks, you will let me know.'

She stared straight back at him. 'I fight my own battles. Without assistance.'

'Attack you and they attack me.'

Sayrid opened and closed her mouth several times. Finally she shrugged. 'As you wish, but I can defend myself. I've never sheltered behind anyone and I'm not about to start.'

Hrolf struggled to keep his temper. He knew that physically she could defend herself more than adequately. But he knew how vulnerable Sayrid was behind the fierce mask she wore. The way he felt about her was far too new to be shared.

'Remember who won the wager!'

She contented herself with crossing her arms and scowling. 'If you wanted a compliant wife, you married the wrong woman.'

'Best do as he says, Say.' Regin gave a smug smile. 'Upsetting a sea king is a bad idea. He obviously has set ideas on how a woman should act. Pity.'

He gave Regin a hard look. The man delighted in causing mischief. 'Put your weapons in the pile as well.'

'I've no wish to fall out with my new brother-in-law,' Regin said, making a mocking bow after he'd placed his sword on top of the pile, a sword so shiny Hrolf doubted if it had ever been drawn in battle. It took all of Hrolf's training not to punch him, particularly when he thought about the scars Sayrid bore and the battered sword she had used in their fight.

Blodvin bleated excuses before they both fled.

'Your brother has seen sense,' Hrolf said between gritted teeth. 'A pity.'

'What is going on?' Sayrid asked as she struggled to control her temper. First Regin appeared with a group of strangers who appeared more inclined to rob than to trade and then Hrolf appeared to want to demonstrate his ownership of the lands and her. Just when she had thought they were getting on better. 'Why are you baiting my brother like that? What great wrong has he done you other than being related to me?'

Hrolf's jaw became even more set. 'Your

brother is a guest under my roof. He must abide by the same rules. It is fair.'

'He lives here. He has always done.' Sayrid pointed towards where Hrolf's men stood with their swords clearly visible. 'Are they to lose their weapons in the interests of fairness?'

'They are pledged to me. I would trust them with my life and the lives of my family. Most women would never question their husband in this fashion.'

Sayrid stared at him in disbelief and growing frustration. 'I married you, but I didn't suddenly become ignorant. You ought to be listening to my counsel, instead of just bedding me.'

He massaged her back. 'Bedding you is more pleasurable.'

She ignored the warm tingle which accompanied his caress. He seemed to think that all he had to do was touch her and she'd go along with his plans. 'Do you want Regin to swear an oath to you?'

Hrolf shrugged. 'It is a matter for him, but I only want warriors who are prepared to fight.' His eyes hardened. 'It must be his decision, Sayrid, without your help.'

'You are a hard man.'

'But I'm alive. What is mine, I keep safe, and that includes you.'

When the last of the weapons were deposited, Hrolf's men led the group off to the hall.

Hrolf and Sayrid remained standing in front of the pile of swords, axes and assorted knives. Sayrid kicked one of the swords with her foot. Hrolf had warned her about the wager, but she'd been so certain. And now she'd lost any chance to train with the men. She had a bad feeling about these guests.

'Your considered opinion?' Hrolf asked, catching her elbow. 'Before you retire to the kitchens to look after the food and ale.'

She started. He was actually asking her opinion. 'I thought you were only interested in one thing from me.'

'Our guests have retired.'

Sayrid assessed him under her lashes. He was playing some sort of game with their guests. But it was her chance to demonstrate her knowledge and make him see that she could do more than simply supervise the women. 'Far too many. And two kept knives down their boots.'

'What else?'

Sayrid studied the axes. 'They are from the East. Known to you.'

A dimple played in the corner of his mouth. 'Perhaps.'

'You had best tell me what you know. Keeping me in the dark serves no good purpose.' Sayrid put a hand on his arm. 'I hate begging.'

'I shall remind you of that later. Sometimes begging can be fun.' His voice dropped to husky note and there was a distinct gleam in his eye.

Her gaze dropped and she saw the evidence of his arousal.

Her face flamed and she glanced over her shoulder. Two of Hrolf's men hastily pretended to be doing something else. 'You delight in speaking nonsense.'

He raised her hand to his lips. 'Only when it brings colour to your cheeks.'

Her heart skipped a beat. She hated that she wanted the unpleasantness of this morning to go. He'd been right about her brother arriving here, but she knew in her heart Regin would never do anything to harm her. 'Hrolf, trust me to do the right thing.'

Hrolf's brow knitted. 'Something is wrong. It is too much of a coincidence. First the sabotage on my ship and then your brother shows up here with a war band, expecting these lands to be un-defended. He is the traitor, Sayrid. All the evidence points to it. I'm sorry.'

She pulled away from his grasp. All the heat leached out of her, leaving her cold. He was deliberately using her attraction to him to bend her to his will. As if a simple touch would make her forget her duty towards her family.

'Trust you to jump to the wrong conclusion about my brother.' She poured scorn into her voice. 'This is all about Blodvin changing her mind about meeting my stepmother and getting cold feet. Blodvin can be very impetuous and only thinks afterwards.'

'Indeed.'

'I have some sympathy with her plight as my stepmother is a strong-minded woman and will be less than pleased that Regin married without a dowry.' Sayrid gave a shrug. 'I suspect she was trying to get Regin away before he actually caused problems and then realized what she was getting into, once Regin sobered up enough to remember what his mother can be like.'

'I wonder what it will take before you see matters how they truly are. Your brother does you no favours.'

Sayrid's mouth went dry. Here she had thought Hrolf might actually care for her, but in reality he had been trying to bind her to him.

The reason for leaving so quickly now became clear. He had expected Regin to behave in this fashion. She didn't know who she wanted to shake more, Hrolf for being willing to believe the worst or Regin for falling into the trap.

'My brother would never do anything to jeopardize the hall or these lands. They are in his blood.'

'But they no longer belong to him. He had an expectation if you died without marrying, but now nothing.'

'He would never make an alliance with Lavrans.'

'Many men have done worse for less.'

'He knows the vengeance Lavrans has sworn against this family. Why would he side with our sworn enemy?'

Hrolf's eyes glittered. 'The enemy of my enemy is my friend.'

'Except in this case you are wrong. Regin knows you are far from the enemy. He knows you have an alliance with Kettil.' Sayrid crossed her arms and stared at the pile of weapons. Hrolf was right. There were far too many for peaceable travellers. And even Regin would have been much more wary about picking up travellers. 'He does have brains.'

Hrolf sighed. 'Your brother has a history of doing ill-considered things which you then have to clean up. You are far too soft with him.'

'I should have behaved more like my father?' Sayrid enquired in a low voice, clinging to her temper. More than ever she wished that she had not hesitated. Hrolf had no right to lecture her in that way.

'There comes a time when a man has to stand on his own two feet.'

Sayrid wanted to hit something hard. Hrolf knew nothing of the history of what Regin had suffered. He should have guessed from her scars.

'You know much about my family.'

'I know more than I did at this time yesterday. People will talk with the right persuasion.'

'You bribed people to learn about my family?' She blinked rapidly.

'It is amazing how many people wanted to

speak up. They all have the same sort of conclusion.'

'Which is?'

'You have done much to bring about the present prosperity this house currently enjoys and your brother rather less.'

'There are reasons for it. I am...was the head of the house.'

'Now I am. Obey me.'

Sayrid gestured towards one of the servants, instructing her to fetch more ale and make the travellers welcome before she exploded. Right now she wanted to shake the lot of them, starting with Hrolf, but continuing on to Blodvin and Regin.

Whatever had possessed the pair of them to behave in such a fashion? They were a couple of naive innocents.

Sayrid paused. Blodvin wasn't that naive. She might pretend, but she knew more about what was going on and how people should behave. Her father, Bloodaxe, was one of the most devious men in the whole of Svear. Her stomach roiled. She'd been blind. Blodvin was up to something.

'Is something wrong? You are still here.'

Sayrid straightened her gown and touched the

keys which hung from her belt. 'Obey you, you said?'

Hrolf glared at her. 'Is that possible?'

'The women have retired to the kitchen to prepare the food. I shall as well. It was the terms of our wager, was it not?'

He lifted a brow. 'Seeing sense at last?'

'As you wish, husband.' She turned her lips up to what she hoped would be an enigmatic smile. Obey him indeed. She would use her banishment to her advantage. She'd find a way to prove Regin's innocence.

Chapter Thirteen

'Sayrid! I thought you never went into the kitchen as a point of principle!' Blodvin exclaimed, rising from where she sat nibbling cakes. The entire kitchen scurried around her preparing food, but not Blodvin. Blodvin rested, looking very pretty and fragile.

Sayrid stood, feeling bigger and clumsier than ever. 'No place is hidden from me, Blodvin. And those cakes which I made yesterday were for everyone.'

'I'll have to have words with Auda for leading me astray. It is good that I arrived when I did. You will need someone to run this house.'

'Why?'

'You'll be too busy, preparing for a war which never comes.'

Sayrid schooled her features. Auda not being

there was all down to Blodvin and her sudden desire to leave. If she and Regin had stayed... And she might not be the best housekeeper yet, but she had certainly made strides. She was proud of those cakes. 'The hall remains standing even though Auda is enjoying a welcome rest with Kettil and his wife.'

Blodvin fluttered her lashes. 'I noticed a few improvements that could be made. I've given servants orders. My mother used to say what a natural housekeeper I was. If you don't mind me saying...the cakes could use a hint more butter.'

'I handle the servants. In the past I've dismissed the task far too readily.' She took the platter from the table and placed it up high on a shelf. 'Hrolf prefers my cakes the way they are.'

'Well...if he does...who am I to say differently?'

Sayrid motioned to the women to keep preparing the food. In many ways it had felt good ordering the food and getting to grips with the housekeeping. It, too, required focus and a thoughtful mind. 'I've heard tales about how Regin behaved at my wedding feast after he gave me a promise.'

Tears shimmered in Blodvin's eyes. 'We've returned to our house if you will have us, after the way Regin behaved. He said some dreadful things about Hrolf at the feast and nearly came to blows with Hrolf's bodyguard. What sort of a man needs a bodyguard? And they are foreign. I got him away the best I could so we wouldn't be murdered in our beds.'

'Regin was foolish,' Sayrid said. 'But it stops. Hrolf is my husband. You are my family. His bodyguard will do nothing as you've no wish to harm him. I will make sure they understand this.'

'You understand.' Blodvin clapped. 'I knew you would. I only have the best interests of my unborn child at heart. I couldn't…couldn't allow anything to happen to Regin.'

'Credit me with a little intelligence, Blodvin.' Sayrid leant forward. 'Why did you and my brother leave so quickly? It looks bad. Auda had to remain behind as surety for Regin's good be-haviour.'

Blodvin led her to a quiet corner of the kitchen. 'Something happened back at the village. I can feel it in my bones. My mother says that my great-great-grandmother was a witch and I just know things.'

'Indeed.'

'Whatever happened, Regin is innocent. He was with me the whole time. It pains me that so many people are quick to condemn him over a few careless words and one single ill-judged swing of the sword.'

Sayrid pulled her arm away from Blodvin, feeling larger and clumsier than ever as she managed to kick a bucket of water across the floor. All conversation and work stopped.

Sayrid marched over and righted it.

'Hrolf's flag ship was damaged,' she said carefully.

'It might have been damaged before and no one noticed.' Blodvin rolled her eyes. 'Honestly, these men. They are worse than children. One little thing is out of place and you'd think Ragnarök was about to arrive.' Blodvin took the bucket and put it to one side. 'My mother said that it was best to keep such things out of the way or warriors would trip over them. Oops! Me and my mouth. You're not a warrior any more.'

Sayrid clung on to her temper. Blodvin did not seem to understand the danger Regin was in.

'Hrolf swears the damage was done in the night, the same night that my brother apparently attacked Hrolf's bodyguard.'

Blodvin's eye turned pitying. 'And you believe him?'

'Why wouldn't I?'

Blodvin drew a little line on the table. 'Sayrid, I thought it would take more than a night spent in a man's arms to turn you into a lump of quivering female flesh. One of the best pieces of advice my mother ever gave me was to maintain a healthy scepticism where men were concerned. It is obvious that he is simply looking for a scapegoat to cover up for something which happened weeks before.'

Sayrid stared at the other woman. Blodvin was behaving as if it were nothing. But she had seen the fresh damage to the ship and knew what the consequences could have been.

For Blodvin to dismiss it in that fashion showed that Blodvin had little idea about ships. The knowledge made her feel better. Blodvin might be beautiful, but beauty wasn't everything. Regin's behaviour was understandable, but misguided.

'I can understand that approach if I was married to your father,' she said instead.

Blodvin's mouth dropped open. 'I was trying to be helpful. And Regin, the poor lamb, never went near that ship. He was with me the whole time after we left the feast.'

Sayrid leant forward. 'Are you willing to swear it to the *jaarl*? It might help.'

The younger woman nibbled her bottom lip.

'It is unseemly for a woman to give testimony about her husband, but I would swear it if you think it would help. But after the baby is born, yes? I've no wish to travel anywhere until then.' She patted her pregnant belly. 'I have my child to think of. Only the best for this little one.'

The muscles in Sayrid's neck eased. Regin had an alibi. 'Thank you.'

Blodvin bobbed a curtsy. 'My pleasure. I do hope we can be friends, Sayrid. The way you are acting, anyone would think you didn't like me very much. Imagine practically accusing me of doing something untoward. And those travellers mean no harm. I'm sure of it. How humiliating to have to give up their swords and be searched for weapons like that!'

Sayrid pinched the bridge of her nose. It was far from Blodvin's fault about their unwelcome visitors or the damage to the ship. And taking her poor temper out on her sister-in-law did no one any good. 'It has been a trying few days. And it is customary to surrender your weapons. They will be returned to the men when they leave. Until then they will be kept in the strongroom under lock and key. It is wise to be cautious where travellers are concerned.'

Blodvin nodded. 'I keep forgetting that you never planned to be married. Is your new daughter a trial? I mean how she behaved at the wedding. It is a wonder you allowed her to come here at all. I would have banished her and that nurse. Up to no good.'

Sayrid tilted her head to one side. Blodvin's mind always seemed to be flitting from one subject to the next.

'Inga? She has an active imagination, but her heart is in the right place. She and her nurse worked on this dress as they thought the colouring suited me better. Why do you think she is up to no good?'

'The instant she saw me, she ran out of the kitchen screaming about ghosts.' Blodvin rolled her eyes. 'As if I could ever be mistaken for such a horrible thing!'

The back of Sayrid's neck prickled. Had Blodvin been by the ship that night? Why would she do such a thing? It made little sense.

Inga delighted in her imagination and creating a stir. There was no way Blodvin would be involved in the sabotaging of the ship. She knew nothing about how ships were made. And what could she hope to gain from it anyway?

It made no sense. Blodvin seemed in favour of the match. And her family had no grudge against Hrolf. After all, Hrolf had nearly married her.

Sayrid pasted a smile on, but silently vowed to ask Inga about why Blodvin was a ghost. 'She called me a frost giant for a little while, but she will come around to the idea of you. She is a lively girl and has a good sense of humour.'

'I'm sure you are correct.' Blodvin gave a decisive nod. 'I don't envy you, though. A daughter like that and a husband with a reputation like Hrolf's.'

'Hrolf has an excellent reputation.'

Blodvin put her nose in the air. 'I have heard tales. Regin is very different. I intend to make something of my husband. I have my baby to think of. You just watch and see.'

'It is well that I married Hrolf instead of you.' Sayrid clenched her fists. Regin might not be a great warrior, but he had other points. She had thought Blodvin had seen those, but instead it sounded like she was already tired of him.

The woman's cheeks reddened. 'I thought we were sisters, Sayrid. You can confide in me. It is fine. I understand how these things are.'

Sayrid kept her face bland. Confiding in Blodvin would mean any secret she wanted keeping being spread with a swiftness that would surprise even the gods. 'I will bear that in mind should I ever have the need to confide anything.'

She walked swiftly from the kitchen and went out to the deserted training area. A lump came in her throat. Because she had totally misjudged Regin and Blodvin, all this was barred to her. She wanted to be a good wife, but she also wanted Hrolf to respect her.

Sayrid discovered Regin in the stables, grooming his horse where he always went if he was troubled.

Thankfully no one else was about.

'Are you going to tell me the truth?' she asked, advancing towards him. 'Why did you have Auda lie for you?'

'Are you going to listen to me? Or are you going to believe what that brute of a husband tells you?'

'Hrolf is…' Sayrid swallowed hard. Explaining about Hrolf when Regin was in this mood was not worth it. Her feelings were too new and Regin was likely to tease her. 'I will listen to you. Why did you leave the village without saying goodbye?'

'Blodvin's idea.' Regin continued to brush the horse. 'Once I'd sobered up, I knew what a terrible idea it was. Think about how my mother will react to Blodvin. She wasn't fond of Blodvin's mother. She wouldn't understand and she'd take it out on Blodvin.'

Sayrid crossed her arms. 'Look at me when you speak to me.'

He glanced up. His mouth was set in a mutinous scowl. 'You know what an utter witch my mother is.'

'And you remembered that when?'

He gave the horse another fierce brush. 'Look, Blodvin was doing her best when she made me depart. I had no idea what she wrote on the rune until later. And then I tried to make it good, but I just couldn't.'

'Do you remember what you did to make Blodvin want to leave quickly?'

Regin turned away from her. 'Is there any point

going over it? I was drunk and upset. I behaved like the worst sort of fool.'

'Yes, you did.' Sayrid put a hand on her brother's shoulder. He shrugged it off. 'You have made things difficult…for everyone.'

'I want it to go back to how it was before. Before he ever showed up.'

Sayrid stared at her brother. Go back? That was the last thing she wanted. 'I'm discovering that I am capable of far more than I dreamt. You should taste my cakes. I've stopped burning them.'

'I thought all you ever wanted was to be a warrior. Cooking was beneath contempt.' He turned back to her with a fierce face. 'You see what I mean. A few days and he has you wrapped around his little finger. Dresses and baking. That is not what my sister does! Where is it going to end? Do you think he could actually care for you? He is using you and you refuse to see it.'

'I will always be your sister,' Sayrid said quietly. A huge ache opened in her middle. 'I'd hoped you'd be happy for me. I've stopped fearing things. I can do more than fight.'

'You always could.' He gave the horse another swipe with the brush. 'It shouldn't have taken a sea king to show you that.'

'You know, I think you are jealous of Hrolf. He has accomplished a lot in his life. He is a better warrior than I am.'

Her brother slammed down his brush. With Regin in this mood, she at last understood why Kettil had his reservations about him and why he wanted a warrior like Hrolf controlling this bay. He was behaving worse than an unblooded youth. She'd hoped marriage and a pregnant wife would bring maturity, but no. Immediately she cursed herself for the disloyal thought. Regin always reacted badly to heavy-handed authority.

'Have a care, Regin.'

'He is arrogant and overbearing. Ordering me about like I was little better than a thrall. I grew up in this hall. I should be welcome here without question.'

'When you get to know him, you will see that Hrolf has many admirable qualities.' Sayrid knew she spoke the truth rather than mouthing simple platitudes. She did admire Hrolf's courage and the way he handled his men and…

'Why did you have to lose, Say? If you'd won, you'd be on your way east.'

Sayrid gave a strangled laugh. She had to wonder if she really knew her brother. 'Trying to get rid of me?'

Regin paled. 'Never. You know how important you are to me. You believe me, don't you?'

That was the trouble. Sayrid found it difficult to know what she believed any more.

Sayrid turned on her heel and left her brother to stew. Regin would come around to her way of thinking. He always did. But there was something about him that left her uneasy as if she were really seeing him for the first time.

'Did you learn anything?' Hrolf paused in his pacing of the bedchamber. He opened his arms, expecting her to walk in to them and lay her head against his shoulder. Thoughts of her doing so had distracted him when he was unsuccessfully grilling the visitors. They still maintained that they were travellers on lawful business and had never been to the East.

'Learn anything?' Sayrid sat down on a trunk, ignoring his outstretched arms.

'I worked out why you retired so easily. You wanted to find out if Blodvin knew anything.' Hrolf put his hands behind his head. 'You can be my eyes and ears where I can't go. A sure benefit to having a wife.'

Sayrid tilted her head to one side. All of Regin's insinuations about being enthralled with Hrolf to the point of stupidity came rushing back. 'I've no idea what you are talking about. Get someone else to do your spying.'

He crossed the room in two strides. His heavy hands went on her shoulders, pinning her to the spot. Her flesh quivered under his fingers. The muscles in his neck relaxed slightly. She wanted him. 'I am giving you credit by believing you were doing what I would do. Interrogating Blodvin. There is something about her story which is off. Have you spoken to your brother? Has he explained why he left?'

Sayrid bristled. She had come in ready to share her knowledge and Hrolf made it sound as if she had to do his bidding. Blodvin's words about being cautious ate away at her soul. 'I'm pleased you credit me with some intelligence.'

Hrolf tapped his fingers together. 'You are one of the most intelligent women I've ever met. I could even have seen you leading a *felag*. Does that satisfy you?'

'You might be able to see me leading a *felag*?'

she enquired in a silken tone, trying to keep a leash on her temper. Talk about damning with faint praise! 'I lost an equal contest of arms to you, but before that I had over five years' experience sailing on the sea and trading at markets. You want all that to vanish like it never happened?'

'I want you to be my wife, properly. I think we are well suited.' He stood stiffly as if he were reciting from memory. 'Men and women have different spheres of influence. It is the way I was brought up, but—'

'I can't be that if all you want is for me to be in the kitchen and in the bedroom,' she cried out before he finished. 'I can't be like my stepmother or Blodvin.' Sayrid wrapped her arms about her middle as her entire body began to shake. 'If you thought anything of me, you would see that.'

Hrolf was silent for a long while and when he spoke, he spoke in measured tones as if he was speaking to a child. 'I want to find a traitor, Sayrid. I don't care who he is. I simply want him unmasked.'

'And if he were one of your own?'

Hrolf froze. He rejected the idea. He trusted his men. They had no reason to betray him, not after all the time they had spent together. 'What did your brother say?'

'He feels aggrieved and that you will condemn him without listening. He knows he was foolish and used ill-considered words.'

'Whom did Blodvin accuse?'

'Being with her always makes my head ache. I can't think what Regin sees in her. But she did ask the question about your men.'

'She has a good pair of breasts and isn't afraid to use them.'

Sayrid's eyes widened. 'Excuse me?'

'A man would have to be dead not to notice. And she made sure I noticed them.' Hrolf rapidly explained about the way Bodvin's cloak slipped.

'Do you ever think of anything else?'

Giving in to impulse, he leant forward and brushed Sayrid's lips. They trembled. A surge of male pride went through him. 'You are jealous.'

She spun out of his grip.

'Of her? Hardly!'

He laughed.

'What is so funny?'

'You looking cross when there is no need to. I noticed, but why would I be interested when someone else graces my bed?'

'You mean you'd be interested if I wasn't here!'

'That is not what I said!' Hrolf's temper flared. Sayrid was being totally unreasonable. Accusing him of wanting another woman when all he wanted to do was spend time with her! 'You are my wife. I've no intention of dishonouring you.'

Her eyes flashed a dangerous blue. 'You mean, so soon after the marriage. I see.'

'You see nothing at all and what are you expecting? Ours could hardly be called a love match. My battle with you was long and hard fought.' He ran his hands through his hair, aware of Sayrid's horrified look. He was going about this all wrong. He'd hurt her and that was the last thing he wanted to do. But the words stuck in his throat. 'Love? Who needs it? We are married and we are compatible. Your family is complicating matters.'

Sayrid bristled. Instinctively she reached for her sword, but instead found the bunch of keys. Tearing them from her belt, she threw them with all her might. They clanked on the floor next to him. 'I am through with trying. I wanted to be a good wife, but I can see that it is impossible. I will never be the woman you want. I like pitting my wits against people and I like fighting.

I'm proud of my strength and what I've accomplished. My family would have starved without me. I was wrong to want more.'

Hrolf stared at her. 'But at what cost to you?'

'I still breathe.' She stood proudly with her head up. 'I can never be the sort of wife you desire. Let us stop this pretence and agree that it is never going to work.'

Without giving him a chance to haul her into his arms, she fled from the room.

Once she had gone, the room became utterly still and lost its vibrancy.

That he wanted to go after her made Hrolf pause. He never chased after women. He had kept the two parts of his life separate. But he didn't want that with Sayrid. He wanted something more. Sayrid had shown him how empty and devoid of meaning his life was. And above all, he wanted to keep her from being harmed. He cared about her. More than he had ever cared about anyone before. The price she was demanding was far too high.

He hit his hand against the table, making the *tafl* pieces jump.

Chapter Fourteen

Sayrid stared at the fish pond, searching for trout in the grey-rose of dawn. Hrolf had not come looking for her all night, even when she'd missed sitting at the high table for supper.

She had hardly hidden, staying in the kitchen to make sure the food was properly served, but she had not gone out of her way to join the men. Their jokes and loud talking had scraped against her nerves and she preferred to listen to Inga's latest attempt at a saga.

She glimpsed Hrolf several times and once she thought he was looking at her, but she couldn't be sure. All she knew was that a large lump of misery had settled in her chest.

Regin had stayed away as well, which was not a good sign. He had to know by now what he stood accused of. She should be pleased that he wanted to stand on his own two feet, but she wanted to give him counsel.

Sayrid tried one half-hearted throw of the spear and missed the fish. She gave a frustrated yell and waded out into the pond to retrieve it. The water soaked the hem of her skirt. She gave vent to her anger and tossed the spear towards the bank where it fell with a clatter.

'Were you aiming that at me?'

Her heart skipped a small beat. 'If I was aiming at you, I would have made the shot.'

Hrolf's laughter rumbled out over the pond. 'Good to know. I'd hate to think your arm is compromised.'

She bent to retrieve the spear. 'I'm fishing. It is best done in silence.'

'Is that what you are doing?'

'Of course.' She drew back her spear and glared at him. 'What else would I be doing standing knee deep in a freezing-cold pond? Or should your wife be doing something else?'

'Good question. I will have to consider it.'

'I intend to keep fishing whether or not I have your permission.'

Hrolf made no attempt to leave. The sunlight hit his hair, turning it golden. No man had the right to look so good. 'I never asked you to stop. Why did you not dine with me last night?'

She gave a half shrug. 'Blodvin does talking at feasts much better than I do.'

'Are you going to come out of the pond?'

Sayrid shook her head. 'I'm trying to fish.'

'Blodvin could put any number of people to sleep. And I thought Inga's mother was bad.' He rubbed the back of his neck. 'I found her stories impossible to follow and she kept going on and on that Regin knew nothing and was not to blame. You've spoilt me for interesting conversation. I want to hear your voice.'

Sayrid carefully retrieved the spear. Hrolf had found Inga's mother boring. 'Truly?'

He gave a half smile. 'Lately I have discovered that I need more interesting companionship.'

'Is this an apology?'

'If you require one...' He shrugged his shoulder. 'Fine, yes, but I was pleased you were jealous. I shouldn't have teased you though.'

Sayrid waded out of the pond. She stopped and released her skirt so it fell about her ankles. 'I'm sorry as well. I feel clumsy and overgrown when I am about Blodvin. It is like my stepmother is whispering in my ear again about all the things

I'm bad at. I took my foul mood out on you. That was wrong of me.'

Hrolf's fingers went under her elbow. 'Hush now.'

She regarded his mouth and impulsively leant forward. He tasted of fresh spring water and summer meadows with a hint of pure Hrolf. The instant their mouths touched, his arms went around her and held her tight.

She opened her mouth and drew him in. She buried her hands in his hair and was surprised to find it damp.

She drew back. 'You had a bath?'

'I went swimming. I had no desire to stay in that room without you. And I knew you weren't in your old sleeping quarters.'

'How did you know that?'

'They were given to our guests. Even you would balk at sleeping amongst those men.'

'I found it impossible to sleep.' She turned her mouth to his. 'But I missed this more.'

He instantly deepened the kiss. Their tongues tangled and teased as their hands roamed freely all over each other. He started to pull her gown up, but she shook her head.

'My time.'

Slowly she traced a line down his throat and chest until she reached his trouser band. She rapidly undid it and allowed him to spring free. Then she stroked his arousal, hot, heavy and just for her.

He groaned in the back of his throat. 'Where did you learn this?'

'I put your lessons to good use. I know what your touch does to me.'

He grew in her hand, pulsating. Slowly she lowered her mouth to the tip of him and traced the head, catching the tiny bead of moisture on her tongue.

'Please.' His hands dug into her shoulders as his body bucked upwards. 'Ride me. Let me be in you.'

They fell to the bank and slowly she straddled him, impaling herself, feeling her body open to welcome the full length of him. His hands cupped her hips, holding her steady. Slowly she began to move, calling the rhythm, faster and faster until they reached the same shuddering climax. She collapsed, spent, on to his chest as he pumped his seed into her hard.

Silently they lay there with his hand gently rubbing her back.

* * *

Hrolf closed his eyes and made a memory as Sayrid slept in his arms with the green boughs above them and the water of the fishing pond gently lapping near them. It was as close to perfection as he had ever experienced on this earth.

It frightened him how much this woman had come to mean to him in the past few days.

Last night, he had kept searching for her, unable to settle. And now she was here. She had awakened so many emotions within him. They scared him. He was fast becoming like his father, dependent on someone else. And when his mother had died, his father had been like a lost child, not eating or drinking properly until they had found him curled in a ball, frozen in the winter snow. His uncle had taken him in and taught him that women should be enjoyed, but not given any power over his heart.

He kissed her naked shoulder. She turned over and her arm went about his neck. He knew then that she had his heart. She had taken it that first night when she defied him by jumping into the river. He needed her in his life, challenging him.

'You appear to be very serious.'

The words spilled out of him about his mother's death, how his father had behaved and his vow about keeping the women in his life separate, but how he no longer wanted that. She listened quietly.

'We won't make the same mistakes,' she said into the silence. 'You're not your father.'

'We need to return. People will be wondering where we are.'

She stretched. 'I'd like to stay here forever.'

He laughed softly in his throat. 'I would as well, but there are others to think about. And I take my duty seriously.'

She rolled off him and started to dress, suddenly all businesslike, and the passion they had shared replaced by another passion. 'Do you think there is a traitor?'

'We will be safe here. Lavrans will make a mistake. He dislikes waiting.'

'You think he will strike Kettil before you.'

Hrolf nodded. 'Bragi is an excellent warrior and the men respect him. He won't let me down.'

'And if he should strike here first?' A cold shiver went down her spine. She had little doubt. 'Even though all the weapons are locked up, I don't trust those travellers who arrived with

Regin and Blodvin. If only Regin would open up like he used to.'

'They will be gone today, probably before we return to the hall. I gave my men strict orders. They are to provide an escort to the edge of our lands. The swords can be returned there.' He put his finger under her chin. 'We will find your brother a farmhouse where he can begin to make a new life. He will speak to you then.'

'You really don't trust them.'

'I stopped believing in coincidences a long time ago. The only thing I thank the gods for is the way you constructed that blockade. Even if Lavrans wanted, without a guide, his ships would run aground.' He put an arm about her. 'I feel like I'm missing something. A tiny piece which will make everything become clear. Was it our marriage that caused Lavrans to make his move?'

Sayrid stared at the pond. 'I know what you mean. Too many things don't make sense. Our marriage cannot have been the catalyst. If these men were on their way here already, then they cannot have been expecting you.'

He cupped her face. 'You may be right. What else are you thinking?'

She put her hands on his face and felt the warm skin under her fingertips. He valued her opinion. 'Blodvin. Inga called her a ghost yesterday but I think she means a different ghost from the one she supposedly saw at the harbour. I never got an opportunity to question Inga about it. It could be her play-acting again. But why would Blodvin be down at the harbour wrecking your ship? She has nothing against you.'

'How long did Regin know Blodvin before they eloped?'

'Several months, long enough for him to get her pregnant,' Sayrid admitted with a rueful smile. 'The pregnancy surprised me. I thought he would have been more cautious. I had warned him, but what can you do in the face of young love? He swore it was only the once. But it changed everything. Abandoning my blood is impossible.'

Hrolf sat up straighter. His face became hardened planes. 'When did the only once happen?'

'At the summer festival apparently. Regin was prepared to swear that neither had had lovers before.' She shook her head. 'I may dislike Regin's choice of bride, but she is too…'

'Too what…honey-sweet? Accomplished in the

woman's sphere?' Hrolf asked. 'You were the one who accused me of prejudice. Be careful that you don't fall into the same trap.'

Sayrid hugged her knees to her chest. 'But why would she do such a thing?'

'About time we asked her.'

A loud shout followed by a long blast from the horn drowned the rest of his response.

Sayrid instantly started to run, but before she had gone a hundred paces, Magda stumbled into the clearing. On seeing Hrolf, she fell to her knees and started wailing.

'What is going on?' Sayrid asked. 'Where is Inga?'

'It is what I'm trying to discover. She keeps going on about the ghost.'

'She means Blodvin. Inga calls her a ghost.'

The woman nodded vigorously and rapidly explained Inga was with Blodvin before she tugged on Sayrid's arm. 'We must go. There is trouble.'

'Trouble?' Hrolf's brow creased. 'What sort of trouble?'

Sayrid saw the smoke begin to rise and her blood ran cold. 'The hall has been attacked. As impossible as it sounds, it has been and it has come from the sea.'

'Regin! I'm sorry, Sayrid.'

Sayrid's stomach revolted. Regin was the only explanation. He had completely betrayed her. Everything she had done for him meant nothing to him. 'I don't understand why he has behaved in this fashion. I would have wagered my life on him. I owe him several life debts. He found me after the beating and saved my life.'

Hrolf's face was like thunder. 'And this is how he treats you?'

The pain in her head increased to a breaking point. She struggled to take deep breaths. Even now, she wanted to believe that Regin had nothing to do with this, but as the smoke billowed higher, she had no other explanation. 'If my brother has done this, then he will pay, but that is for later. Right now we need to regain control of the hall.'

'There we agree. I have faced far worse odds.'

'How can we hope to succeed?'

'They may have attacked early, but they neglected to secure the two most important warriors. Do I have your sword arm, my lady?'

Sayrid returned his smile. 'With pleasure.'

Hrolf turned to the nurse. 'Have any more men arrived? Who of my men remain standing?'

The nurse shook her head and started wailing in Rus.

'Take a deep breath and speak slowly, Magda. I want to understand as well.' Sayrid grabbed her cold hand. 'Where did the men come from?'

Magda gulped air. 'In boats! From the sea. At dawn.'

She then started speaking in Rus and making wild gestures.

'In the North language,' Hrolf commanded. 'Sayrid needs to hear. She knows the hall and its buildings better than I do. Your words may make all the difference to our success.'

From her garbled words, Sayrid gathered that Hrolf's bodyguard had been slain first. When she had seen the sails, she'd gone to find them, but their throats had been slit while they slept.

The others were either dead or captured. The attack had happened while they all slept. Her brother's betrayal was complete.

Hrolf hunkered down and drew a quick map in the dirt. 'They struck in the early morning and must have assumed that we would still be asleep in our bed.'

'They will be searching for us.'

'Not yet. They will be securing the hall and the outbuildings.'

'Then we have to strike before they get settled.'

Sayrid took a steadying breath. The hopelessness of the situation nearly overwhelmed her. There wasn't time to go to the outlying farms. And the men there would not be able to fight against hardened warriors. 'We have a fishing spear and a knife. And I know all the hiding places in the hall and in the outer buildings.'

Hrolf kissed her forehead. 'We will win the land back. I give you my solemn promise. I pledge you my all.'

The sound of a twig breaking made them both freeze.

'Where did that old woman go? Lavrans ordered her death,' one voice shouted.

'As if we didn't have enough to do,' a second voice grumbled. 'Lavrans doesn't want any of them Rus left alive.'

Magda began to openly weep, but Hrolf whispered a few words to her. Her eyes grew big and she nodded. She immediately rearranged her shawl.

Hrolf put his fingers to his lips and jerked his head towards the bushes.

'Opportunity,' he mouthed to Sayrid. 'Need to lure them.'

Sayrid nodded her understanding as her fingers closed around the fishing spear. She crouched low, waiting. Every nerve tingled with anticipation. They had this one chance,

At Hrolf's signal, Magda gave a little yelp.

'Louder,' Sayrid muttered. 'They need to hear you.'

Magda gave her a panic-stricken look, but complied with a deafening wail.

The pair crashed into the clearing. Sayrid rose up on her toes, aimed for the lead warrior and tossed the spear. It seemed to hang in the air for a timeless moment. Then it connected with the warrior's throat. He went down with a gurgle.

Hrolf dashed forward, brandishing his knife. He rolled and grabbed the fallen man's sword in one swift move, but the other warrior was on him immediately. As the other warrior brought his sword down, Hrolf jabbed his knife forward, meeting the sword.

Sword met knife, locked in mortal combat.

Then Hrolf brought his other arm up and dispatched the man. He fell to the ground beside the first.

Hrolf gestured towards the sword and shield. 'You wanted weapons, my lady. Will these do?'

Sayrid retrieved her spear as well as taking one of the swords and a shield. 'Are you still determined to say that I'm not a good warrior?'

Hrolf gave a crooked smile. 'Right now, I give thanks to Odin that we did not have a spear-throwing contest.'

'He was far simpler to catch than the old trout in the pond.'

'I would be honoured to fight alongside my wife.' He gave her a quick kiss.

'What was that for?'

'To remind you that while I shall depend on your skill as a warrior, I know you are my woman and I intend to have you in my bed when this is done.'

A warm bubble of happiness filled Sayrid. He saw her as both. She didn't have to pretend one way or the other.

'Shall we retake the hall?'

'I will help as well,' Magda declared. 'Give me

a knife. I can fight. I want to avenge the deaths of my countrymen.'

Sayrid glanced at Hrolf. He nodded.

'All help gratefully received. I can't do this on my own.'

Chapter Fifteen

Spying the ruins of the hall, Sayrid felt her heart shatter. Flames licked at the great structure and all was confusion where, a short time ago, it had been tranquil peace.

At the harbour's edge, another ship was pulled up. Her mouth tasted of ash and her heart was sick. Regin's betrayal had been complete.

An eerie silence hung over everything. So confident were the attackers that they had left the ship unguarded while they looted and pillaged.

Sayrid clenched impotent fists. After all she'd been through, it seemed unfair that this should happen to the place she loved.

Hrolf put a hand on her shoulder. 'Lavrans.'

'I recognise the sail,' she choked out. 'In my worst nightmares I never thought to see it here.'

'Nor did I.'

'Regin had best hope he dies in battle. That son of Loki is nothing to me.' Sayrid set her jaw as she spied the mutilated body of one of the serving women.

'We will find the truth, I promise. You have no idea if Regin was blackmailed.'

'But right now we take back this land.' Silently Sayrid prayed that some of Hrolf's men were safe.

'I search the outbuildings,' Magda declared. 'If you distract, they will not pay attention to an old woman. Maybe some of your warriors alive.'

Sayrid tossed her the keys. 'Hopefully these will help.'

The woman bowed her thanks and hurried off.

'It seems I have seriously underestimated a number of people,' Hrolf said.

'At least you are able to admit it.'

Sayrid rapidly gathered extra pieces of wood, buckets and an old fork as possible missiles. Hrolf, she noticed, did the same.

He nodded his approval. 'We need all the weapons we can get.'

She bent down and tore a strip off her skirt and wadded it.

'Let me guess—you need to be able to move your legs when you fight.'

'That and I want to block his retreat.' She dipped the makeshift torch in the burning embers and then walked purposefully to the unguarded ship. It was very easy to set it alight.

'Shall we retake this hall?' she asked Hrolf. 'Even though we have no hope of survival, we will retain our honour.'

'We go side by side.' He smiled. 'You have to like the odds.'

'I have faced worse.'

His face sobered. 'But I haven't. You must stay safe.'

'I will if you will.'

At that moment, a warrior emerged from one of the outbuildings, carrying a piglet. When he spied them, he stopped. Sayrid rolled a bucket forward. He went to go over it, but the piglet began to squirm and he toppled over.

Hrolf ran forward and swiftly dispatched him. But at his dying shout, others emerged from the building.

Sayrid engaged the first one, Although he was skilled, he was no match for her. With a few swift strokes, she beat him to the ground. As she finished, another warrior charged forward. This one was more deliberate in his actions, but not any real challenge.

'Watch your back!'

Hrolf's call caused her to pivot and instinctively raise her shield. A bone-jarring thud hit her shield, nearly cleaving it in half. The warrior fell at her feet.

'I owe you a life debt,' she choked out.

'I'll remind you of it later.'

There was a loud cry of 'Hrolf! Hrolf! Hrolf!' His remaining men streamed from their prison and the battle truly was joined.

Sayrid fought hard, but a grizzled warrior took advantage of her tiredness. She was forced on to her back foot as her bottom touched the wall. All her muscles ached and she doubted if she had enough strength to lift her sword.

Suddenly the warrior's face developed a surprised expression. He toppled forward. Sayrid summoned her remaining energy to move out of the way.

'I, too, can fight,' Magda said, brandishing a bloody knife. 'Revenge for my kinsmen.'

'Keep up the good work!'

Sayrid raced back to where Hrolf stood with

his men. Lavrans's ship now blazed bright, lighting the sky.

'Lavrans! Stop sulking! Come and fight like a man!'

'Hrolf Sea-Rider, I have nothing against you.' A large man emerged from the barn. He was handsome in an overly pretty way which had started to run to fat. There was a faint air of Regin about him and she had to wonder if the rumour about Regin not being her father's was true. 'Leave this place. Return to the East. My quarrel is with Ironfist and his children.'

'You attacked my holdings, killed my men and destroyed my hall.' Hrolf slapped his sword against his leg. The lines of weariness were clearly etched on his face. 'I challenge you to a fight to decide this once and for all.'

Sayrid gulped hard. He would need every ounce of strength to fight an opponent like Lavrans.

'A pleasure. This has been coming for some time.'

'For far too long.'

Hrolf glanced at Sayrid. Sweat poured from her brow. Her gown was now splattered with mud and blood. A streak of dirt marred her cheek. But she had never appeared so lovely to him. Bravery, courage and passion flowed from every particle of her body. Finally he knew what he was fighting for. It wasn't land, riches or even glory, but for this woman and the life he hoped to build with her. It wasn't about her putting him first, but about him putting her there. There were so many things he wished he'd said to her. If Odin and Thor were with him, he would tell her tonight while they lay wrapped in each other's arms.

'I fight gladly.'

'Then shall we have to? And don't worry, your wife has no appeal for me, but it might be amusing to see how she waltzes with a bear.'

'My wife is worth a thousand of you.'

Round and round, they circled each other, probing and testing. All of Hrolf's muscles screamed, but he kept focused on his opponent, waiting for him to make a mistake. Then, when he thought he could no longer hold the sword another instant, he heard Sayrid call out. Lavrans turned his head.

In that split instant, Hrolf lunged forward, using the trick Sayrid had used against him. Lavrans ended up on the ground, his sword to one side.

Hrolf did not hesitate 'This is for everyone you murdered.'

He drove his sword home. The cheers of his

remaining men rang out. Lavrans's men hastily signalled their surrender.

'Is it over?' Sayrid asked.

'Yes, it is over.' He wiped the sweat which half-blinded him from his eyes. 'You are safe. I will not allow you to be hurt.'

'And Regin?'

Hrolf's heart squeezed. It gave him no joy to say, 'Your brother betrayed us all.'

Sayrid gave an unhappy nod. 'He is a traitor. If I had any lingering doubts, seeing Lavrans's ship convinced me. I have no idea when or how he turned. He deserves a traitor's death. Just do not ask me to watch.'

'I wish it were otherwise.' His face creased with concern. 'I'd have preferred to meet him in battle.'

'We need to find him.' Sayrid concentrated on the barn. She could barely bring herself to voice her unspoken fear that, having lost his usefulness, Regin was already dead. And she had to know why he had behaved in such a fashion. What could she have done to prevent it? Had it truly been because she had surrendered to Hrolf? 'I must find him.'

'You can stay here in the yard if you wish.'

Sayrid closed her eyes. Hrolf was attempting to be kind. They both knew what could be in that barn. But she was also reluctant to confess that she was afraid of losing him, or of him going in and not coming out again. 'We go together. I will not have it said that I shirked my duty.'

His face closed to hard planes. 'It is your choice.'

The barn held an unnatural stillness. All the animals had gone. Sayrid walked next to Hrolf, not speaking. Hrolf put an arm about her. 'You don't need to see this.'

A single tear ran down her cheek. 'I do.'

'Very well.' He stepped aside and revealed the bloodied body, stretched spreadeagle in the stall where Regin's favourite horse had been stabled. The horse, she saw with a pang, had been slaughtered. It was impossible to tell which was the blood from the horse and which was her brother's blood.

'Regin?' she whispered through cracked lips. 'Are you alive?'

Hrolf placed his weapons down and went over to the body. His face became creased with concern. 'Whatever he hoped to gain, it wasn't this.'

Sayrid forced her feet to move and she knelt

beside the body. 'Why, Regin? Why did you try to destroy us like this?'

No answer. She went to shut his eyes, but his hand grabbed her wrist.

'Say?' Regin said in a barely recognisable croak. 'Say, I made a mistake. I'm sorry.'

Tears flowed down her face unchecked. 'I know.'

'I'm no traitor. I thought you'd just go off adventuring to the East and there'd be no need for this.'

'Who are you protecting?' Hrolf asked in a hard voice. 'Your sister could have died today because of you. Brave men died today because of you. Is that what you wanted?'

'Blodvin.' His hand plucked at the blood-soaked straw. 'Not my baby. Do not trust her. Wicked.'

Sayrid's heart contracted. Not his baby? Blodvin had betrayed them all? Thinking back, she wondered why she hadn't thought of it before. She'd never fully trusted Bloodaxe and she certainly should not have trusted his daughter. Regin had sworn that it had been only the one time. Her brother had been deceived in the worst possible way. 'I'm so sorry.'

'We both are,' Hrolf said.

'Thought I was doing it for my child and the child wasn't even mine,' her brother said, gasping between each word. 'Lavrans...'

'Dead.'

Her brother gave a small semblance of a smile. 'Good.'

'Sayrid...' Hrolf hauled her back against him. 'I will ask Magda to make him comfortable. It is in the Norns' spindles if he lives or dies. His injuries...I have seldom seen a man survive for long with that sort.'

Sayrid rose. She understood what Hrolf was offering. 'I should stay. I have been on a battlefield before.'

Her brother's head thrashed about on the straw. 'Say...go. You need to find Blodvin. She took the little girl. I objected because I don't make war against children and they beat me. Find the girl. Save her. You are good at that.'

The true horror of what Regin was saying hit Sayrid like a hammer blow. She hadn't given Inga a second thought after Magda explained that Blodvin had her. She had assumed all would be well. Blodvin was known to be good with children and that was before she had heard of Blodvin's treachery.

'We need to go. Now. Regin, Magda will make you comfortable. And the Norns willing, I will see you again.'

'Sayrid?' Hrolf croaked, and then she watched as the horror sank in. 'Blodvin has my daughter?'

Sayrid went cold. 'Blodvin won't have hurt her. The woman sheds tears at the slightest problem and she seems incapable of doing anything except looking pretty. She isn't a cold-blooded murderess.'

Hrolf raised a brow. 'You want to believe that. She is capable of far more than you want to think.'

Sayrid put her hand in his. 'I have to believe we can save Inga, Hrolf. I have to believe that Blodvin won't harm her...or at least not yet.'

'Does your brother know where she is?'

Regin shook his head. 'Hiding place.'

He gurgled faintly and collapsed.

'We will get no more from him,' Sayrid said, kneeling beside Regin's body. She could see the faint rise and fall of his chest. He was alive, but barely. 'Don't try.'

Hrolf let out a great roar which echoed around the barn. 'I've no idea where that witch has taken my daughter. I want my daughter found alive!'

Sayrid put her arms about him. 'We will find

her together. There is nothing more that can be done here. But we will find her.'

'Thank you.'

Hrolf called for his remaining men and for Magda. The old nurse took one look and understood what needed to be done, immediately volunteering to stay with Regin.

'Where do we start?' he asked.

'We start with the hiding places for women. My father feared attack. He caused three to be built. I made sure that Blodvin knew about them when we first arrived. I had thought her very nervous the way she kept going on about them, but she had obviously planned this well,' Sayrid said bitterly. 'I've no idea which one she's used.'

'Can you give directions? It will go quicker if we can split up. We know that Blodvin doesn't have any warriors protecting her. It is simply a matter of finding her and Inga.'

Sayrid nodded. 'You are right. It is best to split up. We can send men to the closest two, but it was the farthest she was most interested in.'

'We will go to that one.'

Sayrid gave rapid instructions and two parties of warriors started off towards the nearest hiding places. Each party had strict instructions to blow three blasts on a hunting horn if they found her—dead or alive.

Sayrid hugged her arms about her waist. She refused to think about that little girl being dead or harmed in any fashion. She had to hope that Blodvin wanted to use the girl as a bargaining counter in case the attack went against her lover. 'I never suspected Blodvin would harm her or I wouldn't have suggested going into battle with you.'

'If you hadn't been there, who knows what would have happened to me?' Hrolf ran a hand through his hair. 'For years I wondered if Inga was truly mine, but now I know it doesn't matter. Inga is my daughter and I want her back.'

'She is my daughter as well.' Sayrid quickened her pace. 'I should have known that there was more to Inga's story about the ghost than simple imagination. I was so intent on proving Regin's innocence that I missed the obvious connection. I underestimated her.'

'We all did.'

Sayrid led the way to the furthest and most difficult-to-find hiding place. When they reached it, Sayrid moved the ivy which covered the entrance.

'Blodvin? Inga? Everything is safe.'

The only answer was the wind whistling.

Her heart knocked. She turned towards Hrolf. 'I'd been so sure. It made sense.'

He put his arm about her and she laid her head against his shoulder. He drew her in closer. 'We will find them. They will be in another safe house, waiting to hear the outcome.'

'Of course we will. And Inga will be safe.' She put her hand on his chest. 'I know it.'

'Who are you trying to make feel better?'

'The both of us.'

'I wish I shared your confidence.'

Sayrid stiffened as her eye caught a brightly coloured bead. 'What is that?'

She hurried over and picked it out of the dirt. 'It looks like one of the beads Inga wears.'

'It could have been here for years.'

Sayrid tightened her hand around the bead. It belonged to Inga. She had been here. Recently. And the only person she could have been with was Blodvin. The problem was to find the next clue. On her hands and knees she started to scour the area.

'What are you doing?'

'Searching. Inga is far more capable than Blodvin will give her credit for.' Sayrid spotted the next bead, a rose-and-white one, lying under a tree. 'There! Do you think that one is leftover from years ago as well?'

'Truly remarkable.' Hrolf held the bead in his hand. 'Inga loved this bead. I brought it back to her from Constantinople.'

'Clever girl. She is laying a trail for us to follow.' Sayrid rocked back on her heels. 'Hopefully we will find her before she runs out of beads.'

'I hope we are in time.' Hrolf started off at a slow run, looking left and right. He spotted the third bead and held it up. 'We are going in the right direction.'

'Give it to me,' Sayrid said. 'When we find Inga, we can give the beads back to her.'

'Plus several extra!'

She grabbed his hand and gave it a squeeze. He squeezed back. 'My thinking exactly.'

After the third bead, the fourth and fifth were easy to spot, but the sixth proved elusive until Sayrid spotted it by a pond.

'Of course,' she murmured. 'I know where they have gone.'

'I thought there were only three hiding places.'

'Blodvin is making for the cliff at the top of the headland. She will be able to observe what is happening and make her plans accordingly.'

'If she harms a hair on my Inga's head, she is a dead woman.'

Sayrid stopped abruptly. 'I want Blodvin properly punished, but I also want to find out who else was involved. It is finally our chance to uncover the true traitor, the one who has been telling Lavrans all the shipping secrets.'

'You mean her father.'

'How else could Blodvin have met Lavrans?' Silently she waited for Hrolf to agree. 'The double-crossing swine. I should have known that a man who will cheat on wool will cheat on other things.'

He nodded reluctantly. 'I will do all in my power to bring her to justice, even if my first inclination is to put a sword to her throat. If my daughter is dead, I will not spare the witch.'

'Inga was alive when she dropped these beads. It isn't much, but I hang on to it.'

'I hadn't thought of it in that way.' He put a hand on her shoulder. 'I'm glad you are here.'

Sayrid put on what she hoped was a confident

smile, but inside she knew she would blame herself for the rest of her life if anything happened to Inga.

They rounded a corner and Sayrid saw them, standing at the cliff's edge. The wind whipped Blodvin's hair, making her look quite wild. Inga was pale but resolute.

'There they are. And Inga is alive. See.'

Hrolf threw his arms about her. His face showed utter relief. 'I am in your debt for finding them. I would never have considered a bead trail.'

'Our daughter's doing.'

He started running towards the pair.

'They are too close to the edge,' Sayrid called.

Hrolf immediately checked his movement. Sayrid was right. In his haste to protect his daughter, he had nearly ruined everything. They would need to be coaxed away from danger.

'What do you suggest?

'Get their attention and keep it focused on you. I will go around the other way. We don't want Blodvin getting scared and accidentally jumping off the cliff.'

Hrolf nodded, seeing the sense in Sayrid's words. He wanted to tell Sayrid not to take the risk, but he knew there was no stopping her, just as there had been no stopping her when they had fought off Lavrans and his men earlier. His wife was fiercely loyal and protective. And she had taught him that women were much more than ornaments to be protected and admired.

'Keep safe,' he said as a lump came in his throat. His heart was far too full to begin. 'You're precious to everyone.'

She made a little disparaging gesture. 'I plan on doing that. The same goes for you. When I get close, you distract Blodvin. Once I have Inga, we will worry about that witch.'

Without giving him time to reply, she turned her back and strode off.

He watched as she moved, marvelling once again at the economy of her movements.

'Inga!' Hrolf shouted when he figured that Sayrid had nearly reached the place where there was no cover. 'Come here. Come to your father. All the bad men are gone. We want you to come home now.'

Blodvin turned towards him. Her blonde hair whipped in front of her face in snake-like tendrils. Suddenly her face transformed and became simpering.

'Hrolf! Thank Sif and all the goddesses, you

are safe. Someone has attacked the hall. Inga and I—'

'Don't believe her, Far! She is a troll wife!'

'Ha! Ha! Your daughter and I are playing a little game.' Her smile became wider, but he noticed she gripped Inga's wrist. 'You understand? A game to pass the time while we waited? A most enchanting child. Full of stories about ghosts, witches and trolls.'

'It is over now, Blodvin.' Hrolf advanced steadily.

Inga struggled against Blodvin's grip. 'She is lying. She is a troll wife!'

'You see what I mean.'

'Release my daughter, Blodvin. Lavrans is dead.' Hrolf advanced slowly towards them. He had never killed a pregnant woman before and he had no intention of starting, but if she put Inga or Sayrid in any more danger, he refused to be held accountable for his actions.

The woman shook her head. 'He can't be. He is…is invincible.'

'I killed him in a fair fight.' He gauged the distance. 'The game is over, Blodvin. We know what you have done. I found Regin.'

'You know nothing.' The woman took a step backwards towards the cliff edge. Several rocks tumbled down. Blodvin lost her balance and began to circle her arms while Inga started screaming.

'No!' The raw sound emerged from Sayrid's throat. She dashed forward just as Blodvin took another step backwards off the cliff. With one flying leap she grabbed Inga's ankle before the little girl was dragged off.

Blodvin's and Inga's screams rang in her ears. She fought to pull the pair up, but her muscles screamed in protest. She felt Inga's ankle begin to slip from her grasp.

In a heartbeat Hrolf was beside her. 'We will save you. Hang on!'

'I'm trying, Far!'

Hrolf's large hands closed about Inga's legs. 'I have you. Sayrid and I have you, Inga.'

'Hold on, Blodvin,' Sayrid shouted. 'We can save you and your baby.'

The only answer was a piercing shriek, but she kept hold of Inga.

Working together, they pulled the pair back up. Sayrid was half an inch from Blodvin's hand when the woman shook her head.

'No, I can't do it. I can't live if I've lost everything.' Very deliberately she let go of one of Inga's wrists.

Sayrid leant a few extra inches. Her fingers clamped about the woman's wrist as Blodvin dug her nails in, scratching and clawing at her. 'You are not getting away that easily.'

Hrolf bent down and hauled the woman up. 'Bind her arms.'

'But…but…but…' Blodvin spluttered. 'I'm pregnant.'

'That will be something Kettil will take into consideration when he decides your fate,' Hrolf replied. He reached into his pocket, retrieved the horn and blew three blasts. 'We will wait here for the others to arrive. You are my prisoner now. Sayrid, look after Inga.'

'My pleasure.'

Hrolf tied Blodvin up. All pretence to gentility had vanished. Blodvin fought him until he secured her hands behind her back and tied her feet.

In very little time, several of his men appeared and took charge of the now-deranged prisoner.

'You're safe,' Sayrid murmured against Inga's hair as they set off towards the ruined hall. 'My brave daughter, you are safe.'

The girl turned a tear-stained face towards her. 'I was brave like you. Do you think my father will love me now like he loves you?'

It was on the tip of Sayrid's tongue to tell her that Hrolf had no great feelings for his wife and that it had all been about the land. But she swallowed the words. The little girl needed her illusions of romance. 'Your father loved you before. After all, he brought you to this land so that you could be near him.'

Inga's brow knitted together. In that instant, Sayrid saw a female version of Hrolf. 'I never thought about that.'

'You look very like your father when you frown like that.'

Inga coloured. 'Do I really?'

Hrolf picked his daughter up. 'How you could ever doubt I love you, Inga, is beyond me. And Sayrid is right. You take after my late mother, a very brave woman who loved her family. I never saw that before. Remind me to tell you about her sometime.'

Sayrid noted with a pang that he said nothing about loving her, his wife. She was wrong to hope. But it was a start. He was speaking about his mother.

'And Blodvin?' Inga asked.

'Going where troll wives go,' Sayrid answered shortly. 'She will never bother you again.'

'Good.'

Hrolf watched his wife stand slightly apart with her ash-white hair blowing in the wind. Her dress was marked and torn. Her face was covered with a mixture of soot, dust and sweat, but she had never looked more beautiful.

This was what she was born to do. And he was wrong to think otherwise. She needed to be able to visit other lands and be the sort of woman she was meant to be.

He'd been wrong to try to change her. He'd been wrong to try to tame her.

'Sayrid,' he said, intending to tell her some of it.

She shook her head. 'I know...I know...we need to get back. There is a lot to do to secure the remains of the hall.'

She started to move brusquely down the hill. Hrolf sighed.

'You should tell Sayrid that you love her,' Inga said, snuggling her head down on his shoulder. 'It is the sort of thing ladies like to hear.'

Sayrid stared at the smouldering pile of wood that had been her childhood home. Tomorrow would be soon enough to start rebuilding. She dreaded to think what had been lost, but it was nothing compared to what had nearly been lost.

A bone-tired weariness swept over her. She wondered if she'd have the heart to start again. She'd missed what must have been obvious to everyone, that her brother was a traitor. She had to wonder what else she'd missed. And how could Hrolf feel anything for her now? She had put his beloved daughter in danger. Her blind refusal even to consider the possibility of her brother's guilt had nearly destroyed them all.

She started to move some of the wood.

'Leave it, Sayrid,' Hrolf said, coming to stand beside her. The setting sun turned his hair golden. 'There will be time for that tomorrow. You look absolutely exhausted.'

'Magda reported that she thinks my brother should survive,' she began before he could say anything more damning. 'She has given him a sleeping draught. I know I said earlier that it would be easier if he died, but he is my brother.'

'It is good to know.' His brow creased. 'He will have to face trial with Blodvin, but I will speak in his favour.'

'You will?'

He nodded slowly. 'A man will do a lot for

the woman he loves and his child. In the end he tried to do the right thing and he certainly did not know the extent of their plans. It is thanks in part to him that we were able to save Inga.'

Sayrid dropped the wood with a loud clunk. It amazed her that Hrolf was willing to forgive her brother even a little bit. The ache in her heart was too raw.

'I wanted to apologize,' she said before she lost her nerve. 'You were right and I didn't want to see it. I never considered my brother to be capable of such a thing.'

'It is a measure of how much you love your brother and sister that you couldn't. I see that now.'

Sayrid nodded.

'Blodvin confessed everything while you were with your brother.' He shook his head. 'Once she started talking, she found it impossible to stop. I made sure that three of my men also heard the confession. She and Lavrans planned it all. They were going to murder you and your brother and claim the land through the baby. I underestimated her cold-bloodedness.'

'We all did.' A shiver ran down Sayrid's back. She had unknowingly harboured a viper. She had come so close to death. And she was as guilty as Hrolf about underestimating people. She had assumed that because Blodvin played the pretty and helpless female that was what she was. 'Where is she now?'

'I have sent her under guard to Kettil. It is over, Sayrid. You will not have to suffer from that troll wife again.'

'I see where Inga gets her colourful language.'

'Inga is right about her. Troll wife fits.'

'How did Blodvin know Lavrans?'

'Her father has been in his pay for years. You were right about that.'

'But why did he want you to marry Blodvin? Surely he knew what would happen!'

'They had a falling-out over Blodvin as her father wanted her to be Lavrans's wife, not his concubine. Lavrans disagreed.' Hrolf's face became grim. 'From what she said, they became lovers shortly before Blodvin seduced your brother. Lavrans wanted to exact his revenge on your family in the most horrible way imaginable.'

Sayrid shook her head. The knowledge gave her no pleasure. 'Poor Regin. He had terrible judgement when it came to falling in love.'

Hrolf stood awkwardly at her side. 'Love will

make a man do many things. It makes what I have to say awkward.'

Sayrid put a hand to her head. Her heart splintered into a thousand shards. The events of this morning should be pulling them closer together, but all she could think about was how her brother had betrayed them and how her husband had very nearly lost his daughter.

She'd once scoffed at Regin about love, but she understood now how one person could take over your life. 'Awkward?'

He pulled her closer, preventing her from moving. 'I've done you a disservice. I thought that you needed taming and that no woman could ever enjoy battles. That women needed protecting.'

'It is what I'm good at. Far better than sewing.' She wrapped her arms about her waist. 'Once I thought it would be my whole life and now...I see that I allowed fear to rule me. I am capable of many things. All I had to do was to try. You gave me the courage to do that.'

'Did I?' His face suddenly became very hopeful. 'Do you want something more, Sayrid?'

'Why are you here, Hrolf?'

'I was coming to apologize and to offer you a place on my next *felag*.'

'Your next *felag*?' Sayrid's heart pounded. He was going to leave. His alliance with Kettil had been to guard against Lavrans and now that the sea king was dead, there was nothing to stop Hrolf from going back east. And she hadn't even begun to conquer the womanly arts like they had agreed. 'Where are you going?'

'I was thinking about Constantinople. I believe you expressed an interest in going there.' He caught her hand and brought it to his lips. 'If that is where you want to go, it is as good a destination as any.'

Sayrid stared at him. Her heart pounded so rapidly that she was certain he must be able to hear it. 'When the time is right, I would love to go to the East, but not for glory or gold. I want to honour your bodyguards and see where Inga came from.'

'When the time is right? Sayrid, I want you as you are, not some perfection of womanhood.'

A lump came into her throat. He was offering her the chance but she looked around her and knew she couldn't. 'I can't abandon everyone here, you understand. I love my home even when it is a smouldering wreck, especially when it is a smouldering wreck. I am good at organising things as well as fighting. You've shown me that. So you go and I will stay here, making sure this estate prospers.'

Hrolf's face swam in front of her. She was aware that he still had her hand. She tugged, but his fingers held her tighter. 'Hear me out, Sayrid, and then decide.'

She nodded briefly.

'I told you a lie the other day. I told you that I could never love and I was wrong.' He pulled her close. 'I was wrong about many things and I'm sorry. I want you to be happy and if that means taking you off on a *felag*, then that is what I want. If it means staying here, rebuilding and bringing up our children, then that is what I want, but I want to be with you. Always to be with you.'

Her heart stopped in her throat. Hrolf was speaking of love. A tiny seed of hope grew within her breast. 'You love Inga, that much is obvious.'

'I can admit to loving Inga because one very maddening woman taught to me to love.' He brushed her hair away from her forehead. A flame flickered in his eyes. 'Today I died a thousand deaths because you were in danger. The reason I fought so hard was because of you. And I bitterly regret changing your life so much. You are a great warrior, Sayrid. One of the best I have ever fought alongside. And I should be proud of that. But I want a wife, a woman in my bed as well. Is that greedy of me?'

'Which woman?'

He leant forward and nipped her nose. 'You, but you how you are. I don't care if you burn food or mix up threads as long as you are there for me. You make me think. I fell in love with you the instant you escaped from me and swam out to that blasted boat. You have been in my dreams ever since.'

'You dreamt of me?'

'I'm happy to say that the reality of you far outweighed any dream. You are the only woman I want. You are the heart of my life.'

'I want to stay here with you. I want to rebuild this hall and make it a place of prosperity so that our children do not have to raid. And then I want to visit the far places I've dreamt about with you.' Sayrid placed her head on his shoulder, marvelling at his words. Hrolf loved her, truly loved her. 'Once, my ambition was to be a great warrior above all things, but now I want to be a wife and mother. I might be the heart of your life, but you are the one who gives me life.'

'Just as I want to be a husband and a father before being a warrior.' He traced the outline of her lips.

'We can work together to create a household where all are valued.'

He brushed his lips against hers. 'Sayrid Avildottar, will you be my shield maiden forever?'

'I would rather be your wife.'

'You are both.' He captured her lips and for a long time, they allowed their bodies to express their love for each other.

Epilogue

Two and a half years later

In the dim light, Sayrid sat next to the double cradle, absently rocking her sleeping babies as she listened to the dying sounds of the feast.

Earlier, the rebuilt hall had rung with applause when Inga had recited her first saga in honour of Auda's marriage. Sayrid thought the saga owed a lot to the events surrounding her own marriage to Hrolf, but Inga swore that no one else would notice. Inga also included a bit from the journey they had taken a year ago down to Constantinople.

Sayrid was very glad that she hadn't realized about her pregnancy until they were nearly home. Once he knew, Hrolf had worried about her all the time.

It had done her heart good to see Auda settled

with a younger warrior whom she had met on the trip to Constantinople. It was clear that they loved each other very much. Hrolf, in his new role as *jaarl*, had settled some of the land that had once belonged to Blodvin's father on the couple as a wedding gift.

'I thought I'd find you here with our sons.' Hrolf came into their private chamber, holding two goblets.

'I wanted a bit of peace after today's events.' Sayrid gave a small laugh. 'My stepmother's decision to stay away because Auda's chosen groom wasn't worthy did not detract from the day one bit.'

'It amazes me that you could forgive her.'

'Holding bitterness in my heart helps no one.' Sayrid shook her head. 'I refuse to become bitter and twisted like her. Auda made such a lovely bride.'

'The loveliest bride I have ever seen was my wife, who wore a crown of wilting flowers and a dress which revealed far more than it concealed. I wanted to slit every man's throat who looked at you that day.'

'You like to exaggerate.'

'I never exaggerate where you are concerned.'

Hrolf handed her a goblet. 'I've brought you some of the Frankish wine which Regin sent in honour of Auda's marriage.'

Sayrid tasted the sweet wine. From its honeyed taste, she knew Regin had sent the very best, along with a gift of gold for their sister. 'Did Bragi say how he was doing?'

'He thrives.' Hrolf came and put his arms about Sayrid's waist. Sayrid leant back against his firm body, drawing comfort from it. 'There was no place for him here. He welcomed the banishment. It gave him a chance to rebuild his life after what happened. And he is well thought of.'

Sayrid nodded. She understood why her brother had made the decision, but she wished life had been kinder to him. 'I wish the baby had lived. Despite everything, Regin would have claimed it as his own. My brother is like that.'

'It came too soon.' Hrolf shook his head. 'Blodvin's death was one of the reasons why I worried when you were pregnant.'

'You would have been worse if you'd realized that I carried twins.'

He kissed her neck. 'The gods were kind to me. I have healthy sons and a wife I love. Once I thought love was something to be feared.'

'And now?'

'You and my children are my life. You hold my heart in your hands and I've learnt that my life is better with a strong woman by my side.'

For a long time neither spoke as they watched their twin sons sleeping peacefully in the cradle.

* * * * *

Historical Note

Did shield maidens really exist? Scholars are divided. For many years, shield maidens were dismissed as pure fantasy, particularly as weapons were very rarely found in women's graves.

Until recently such finds were interpreted as gifts or as having a symbolic value. I personally suspect that it might have been men making such assumptions. Who is to say why something has been placed in a grave? Why should a woman have it as an unused gift and a man have it as a tool he used? The vast majority of weapons found in female graves were of a projectile nature. In other words, they were weapons which did not require a great deal of upper-body strength. I personally think women used the weapons.

Recently, there has been a reappraisal and it is

beginning to be accepted that a very few women might have served as warriors.

While a number of sagas mention Valkyries and shield maidens, there are few credible references to women warriors in reliable historical sources. However one is a description of a Byzantium campaign against Scandinavian Rus in 970, which tantalisingly mentions that the Rus had armed and armoured women amongst their warriors. Another brief mention is from the Irish *Cogadh Gaedhel re Gallaibh* which gives a list of Viking fleets that attacked Munster in the tenth century. Last in the list is the fleet belonging to Inghen Ruaidh or the Red Maiden, but there is nothing else about her.

In the sagas, once a shield maiden married, she put away her male clothes and settled down, normally making a good wife. The sagas also mention some of the problems women warriors found—lack of respect being the chief amongst them.

But because of the lack of primary sources dating from the actual period, it is doubtful if we will ever learn the full truth. Still, it is fun to speculate.

If you are interested in learning more about the

Vikings—warrior women or otherwise—these books might prove useful:

Ferguson, Robert, *The Hammer and the Cross: A New History of the Vikings* (2010, Penguin Books, London)

Jesch, Judith, *Women in the Viking Age* (2005, Boydell Press, Woodbridge, Suffolk)

O'Brien, Harriet, *Queen Emma and the Vikings: The Woman Who Shaped the Events of 1066* (2006, Bloomsbury, London)

Magnusson, Magnus KBE, *The Vikings* (2003, The History Press, Stroud, Gloucestershire)

Parker, Philip, *The Northmen's Fury: A History of the Viking World* (2014, Jonathan Cape, London)

Roesdahl, Else, *The Vikings revised edition,* translated by Susan Margeson and Kirsten Williams (1999, Penguin Books, London)

Williams, Gareth, Pentz, Peter, Wemhoff, Matthias, eds, *Vikings: Life and Legend* (2014, British Museum Press, London)

MILLS & BOON®

Why shop at millsandboon.co.uk?

Each year, thousands of romance readers find their perfect read at millsandboon.co.uk. That's because we're passionate about bringing you the very best romantic fiction. Here are some of the advantages of shopping at www.millsandboon.co.uk:

* **Get new books first**—you'll be able to buy your favourite books one month before they hit the shops

* **Get exclusive discounts**—you'll also be able to buy our specially created monthly collections, with up to 50% off the RRP

* **Find your favourite authors**—latest news, interviews and new releases for all your favourite authors and series on our website, plus ideas for what to try next

* **Join in**—once you've bought your favourite books, don't forget to register with us to rate, review and join in the discussions

Visit **www.millsandboon.co.uk**
for all this and more today!